**His research was strictly confidential. How could word have gotten out?**

Thompson looked at Jason, took a deep breath, looked around at the other tables, and continued in a more muted tone, "I've heard that you recently discovered a molecule that has great potential in curing pancreatic cancer. Apparently, your results in animal models were spectacular."

Jason flushed, and his heart began to pound.

"I would be grateful if you would let my company partner with you in developing and testing this molecule. We would do a great job for you, and, if successful, it would turn our company around. I have a check in my pocket for two hundred thousand dollars made out to you that I will give you in return for your cooperation."

Jason's heart continued to pound, and he knew that his face was now beet red. How could this man possibly know anything about their discovery? None of the in vitro or animal studies had been published. Jason had already contracted with a large pharmaceutical company and a firm specializing in clinical trials to begin human studies. There would be no way that Evan Thompson could know about this research unless someone in the Glassman lab or one of these two companies had leaked information, and the contractual relationship with these two companies strictly prohibited releasing any information to any unauthorized individuals.

"Mr. Thompson, I'm very sympathetic to your situation. And I wish that I could help you. But I'm afraid it would be impossible to help you in this instance." Jason wanted to get up and leave, but he also didn't want to offend this man who apparently was of some importance to Sinai Medical Center.

Jason and Philip have just celebrated their fifth wedding anniversary. They have a four-year old daughter and the perfect marriage. Then Philip is tragically killed in an automobile accident. As Jason struggles to deal with the terrible agony of Philip's death, he discovers that one of his confidential research projects has been leaked to an unscrupulous CEO of a small struggling biopharmaceutical company. Now Jason is being threatened with having his career destroyed and being framed for murder if he doesn't agree to partner with the biopharmaceutical company for clinical trials stemming from his research. Jason knows he can't give into extortion, but refusing could cost him everything he holds dear...

KUDOS for *Second Chances*

In *Second Chances* by John S. Daniels, Jason Green is a medical doctor and researcher at Sinai Medical Center in New York. His husband Philip Olson is killed in an auto accident and Jason is devastated. After Philip's death, Jason throws all his energy into his work and his four-year-old daughter Julie. At work, he discovers a possible cure for certain types of cancer, but again he is devastated to learn that his research data has been leaked to an un-scrupulous CEO of a bio-tech company. Now Jason has to decide what to do about the CEO who is trying to bribe Jason to partner with them, as well as discover who leaked the data. In addition, an old acquaintance reenters his life wanting to start a relationship, now that Philip is dead. But is Jason ready to start over with someone new? The story is intense, fast paced, and intriguing, the science easy even for a lay person to understand. A really great read. ~ *Taylor Jones, The Review Team of Taylor Jones & Regan Murphy*

*Second Chances* by John S. Daniels is the story of Jason Green, a gay doctor and medical researcher in New York. Jason and his partner Philip married a month after same-sex marriage became legal in New York in July 2011. But they had only been married five years when Philip is killed in an auto accident, leaving Jason and their four-year-old adopted daughter, Julie, devastated. As Jason struggles to put his life back together and move on, he receives another blow when he discovers that data from his research on cancer has been leaked to the head of a struggling bio-tech company. Jason is also dealing with a new man in his life, Kevin O'Malley, someone he met over a decade before who still carries a torch for him. Jason doesn't think he is ready to start dating again, but

Kevin is determined that Jason will no longer be the one who got away. With marvelous, complicated, and well-developed characters; a solid well-thought-out plot; plenty of suspense and fast-paced action, Second Chances is one that you won't want to put down. ~ *Regan Murphy, The Review Team of Taylor Jones & Regan Murphy*

# ACKNOWLEDGMENTS

With thanks to Black Opal Books for their support and particularly to Faith C. for her intelligence and diligence in helping me edit this manuscript and its preceding novel, *The Intern*. Thanks to my many friends and colleagues who inspired much of the story in *The Intern* as well as *Second Chances*: David Kipnis, William Daughaday, Kenneth Ludmerer, Donald Skor, Michael Berk, Susan Nash, Michelle Summers, Sally Bondi. And thanks to the many individuals who have enriched my life and who have demonstrated their commitment to human rights, including Rachel Maddow, Chris Hayes, Lawrence O'Donnell, Barbra Streisand, Andre Aciman, Barrack Obama, Joe Biden, and so many others.

# SECOND

# CHANCES

## JOHN S. DANIELS

*A Black Opal Books Publication*

GENRE: GAY ROMANCE/SUSPENSE

SECOND CHANCES
Copyright © 2018 by John S. Daniels
Cover Design by Jackson Cover Designs
All cover art copyright © 2018
All Rights Reserved
Print ISBN: 978-1-626949-33-1

First Publication: JUNE 2018

Published by Black Opal Books **http://www.blackopalbooks.com**

# DEDICATION

*This book is for Werner and Claire Daniels, Susie Knopf, Jeffrey Daniels, and for Lance, Lauren, Melissa, Julie, Zoe, Aaron, Alex, and Caroline.*

# CHAPTER 1

Jason Green sat in the oversized leather chair, dazed, his cheek pressed against the cheek of his four-year-old daughter who was fast asleep in his arms. The Olsen mansion in Wilton, Connecticut, was filled with family and friends in subdued conversation, although Jason heard none of it. The emptiness he felt was unbearable. Jason remembered that same empty feeling when he had lost his mother sixteen years previous, but the depth of this void dwarfed those feelings. Guilt invaded his emptiness: Why would the loss of Philip be more traumatic than the loss of his mother? He had loved his mother so much. She had been the perfect parent. When he was thirteen, he told her that he was gay. She held him and told him that he was not only the perfect son but also an amazing human being. Jason had always been told that even looked like his mother. "As strikingly handsome as your mother was beautiful," his family and friends would say. But that profound emptiness he had experienced when his mother died seemed miniscule compared to how he now felt. Perhaps it was age, or maybe that's the way it was supposed to be.

Jason and Philip married two months after same sex

marriage had become legal in New York in July of 2011. Jason had made it his mission to develop the perfect relationship with Philip after a tumultuous courtship. It took little effort. They were perfect companions. They were perfect lovers. Tears trickled down Jason's face as he recalled his toast to Philip on their fifth wedding anniversary only a few months previously at Trattoria Del'Arte, their favorite restaurant. '*I cannot imagine a more perfect marriage than ours. I cannot imagine a deeper love one human being can have for another than the love I have for you. I cannot imagine a greater feeling of contentment than I've had these past five years. Here's to fifty more years of love and contentment.*'

Philip's exquisite smile and that rare hint of tears in his eyes after Jason said those words remained a vivid memory. Philip had never been one to easily express his emotions, but Jason knew his feelings were mutual. Jason sat almost catatonic as his tears channeled onto Julia's cheek.

Not that his marriage had been one of traditional perfection, Jason pondered as he held Julia more firmly, feeling her heartbeat against his chest. There had been the occasional serious disagreements about Julia's nurturing and education, particularly regarding religion. And Philip had tried to confess, on more than one occasion, sexual encounters that he had while serving as a visiting professor at other medical schools. Jason would quickly stop his confession each time, protesting that whatever he did was unimportant and that Jason was not interested. Despite those imperfections—or what others would regard as imperfections—Jason had meant and felt every word of that anniversary toast. Jason would frequently remind himself that the concept of perfection was nebulous—a lover of a Brahms piano concerto might consider a Schoenberg piano concerto severely flawed, although both are perfect in their own realm. In his own, realm Jason had regarded his marriage as perfect and Philip as complete perfection.

Philip's mangled body had been flown back from San Francisco only the prior day. Although Jason had power of attorney over all of Philip's affairs, he was extremely close with Philip's parents, brother, and sister and gratefully allowed Philip's father to make all of the funeral arrangements and burial in the Olsen family plots in Wilton. Philip would have wanted that, Jason thought, although Jason and Philip had never talked about where they would be buried. Their life together was just beginning, and mortality had never been a consideration. They had both bought life insurance policies when they adopted Julia, but buying those policies had been an afterthought, and the idea that a claim would ever be made seemed ludicrous.

Jason had begged Philip to cancel his trip to San Francisco on Sunday, only three long days ago. But Jason knew that Philip needed to go. After all, he had established himself as an internationally prominent orthopedic surgeon, and because of his innovative surgical techniques in spinal cord surgery, he was frequently asked to be a visiting professor at outstanding academic medical centers all over the world. Jason made him promise to accept only four visiting professorships every year. He couldn't bear being separated from Philip. And Jason knew that Philip hated being away from him and Julia. There would be at least five FaceTime phone calls daily from Philip when he traveled. Jason recalled the sweet kiss Philip had given him as he left their home at five a.m. for his trip to San Francisco. "Give Julia a hug and kiss for me. I'll call you when I get there." Then the sweet and tender kiss, and "I love you." The smell of Philip's aftershave was still fresh in Jason's memory.

A police officer had knocked at Jason's seventeenth-floor condominium at four p.m. that Sunday. Philip had been picked up at the San Francisco airport by an orthopedic surgery resident, and, on their way to the medical center, their car was stopped at the back of a traffic jam on I-280. An eighteen-wheeler plowed into the back of their car, killing Philip and the orthopedic resident instantly. Eyewitnesses stated that the truck had been traveling at least sixty miles per hour and had not even attempted to slow down when the truck struck Philip's car. The truck driver was seriously injured and was found to have an undetectably low blood sugar in the emergency room. He was an insulin dependent diabetic. Jason vomited as the officer finished relating the details. He asked the officer to notify Philip's father. Jason could not fathom giving John Olsen this news.

Jason gave little thought to those awful details. The last three days had been a blur. He could only think of the emptiness he felt and worried whether he would have the strength to go on for the sake of his daughter. Julia, whom they had named after Jason's dead mother, sweet Julia. Jason's tears began to flow uncontrollably from his cheeks onto Julia's cheeks, causing her to stir.

Jason suppressed sobs as he thought of Julia. Jason and Philip had adopted Julia a year after they married. She had been born to a seventeen-year-old Florida girl, and with the help of Philip's father who had powerful political connections, Jason and Philip adopted the infant. Both had immediately bonded with her, and she quickly became the pivot of their personal life. She was a beautiful and happy baby with light blonde hair just like Philip's, and with blue eyes and a beautiful face, just like Philip's. Jason thought about how he had often teased Philip that he must have had had an affair with the natural mother because of their similar physical features. Both fathers had been surprised at the profound love they had developed for her. Jason adored watching Philip play with Julia and was stunned as well as fascinated by the deep bond between the two. Philip was gone only seventy-two hours, and already Jason fretted about how Julia would handle this loss. Tears continued to flow as Julia, still asleep, wiped Jason's tears from her cheek.

Sophia gently wrested Julia from Jason's arms, at first with unconscious resistance from Jason. Jason looked up at Sophia and smiled sadly, tears still flowing from his eyes. "Jason, sweetheart, I'll put her to bed. She's had a long day." Jason handed his daughter to Sophia and unsuccessfully tried to smile. Sophia Gallardo had been Julia's nanny for the past four years and had become an integral part of Green-Olsen family.

Jason had always recognized a subtle sadness in Sophia's eyes, although her pain was now unambiguous. Sophia had confided her personal history to Jason, bit by bit, over the past four years. As an infant she and her parents had escaped Castro's Cuba shortly after Castro seized power, immigrating to France where Sophia's father had relatives. Both of Sophia's parents were physicians, but her father was a brazen womanizer. Finally, by the mid-1960s, Sophia's mother had had enough of her father's philandering, and Sophia and her mother moved to New York City. Sophia married immediately after college and gave birth to a daughter whom she had raised alone after her husband abandoned them. Sophia was so quietly proud of her daughter who had just completed an oncology fellowship at Columbia University after graduating from medical school with honors.

Sophia had worked for twenty-five years as an executive secretary in Sinai Medical Center's Orthopedic Department. Philip had first met her as a resident in that department, and, after Philip had become a full professor, he requested that Sophia become his personal secretary.

Over several years, Philip had become very close to her, and Sophia had come to love Philip as a son. When Philip approached Sophia soon after they had adopted Julia and made her a very attractive offer as a full-time nanny, she immediately agreed. Employing a nanny was not a luxury but a necessity, since both Jason and Philip had demanding jobs and worked long hours.

Sophia wrapped her arms around Julia as she turned to carry her upstairs to her bedroom, tears still streaming down Jason's cheeks. Jason was thinking how fortunate for him at this time to have Sophia, although her employment had turned out to be an expensive necessity. Jason looked over at Philip's parents. As a wedding gift, Philip's parents had given Philip and Jason their spectacular seventeenth-floor condominium that they had owned for over three decades and that overlooked Central Park. It had two bedrooms and was very spacious, but there was no accommodation for a nanny. A small one-bedroom unit on the second floor of their building had been for sale, and Philip and Jason bought it for Sophia to use. It cost over a million dollars. In addition, they paid her one hundred thousand dollars yearly for taking care of Julia Monday through Friday and on occasional Saturdays. But as expensive as that was, Jason thought, Sophia had actually been a bargain. She was in the seventeenth floor unit by five-thirty a.m. every day, made breakfast for all three, kept their home spotless, cooked their supper daily, and took care of Julia until both Jason and Philip arrived home in the evening.

Jason watched Sophia as she slowly climbed the staircase with Julia. Sophia and Julia had become very attached to one another, and there had even been a phase during which Julia would throw tantrums when Sophia left for the evening. She taught Julia to read and speak both English and Spanish, and by four years of age, Julia was fluent in both languages. Sophia took her to nursery school daily and made certain that the very expensive school was performing as advertised, often staying to observe, and complaining to the headmaster if the school did not meet her expectations.

Those memories brought a sad smile to Jason's face. Sophia also took Julia to the zoo, the art museums, the natural history museum, and spent time with other the other children and their nannies in the neighborhood. Jason knew that Sophia had been an indispensable blessing for Philip and him.

It was seven p.m., only a few hours after the heart-wrenching funeral. Jason had prepared a eulogy to be given at the graveside, but he had been unable to deliver it. In fact, he had been unable to say more than a few words to anyone since the news had been given to him. At the graveside, his father had taken Jason's hand-written eulogy from him and read it. Jason did not hear his words. He only held Julia tightly and stared at the casket. Jason saw Philip's father and Paul Olsen, Philip's younger brother, speaking at the graveside, but too their words passed unheard.

Jason took a deep breath and wiped the tears from his cheeks with his shirtsleeve. He looked around the house and saw hundreds of familiar faces. He thought it was time to climb out of this deep, dark hole and be strong for his daughter and Philip's family. Seth and Sheri Goldberg approached him as he slowly got up from the leather chair that he and Philip had sat in together so many times over the past ten years.

Seth was Jason's closest friend and his first resident when he arrived at Sinai as an intern eleven years ago. He was now a Professor of Cardiology at the Sinai Medical Center and had become a very prominent researcher and clinician. Jason had been instrumental in fixing Seth up with Sheri, and Philip and Jason had been godparents to their two children.

Seth took Jason in his arms and hugged him tightly, not letting go for some time. Jason saw the pain in Seth's puffy eyes. "Jason, there is nothing I can say, except that Sheri and I are here for you and that we love you. You have to be strong and get through this. Julia needs you, we all need you." Sheri was crying as Seth continued after a pause. "We're going to head back to the city. When will you be coming back?"

"Probably tomorrow." Jason's answer was flat. "I want Julia to get back to her routine and make things as normal as possible for her. And I have to make sure everything is going smoothly at the lab." Seth put his hand on Jason's face, and both smiled sadly at one another. Seth and Sherri left as Paul Olsen, Philip's younger brother, approached Jason.

Jason had become very close with Paul and his wife Amy over the years, but it was painful for Jason as he watched him approach. He reminded him so much of Philip. Like Philip, he was tall with blond hair and a beautiful face. Paul had graduated Yale law school and had entered his father's law practice, and like Philip, Paul was brilliant and hardworking, perhaps a bit more outgoing than his older brother. Jason and Paul hugged each other and stood, looking at each other, both knowing the deep sadness each was suffering. Jason broke the silence. "How are you holding up?"

"It's a nightmare." Paul grimaced to hold back tears and paused. "I worshipped him." Another pause. "I can't imagine what you're going through. And I can't believe how strong Mom and Dad are, at least on the surface."

"We should go be with them." Jason took Paul's arm, and they walked toward the living room, where John and Evelyn Olsen and Jonathan Green, Jason's father, were standing together in quiet conversation. Each time Jason looked at Philip's parents was a glaring reminder to him of the importance of genetics. Both parents were tall, blond, and physically beautiful people, and it was obvious how Philip, Paul, and their sister, Anna, each acquired their stunningly good looks.

"Where is Julia?" John Olsen asked Jason with a sad smile.

"Sophia is putting her to bed," Jason answered as he hugged Evelyn Olsen, moisture returning to his eyes.

"Jason, I know you're wanting to go back to the city tomorrow, and that's fine. But we have a lot to talk about. Is it okay if we come in this weekend and spend some time together?" John asked with genuine anxiety.

"Of course. I don't want our relationship to change. I'm your son, and Julia is your granddaughter," Jason spoke in his deep southern accent, which remained undiminished despite living in New York City for eleven years. Once again tears trickled down Jason's cheeks. He had always cried easily. Jonathan Green took his son's arm and held him close. Over the next hour, the scores of family and friends filed past, giving parting condolences to Jason and the Olsen family, including Anna, Philip's younger sister, who had joined them. Anna had been particularly close with Philip and was having difficulty coping, frequently disappearing for ten minutes to regain composure.

After everyone parted, John and Evelyn, Paul and Amy, Anna, Jason, and Jonathan sat in the lavish living room around the fireplace at a loss for words. After several minutes of silence, Jason spoke in a quiet voice. "I'm sorry I couldn't speak this afternoon. I don't have words to convey how close Philip and I have been. We were perfect." He paused. "At this moment, I don't see how I can go on. I know I have to, for Julia, if for no one else. I guess, Dad, you went on after Mom died because of Susie and me." Jason looked at John and Evelyn, sitting next to each other on the couch. "And I cannot, even in my wildest imagination, begin to know how it feels to lose a child. I'll do anything to make it easier for you both."

Without hesitation and with a deliberate tone, John said, "Jason, we will go on, because we have no choice. Evelyn and I were both so close to Phil, as we are to Paul and Anna. But Phil shared everything about his life with us. And I can tell you that his life was fulfilled because of you. Even in my profound sadness, I feel a sense of happiness and consolation that I saw him as a fulfilled and happy person. So I'll be forever grateful to you." The only sounds were the crackling of the burning wood, the clanking of dishes that the caterers were cleaning in the kitchen, and Jason's muffled sobs.

On Thursday morning, Jason, Julia, and Sophia had breakfast with the Olsen family, and, after long embraces, Jason strapped Julia into the car seat, and the three drove back to the city in Jason's Murano. Sophia looked back at Julia and talked frequently to her in English and Spanish. Julia had not yet asked for Philip. Jason wondered whether she knew he was not coming home. Perhaps Julia and Sophia had talked about it. Jason took Sophia's hand and held it for the sixty-mile ride back to their home across from Central Park. They arrived at the condominium at ten-thirty a.m. and were greeted by the concierge with a sad smile.

The three-thousand-square-foot condominium was on the seventeenth floor and had a spectacular view of Central Park. Most of the furniture was the original furniture that Philip's parents had purchased almost thirty years ago. The furnishings were expensive and elegant, and the walls were decorated with very expensive artwork that had been part of the Olsen family for several generations. Several of the oil paintings were museum quality by early twentieth-century American artists. Philip and Jason had tried on numerous occasions to return the paintings to Philip's parents after they married, but their offers had always been refused. The only additions Jason had made were an expensive stereo system with Macintosh speakers and a beautiful Roland grand digital piano, which fit perfectly in a corner of the living room.

Julia ran to her room and returned to the living room with her iPad to which she had become addicted. Jason and Philip had limited the time she could use it, but today Jason would let her use it as she wished. Jason went to Sophia and hugged her tightly. "Sophia, I hope you will continue to stay with us. I know how close you and Philip were. But Julia and I need you more than ever."

"Sweetheart, I'm here with you till you kick me out. I'll miss Phil terribly, but I love you and Julia equally. I was worried you would not want me to stay." She touched Jason tenderly on the cheek and then started cleaning the condominium. Jason spent the rest of the day playing with Julia, reading to her, playing the piano with her, and playing games on her iPad with her. At one point, she asked when her daddy would be coming home. Jason answered that he had gone on a very long trip and would not be home for a long time. She looked at Jason for an unusually long moment when he said that, as if she knew that he was lying or that something was amiss. She then asked, "Daddy, are you going on a long trip?" Jason answered that he was never going to leave her.

Jonathan Green, Jason's sixty-four-year-old father, joined them for a pot roast dinner that Sophia had prepared. Jonathan had sold his department store in Mississippi and moved into a condominium only a few blocks from Jason and Philip soon after they had married. He had grown close to the Olsen family and loved Philip as a son. Jason sensed the great pain his father was quietly suffering, much like he remembered when his mother died. He had said little to Jason since the news. What was there to say?

Julia had become very attached to Jonathan, whom she called Papa, and Jonathan took great delight in reading with her, frequently telling Jason and Philip how much it reminded him of his early years with Jason. Jason watched as Jonathan sat with Julia on the couch after supper reading *The Paper Bag Princess*.

Jason and Sophia quietly cleaned dishes. When they finished, Sophia put her hands on Jason's face, smiled sadly at him, and said, "Sweetheart, life goes on. I'll be here in the morning. I love you." They hugged, and Sophia left him to return to her second floor home. Jason stood in the kitchen listening to Julia read to his father. He was gentle and patient, just as he remembered him as a child. Jonathan took Julia to her bedroom for a final bedtime story, and Jason went to his digital piano, plugged in the earphones to mute the external speakers, and began playing Moonlight Sonata. Jason had always turned to his music when stressed or sad, although it had been years since he needed his music for that purpose. His life with Philip had been as perfect as life could be.

Jonathan put his hands on Jason's shoulder, startling him. "She's asleep. She is precious and smart. Her reading is almost as good as yours when you were that age," he said. Jason got up, hugged his father, and began to quietly cry once again. Jonathan wiped the tears off of Jason's cheeks with his hands. "Jason, it gets easier with time. That's the only consolation I can give you. It does get easier. You have Julia and a loving family, and you're an amazing and greatly admired scientist. You have a full life ahead of you. It will get easier."

Jonathan cupped his hands on Jason's face, just like

he did growing up, kissed him on the forehead, smiled sadly, then turned around and left Jason alone.

Jason checked on Julia, who was sleeping soundly. He undressed and crawled into the empty bed. He could still smell the lavender from the soap that Philip used and that had rubbed off onto the sheets and pillowcase. Sleeping with Philip had been one of the most surprising aspects of their relationship. He had never talked about that with Philip or confided in his father or Seth—it had been, and remained, such an inexplicable wonder to him. From the very first time they had slept together, Philip would turn his back to Jason. Jason would place his pillow perpendicular to Philip's pillow, making him slightly higher than Philip in the bed. He would then put his left leg in between Philip's two legs, wrap his arm over Philip's chest and hold his left forearm. The two men would then fall immediately into a deep sleep. Most days, the two would awaken after seven hours of sleep in exactly the same position. Occasionally, Jason would awaken during the night and find himself turned around. He would immediately reposition himself and quickly return to contented sleep. When Philip was away on a visiting professorship, Jason slept poorly. Philip's return always remedied his insomnia. Jason could not explain, but was fascinated by the contentment that he felt sleeping in the same bed with Philip. He knew that he would miss that part of their relationship even more than looking at his beautiful face, listening to his operating room stories, watching him play with Julia, or having sex with him. Tears returned as Jason fell into a restless sleep.

# CHAPTER 2

Jason woke, exhausted, at five-thirty a.m. to the sounds of Sophia making breakfast in the kitchen. He put on his warm running clothes after shaving and brushing his teeth, greeted Sophia with a warm hug, and went on his six-mile run around Central Park. It felt good to be running again. Jason thought the runner's high might ease his sadness. When he returned, he quickly showered, ate breakfast, and went into Julia's room. She was sleeping soundly as Jason kissed her on the cheek.

"Sophia, could you please tell the people at her school not to mention anything about what happened. I'm not certain how much Julia understands, and I don't want her getting upset at school."

"Of course, sweetheart. They're very good about those kinds of things. I'll see you this evening." Sophia gave Jason a tender pat on his cheek, and then Jason left for his laboratory at the Olsen Research Center. It was Friday, the day that he had his weekly conference with all of his postdoctoral fellows and PhD students, and he intended to catch up on all of the activities that had occurred during the past four days.

As he walked the two miles to The Olsen Research

Center, Jason recounted his academic years. He had graduated from his home state medical school, the University of Mississippi, first in his class. He knew that he had been labeled as a genius by his professors, although he never took that description seriously. He decided on Sinai Medical Center for his internship and residency in internal medicine because of Harvey Glassman, a Nobel Prize winning researcher whose writings on cancer research and protein chemistry had caught Jason's attention during his college years but particularly after his mother had died of breast cancer during his second year of medical school.

Jason remembered how difficult it had been to convince an aloof Dr. Glassman to let him join his laboratory during his internship and residency years. Dr. Glassman had at first dismissed his request, replying that interns and residents simply had no time to devote to research activities. However, not only did Jason perform brilliantly in his clinical training, but he was also instrumental in developing new research techniques and making important discoveries in Dr. Glassman's laboratory during those clinical training years. Jason was aware that his work had surprised, if not astounded Dr. Glassman as well as the other researchers at Sinai Medical Center, and by the end of his clinical training, Jason's research accomplishments had been so substantial and his research thesis so well-written and defended that the faculty awarded Jason a PhD. Such an accomplishment during a clinical training program was, as far as Jason knew, unique on the planet.

Jason also knew that Harvey Glassman had been a very demanding mentor to hundreds of postdoctoral fellows over several decades—men and women who had completed PhD programs or combined MD/PhD programs and who wanted to continue training with the famous Nobel Prize winner. Typically those postdoc fellows would go on to establish their own laboratories at other outstanding academic institutions or in industry. A postdoctoral fellowship with Harvey Glassman was a ticket to success in research. However, rarely, if ever, did Harvey Glassman develop close personal relationships with his fellows. He was relentlessly demanding and even insulting when a fellow made an error, and although his postdoc fellows were grateful for the opportunity to work under his tutelage, they rarely left with fond feelings for the famed researcher.

Jason Green knew that he was an exception, possibly the only exception, in Harvey Glassman's long career. Jason did not hesitate to correct Dr. Glassman when he was wrong, something never dared by other fellows, and at times he defended other postdoc fellows whom Dr. Glassman was disparaging. Jason was uncertain why Dr. Glassman tolerated his frequent challenges, but he had always suspected that it was because of his relationship with Philip and Philip's father who had given the money to build the Olsen Research Center and specifically the monies to fund Dr. Glassman's laboratory.

That belief was quashed when Mrs. Glassman gave Jason a letter written by Harvey Glassman on his deathbed shortly before he died of pancreas cancer in 2010. The letter made clear that Dr. Glassman had always considered Jason much smarter than he, that he loved Jason as a son, and that he would be greatly honored and relieved if Jason would consent to taking over his position as head of the Glassman laboratory. Dr. Glassman had made arrangements and received approval for Jason's transition to this powerful position soon after he had been diagnosed with cancer, but he had never discussed this possibility with Jason, probably, Jason thought, because Dr. Glassman had difficulty expressing emotions. When

Jason received that letter, he had been profoundly moved and stunned, and rarely a day passed that he did not think of his mentor and how important he had been to him personally and professionally.

Jason's transition was seamless. He insisted that the laboratory be formally named the Harvey Glassman Research Laboratory. He had been working in the lab full time for a year when Dr. Glassman died, and with Eric Adelman had already expanded the bioinformatics section of the lab into the largest and most sophisticated bioinformatics lab in the country. The amount of data they were able to process from the other postdoc fellows as well as from hundreds of other labs scattered across the country and Europe was astounding, even to Harvey Glassman. In addition, Jason and Eric had developed innovative computerized programs that were able to model proteins that were important in cancer research and treatment.

Now, Jason Green, MD, PhD, felt proud but very humble, even in his profound sadness, as he walked towards his lab. He headed one of the largest and most successful research programs in the country. Already at the young age of thirty-eight, he had been elected to the National Academy of Sciences and awarded many honors by various research organizations. He had appeared the year before on the front cover of *Time Magazine* in an article entitled "Research Pioneer." Jason typically shunned all of the awards and honors bestowed upon him. In fact, the retiring head of the Department of Medicine, Henry Stern, prevailed upon Jason to consent to the *Time* article that Jason had initially refused, accusing Jason of being selfish by denying important publicity that such an article would bring to Sinai Medical Center. Jason vividly remembered his response: "Dr. Stern, sir, this is the final time I'll let your Jewish guilt affect me." Dr. Stern had laughed and said, "Jason, it's time you start calling me Henry." To which Jason responded in typical fashion, "Perhaps one day sir."

During the first year after Harvey Glassman's death, Jason instigated a fundraising drive to raise three million dollars in order to establish the Harvey Glassman Distinguished Professorship, an important custom in the academic world to memorialize an important figure. The money was raised within a few months. Jason had already been promoted to a full professorship, the youngest full professor in the history of Sinai Medical Center, and in an emotional ceremony with the entire faculty and Glassman family in attendance, Jason was installed as the first professor to occupy the Harvey Glassman Distinguished Professorship.

As he approached the Olsen Research Center, Jason shook his head in disbelief at the successes emanating from the Glassman lab since his takeover. As a result of these successes, Jason had won numerous additional grants from the National Institutes of Health and various research foundations, as well as large amounts of money from the pharmaceutical and agricultural industries. He was the principle author of several hundred original research papers published in the most prestigious research and medical journals. Jason had also added seven more postdoctoral fellows, and in addition to the entire seventeenth floor had taken over the entire sixteenth floor of the Olsen Research building. Jason now had responsibility for fourteen postdoctoral fellows, twenty PhD candidates, and an annual budget that exceeded forty-six million dollars. Jason reluctantly admitted to himself that these successes were somewhat unique.

In addition, there were over four hundred applications every year from postdoctoral and doctoral candidates wanting to join the Glassman lab, and Jason

Green's reputation and prestige drew the finest applicants from the best academic centers in the country.

In short, even though Jason was not concerned with status, he did understand that he had become one of the world's preeminent researchers. Like Philip, Jason had been asked to serve as a visiting professor at the best research institutions all over the United States, Europe, and Asia. But unlike Philip, he had shunned virtually every request, and despite pleas from the political powers at Sinai Medical Center, Jason was adamant that he would not leave his laboratory for those types of activities. However, Jason's primary reason for not accepting those invitations was simply that he did not want to leave Philip and Julia. He knew that Eric Adelman, his close associate who headed the bioinformatics lab, was perfectly capable of running the lab in his absence, as he had done this past week since Philip's death. But Jason could not bear being away from his family, and the considerable financial rewards and prestige from such activities had never given Jason a second thought.

Jason had continued operating the lab in the same tradition as Dr. Glassman. He had fourteen separate research labs, each of which had its unique project, although many of the projects overlapped and complemented one or more of the other laboratories. A postdoctoral fellow headed each lab, and one or two PhD candidates were assigned to each postdoc fellow in addition to two or three research assistants. Jason determined the budget of each lab, and because he was so well organized, having all financial data updated daily on a computer program that he and Eric Adelman had developed, every postdoc fellow learned very quickly that virtually nothing escaped Jason's observation.

Jason had surprised himself regarding his own management style. He had initially tried to be informal with

his postdoc fellows, asking them to call him by his first
name. However, although very young, he was nevertheless unintentionally intimidating, and from the very beginning of his directorship, he had always been addressed
as Dr. Green by everyone in the lab with the exception of
Eric Adelman. Jason had also learned very quickly that
he needed to be demanding of all of his postdoc fellows
and PhD candidates. Despite the fact that they were all
highly motivated; ambitious; and, in most cases, brilliant,
it was common for these individuals to perform
suboptimally if Jason did not push each of them on an
almost daily basis. Jason was almost always polite and,
unlike Dr. Glassman, was not aloof but instead very ap-
proachable. But his researchers knew that when he talked
or made requests, he meant business and that he would
not tolerate any efforts that were not of the highest order.

Jason also knew that he had been blessed with unusual memory skills and that he surprised, even astounded,
virtually everyone who worked in the Glassman lab by
knowing every detail of every experiment in every lab.
Jason always enjoyed seeing their surprised looks when
he cited even insignificant details of an experiment, and
the postdoc fellows and PhD students rarely left a Friday
conference not completely astonished by Jason's command for details and even more importantly, for his ability to ask the questions that kept the researchers on the
proper course.

Jason had learned early in his clinical training as an
intern, as well as in his research with Dr. Glassman, that
the most important element in successful problem solving, whether in caring for patients or in the research laboratory, was the ability to ask the right questions. It had
always befuddled Jason how difficult it was for even brilliant individuals to learn this lesson. To that end, he required each postdoc fellow to write down the fundamen-

tal questions that he or she was trying to answer in their research, and present those questions every Friday at the start of their presentations. When a question had been answered or a question was added, the fellow would be required to explain the change. Frequently Jason would point out that it would be impossible to answer a particular question without asking and answering other questions first, and he would prod the fellow until the pertinent questions were being asked. Jason understood that his ability to redirect the thought processes of his postdoctoral fellows and PhD students, to teach them to ask the right questions, would ultimately determine whether their future careers would be successful or not, and Jason deeply felt that with the exception of his daughter, the future successes of his fellows would be his true legacy.

Jason arrived at his lab at seven-thirty after walking the two miles and stopping at the Starbuck's on his way. He had slept poorly the night before, and on those rare nights that he slept poorly, usually when Philip was away on a visiting professorship, he would stop at Starbucks and buy the strongest brew. The kick he got from the caffeine was not particularly pleasant, but it seemed to help him get started.

Eric Adelman was sitting across the elevator waiting for him. "Jason, how are you feeling?" Eric stood and walked with Jason to his office. Jason's office was the same office that Dr. Glassman had used, and he left it unchanged except for the pictures and a larger desk that could accommodate three computer screens. The walls were lined with shelves containing books and journals, the same ones that Harvey Glassman had, in addition to those that Jason had since added. The familiar smell of old books and journals had always brought a sense of calm to Jason.

"I'm fine. The lab will take my mind off of it." Jason

sat down in his office chair behind the desk, and Eric sat across from him. On the desk was a picture of Philip that Jason had taken when he was an intern and Philip was chief resident in orthopedics. The picture was of Philip with an impish smile, in his scrub suit, his chin resting on his palm. On the credenza behind the desk were pictures of his father, mother, sister, and several of Julia. "So what did I miss?" Jason continued as he stared at Philip's picture, his beautiful face, surprised that tears did not form. Perhaps, he thought, there were no more tears to shed.

"Everyone is pretty torn up here. I had a meeting with them on Monday and told them that the best thing they could do for you would be to continue their projects with enthusiasm. The postdocs came to the funeral. I wouldn't let the PhDs go, and they were mostly pissed off at me."

Jason continued to stare at Philip's picture. "Eric, I couldn't tell you who was at the funeral and who wasn't. It's a complete blur. In any case, I appreciate that. It was exactly the right thing to tell them. So any news here?"

Eric shook his head. "Everything has continued smoothly. A large container of sequencing enzymes has gone missing from Keller's lab, but that's all."

Jason started punching keys on his computer, and, after thirty seconds, he looked at Eric. "Please go get Miller, Cook, and Liu in here, and tell them to bring their containers of polymerase with them." Eric frowned and started to say something. "Please, Eric, just do it for me now," Jason insisted.

Eric left and returned a few minutes later with the three postdoc fellows, each holding their containers of enzymes. Dr. Cook spoke softly, "Dr. Green, we are all so sorry for your loss. We don't know what to say."

"Thank you for that, William." Jason continued to look at the computer. "Let me see each of your containers." He took each container, studied the labels, and then looked up. "Dr. Liu, someone in your lab took this bottle from Keller's lab. Find out what happened, and let me know as soon as you know something."

Dr. Liu's eyes widened. "Dr. Green, I'm so sorry. I'll find out straightaway." His British accent was in stark contrast to Jason's southern accent.

The three postdoc fellows turned and walked out quietly. Eric just smiled and shook his head.

"What's going on in your lab?" Jason continued.

"We're having a hard time keeping up with all of the data pouring in from all of these labs. I really think we should hire a few more computer geeks to enter all of this data. We can afford it. Money is pouring in from over two hundred labs now to analyze their data. We have enough money to do a major expansion of our computers. Also, I have eighteen new papers from our postdocs to be submitted to various journals that I need you to critique. I'm not trying to pressure you. You should take your time." Eric paused, and his eyes moistened. "Jason, I'm heartbroken for you. I'm sorry to put all of this on you now."

Dr. Liu knocked on the door, and Jason waved him in. Stephen Walker, one of two PhD students assigned to Dr. Liu, walked in behind. He was in his second year of doctoral work after having graduated from MIT with honors in molecular biology. Both stood silently, and then Mr. Walker said in a quiet voice, "Dr. Green, first, I'm so sorry for your loss. We're all very upset. And I'm sorry for what I did. I accidently contaminated the en-zymes, and I didn't know what to do. I became scared because I know how expensive it is, and so I took a bottle from Dr. Keller's lab. I didn't want to get in trouble. It was wrong. I'm very sorry."

Jason stared at the frightened young man for an uncomfortably long moment, and in his deep southern accent said, "Mr. Walker, what concerns me most is the possibility that deception could become a stratagem that you use in your professional and personal life. You've never impressed me as that kind of person, although I don't know you that well. I can assure you that life will not be pleasant for you if deception is a way that you deal with difficult situations." He paused again for a long moment as he continued to stare at Mr. Walker. "I want you to apologize to Dr. Keller and return the container. You can ask him if it would be okay to use some of his enzymes until another supply arrives for your lab." Another pause. "I want you to apologize to Dr. Liu. This episode reflects badly upon him. Your future evaluations from Dr. Liu had better be nothing but stellar." Another pause. "And I want you to carefully read *The Adventures of Huckleberry Finn* by Mark Twain this weekend. I expect a two-page written essay on my desk within a week on how that story relates to your behavior." He paused, still staring at the red-faced young man, and then in an uncharacteristically aggressive voice said, "*Now get out,*" and waved them out.

The two men turned and walked quickly away.

Eric looked at Jason with a puzzled expression. "Huckleberry Finn?"

"Yeah," Jason said with a forced smile. "Haven't you read it? The book is mostly about lies and deception. It's a classic."

For the rest of the morning, Jason worked on clearing his desk, piled high with papers, journals, and letters. There were hundreds of condolence cards that he put into his briefcase without reading them. He would read them at home after putting Julia to bed. There were numerous communications from other principle investigators from labs across the country and Europe, and he dictated replies to each letter. There were several invitations to give keynote addresses at various scientific meetings, including the National Academy of Sciences annual symposium. He respectfully declined all of those invitations. The Chancellor of the University of Mississippi sent a handwritten letter asking Jason to attend graduation ceremonies the following May in order to receive the Distinguished Alumnus Award, the highest honor given by the University to an alumnus. Jason thought that he would have to strongly consider that invitation and set it aside. He studied the financials of the fourteen labs and dictated memos to each of the postdoc fellows, asking in some cases for clarification of certain expenditures. It was noon, and a knock at the door interrupted his concentration.

"Hey, old man. How about dragging yourself away from here for a bite of lunch." Seth Goldberg was standing at the door with a smile on his face. Jason could see the sadness in the smile, but a smile nevertheless. Jason stood and returned the smile. They hugged and walked to the cafeteria.

"How are Sherri and the kids?" Jason asked.

"Oh, they're great. Sherri wants to go back to work. The kids are both going to be in school next year, so I guess she will. The question is how you're doing?"

"I'll be fine. The lab is very busy. I'm worried about Julia. I think she knows. The only thing I've told her is that Philip went on a long trip and won't be back for a long time. She gave me a funny look." Jason paused with a frown and looked down. "I think she knows. She's very smart. Anyway, Philip's family is coming in tomorrow afternoon to talk and have dinner. I'm going to have to give them the condo back and move somewhere. It was really Philip's condo, and it should stay in their family, and I can't afford to buy it from them. It's probably worth ten million on the market. Anyway, I'll deal with it."

The two made small talk the rest of the lunch break. Jason could sense that Seth avoided talking about Philip. It was too soon to reminisce. Jason knew that Philip's death profoundly affected Seth. They had been close friends for many years, long before Jason and Philip had met. It was, in fact, Seth who had introduced Philip to Jason.

Jason returned to his office and, over the next ninety minutes, reviewed and critiqued four of the eighteen research articles that had been written by the postdoc fellows and their PhD students. He was very pleased with the articles, although they all required revision before he would allow them to be submitted to the various journals. Jason's critiques were true to his character and style. Most of his comments were actually questions that resulted in the writers rethinking and revising their paper. Jason had made it clear that he welcomed challenges from everyone, but it was only on rare occasion that Jason did not prevail. And when a postdoc fellow or PhD student did successfully make his or her case, Jason would always smile, give a pat on the back, and say, "Good job."

At two-thirty p.m., the fourteen postdoc fellows and twenty PhD students crowded into the conference room as they did every Friday. The fellows sat at the large mahogany conference table with Jason at one end, Eric Adelman at the other end, and plenty of cookies and drinks scattered about the table. It was the same table that Jason was seated at eleven years previous, only six weeks after he had graduated from medical school, a seemingly typical intern, attempting to convince an aloof Dr. Glassman to let him work in his lab. The twenty PhD students sat on chairs lining the walls of the conference room, and there was a separate corner table with cookies and drinks for them. Although the PhD students were not required to attend, it was rare that all twenty were not present. Jason noticed that Stephen Walker carried a notepad and *The Adventures of Huckleberry Finn.*

Each fellow was allowed five minutes to provide updates for the week. They all knew that Jason would cut them off if they exceeded the five minutes, and so they learned to be very efficient in their presentation. They also knew that the update was to always begin by presenting the major questions that the lab was trying to answer. After the five-minute presentation, a discussion among the postdoc fellows and Jason would ensue. Jason would almost always start the discussion by asking a methodology question or a question that fundamentally challenged the direction of the research. The question would usually rouse a discussion among the other fellows, and when the fellows started asking the questions that would ultimately help the presenter's research effort, Jason would smile to himself, although his approval was obvious to everyone in the room. Exactly at ten minutes, Jason would interrupt. "Next!"

Jason's ten-minute limit forced each fellow to be focused and efficient in his or her presentation and prevented any one fellow from dominating the conference. However, his real motivation was more practical. There were fourteen presenters, and Jason was determined to leave the laboratory on Fridays by five p.m. to be home with Philip and Julia—now, just Julia.

Jason waved at Stephanie, a second-year postdoctoral fellow who received her PhD from Washington University in Saint Louis in translational genetics. "Okay, Stephanie, you're up."

He had been impressed with her work, she was brilliant with common sense, and she had a wonderful outgoing personality not typical of his postdoc fellows. Jason also had a bias for Washington University. Both of his parents had graduated from that school, where they met and fell in love.

"Dr. Green, I'm speaking for everyone here to let you know that we are deeply saddened for your loss and that anything we can do to ease your pain would be an honor."

Jason smiled sadly. "Thank you for that, Stephanie."

Stephanie continued, "What peptides on the human melanoma cell surface decrease the immune response of the host? What are the structures of those peptides, what is the mechanism of action of each peptide, and where are the genetic mutations accounting for these peptides?" She went on to concisely review a peptide on the surface of melanoma cells that her lab had discovered and had been shown to stimulate the production of immune checkpoint modulators, proteins that suppress the immune response of lymphocytes that have the ability to destroy cancer cells. She reported that they had successfully purified the peptide and were in the process of doing an amino acid sequencing of the peptide.

Jason interrupted. "Thank you, Stephanie. That is an exciting development. What will you do with that sequencing information and how will you prove that the sequence you got is not a contaminant but rather the true peptide?" A vigorous discussion ensued with five of the other postdoc fellows asking questions, Stephanie answering usually without hesitation and taking notes at the same time. Jason smiled and said, "Next."

For the next ninety minutes, each postdoc fellow gave his or her five-minute update, followed by one or two questions from Jason, which always resulted in a vigorous discussion of the project. The level of inquiry and the amount of information exchanged was enormous, and Jason sensed that every postdoc fellow and PhD student was stunned at the value that these conferences had in focusing their research efforts. Dr. Liu presented the final update, describing a novel mutant peptide that had been discovered on the cell surface of seven disparate human cancers, including colon, renal, lung, and pancreas. They had been trying to isolate the peptide in order to determine its structure, but there was a protein contaminate that was preventing the isolation process in every case. Jason asked, "How do you know that protein is a contaminant? Have you identified it?"

Dr. Liu was completely silent and, apparently, stunned. That question was such an obvious and fundamental question, and yet it was a question that had not occurred to him. After a long pause, he said in his British accent, "Thank you, Dr. Green. That is the next question we shall attempt to answer. I think with your permission we shall name the protein 'the Green factor.'"

Jason laughed. "Dr. Liu, should this protein be one with evil intent, or should it be just an innocuous contaminant, I would rather not have my name attached to it. But thank you for the thought." Everyone laughed, and Dr. Liu's face turned bright red. "Good job today, ladies and gentleman. Have a good evening."

Jason was the first out of the room. He walked quickly to his office to gather his briefcase and Bogner coat. His black leather TUMI briefcase had the initials JIGO embossed on one of the pockets, identifying his legal name after marrying Philip: Jason Itzhak Green-Olsen. Philip had given him that particular briefcase because it had meaning on several levels, but primarily because a similar briefcase contributed to the resolution of Philip and Jason's tenuous courtship. An empty feeling returned to him as he turned to leave his office.

Eric was standing at the door. "Jason, you were once again amazing in there. All of them are talking about you out there. All is going well here. I'll be here tomorrow, so please don't come in."

"Thanks, Eric. I'm bringing the articles that I need to critique home with me, so I'll stay home this weekend." They walked quietly to the elevators together, many of the postdoc fellows saying "Goodnight Dr. Green" as they passed by. "Eric, thanks for being such a great partner and friend to me." Jason patted Eric on the shoulder and disappeared into the elevator.

Jason caught a taxi for the two-mile ride home. He usually walked it in thirty minutes, but the twenty minutes he saved this evening was important to him. He walked into his home and Julia, who was sitting on Sophia's lap in the living room reading, jumped up and ran to Jason yelling, "Daddy!"

Jason scooped her into his arms and held her tightly. "What are you reading, sweetheart?" he asked her.

"*The Princess and the Pony*." She hugged Jason again and then wiggled her way down and ran back to Sophia.

Jason walked to Sophia and kissed her on the cheek. "How did everything go today?" he asked in a concerned voice.

"Everything went well. There were no problems at school, and everyone was very sensitive to the situation."

There was a knock on the door, and Jonathan Green walked in.

"Hi, Dad." Jason walked to him and kissed him.

"Papa!" Julia once again jumped up and ran to her grandfather, hugged him, and then ran back to Sophia.

In Spanish, Sophia said to Julia, "Your daddy is going to read the rest of the book with you. I'm going to go finish making supper." Jason understood, sat down with Julia on his lap, and she continued reading the book. Jason was impressed with her reading skills. His father had read with him from an early age, and he planned on continuing that tradition with Julia.

Jason saw the Sabbath candles that Sophia put on the dining table every Friday night, although Jason had always resisted continuing that tradition. Both Philip and Jonathan had argued with Jason that it would be good for Julia to have some religious tradition. But Jason was an atheist, and although he grew up lighting Sabbath candles every Friday with his family, he didn't see the point. Perhaps, Jason thought, he would reconsider, as he sat down with Julia, Sophia, and his father. The four had a wonderful supper of a Spanish chicken casserole with roasted vegetables. Jason and Jonathan were delighted when Sophia and Julia conversed in Spanish during the supper conversations.

After supper, Jonathan continued reading with Julia while Jason and Sophia cleaned. Jason listened to Julia reading to his father, thinking what a blessing it was to have him so near, both for Julia and for himself. Rarely a day went by that Jonathan did not spend time with Julia, picking her up from day school, taking her to a museum, or reading with her.

"Sweetheart, I'll be here tomorrow afternoon," Sophia said. "I know Mr. and Mrs. Olsen are coming in, along with Paul and Amy. I told them I was going to cook and they were delighted. I don't think they wanted to go out for a meal."

"Thanks so much, Sophia. I won't ask you to spend your Saturdays doing that again, I promise." Sophia touched Jason tenderly on his cheek, said goodnight to Jonathan and Julia, kissing Julia and touching Jonathan's cheek, and went to her home on the second floor. Jason sensed that there could be a relationship developing between Jonathan and Sophia. Jonathan had been in New York City for over almost five years, and, as far as Jason knew, he had not gone out with any women. Jason always encouraged him to get involved in social events, but Jonathan always dismissed Jason's suggestions. Jason did notice, however, that Sophia and Jonathan frequently talked quietly together, laughed often, and had even gone to movies together several times, always on a Sunday. Jason never inquired, but he was happy and hopeful that his father had found a new companion or perhaps even a deeper relationship.

Jason took Julia from his father, bathed her, dressed her in her pajamas, and as was the usual custom, told her a story from memory sitting on her bed next to her. The story would usually come from *Aesop's Fables* or *Hans Christian Andersen*, or *Snow White, Cinderella*, or *The Ugly Duckling*. Tonight, he told her the story of *Thumbelina*, and Julia smiled and occasionally laughed, particularly when Jason sang. Philip had tried telling Julia stories, but he could not compete in storytelling with Jason, and so, only on rare occasions, did Philip put Julia to bed. Jason was grateful that this important part of her day would not change.

Jason sat with his father after Julia fell asleep, and they talked about everything but Philip. Jason talked about his first day back in the lab. He mentioned that he might go back to receive an award from the University of Mississippi in the spring. That surprised Jonathan. "You've turned down every single invitation to give talks and get awards. Why accept this one?"

"I don't know. I feel an obligation to the university. They gave me a medical education for next to nothing and were very good to me. I think I owe it to them. Dad, I hope you will come tomorrow afternoon. You know the Olsens are coming and we're going to have a big meal here."

Jonathan replied, "Of course, I'll be here with you."

"I'm sure Philip's dad is going to want this condo to go back to them, and I've already found another place actually in your building that has been redone and is very spacious. It also has three bedrooms, so Sophia could stay with us. I couldn't afford to keep Sophia's place. We have a pretty large mortgage on it." Jason looked very serious, and his eyes became moist. "I just don't want Julia to feel she is being uprooted. I don't really know how much she understands."

"Son, I think she is smarter than you know. But didn't Philip have any life insurance?"

"Oh yes, we both bought policies. And it's a lot—two million dollars. But that's all going into a trust for Julia. I won't touch it. I make a good living, and I've invested wisely, but I don't have enough to afford this home. Anyway, I have it all worked out, let's change the subject." Jason insisted they not talk any further about personal finances, and so they discussed the economy, Jonathan relating some recent articles that he had read regarding the bond market. Jason asked him a number of questions related to credit markets in the automobile and student loan industries, and at ten p.m. Jonathan got up, gave Jason a hug and kiss, and said goodnight. Jason stood at the window overlooking Central Park. His time with Philip had been an unexpected miracle, but living with Philip and Julia in this condominium had been almost implausible. He would miss being here, and all the memories that came with it.

# CHAPTER 3

Jason awoke at four-thirty a.m. after another restless sleep. He critiqued four more research papers, and, at six-thirty a.m., Sophia unexpectedly walked in. She did not usually come on Saturday or Sunday mornings because either Jason or Philip, or sometimes both, would stay with Julia the entire day.

"Sophia, what are you doing here? Go home, I'm here all day." Jason sounded insistent.

"Sweetheart, I know how much you like to run. Go run. I'll make some breakfast for you and Julia, and, when you get back, I'll go home and rest until this afternoon."

Jason smiled and didn't protest. He was grateful. He despised missing his early morning runs. He quickly put on his warm running clothes and ran his six-mile course around Central Park. He returned to the smell of eggs and Canadian bacon, quickly shaved, showered and dressed, and went into the kitchen. He hugged Sophia just as Julia ran in and grabbed Jason's leg. Jason scooped her up, gave her a kiss and tickled her neck with his nose and lips, making Julia laugh hysterically as usual.

After breakfast, Sophia left, Jason dressed Julia, and the two went for a walk in Central Park. Although it was a clear cold late November day, the park was crowded with people going to the zoo, runners, ice skaters, sidewalk artists, and musicians playing their instruments for donations. They saw the sea lions at the zoo, Julia's favorite, and then they walked to FAO Schwartz. Jason bought the Lego set from the movie *Frozen*, her favorite movie. Julia could sing all of the songs from that movie which had amazed and delighted Jason. They stopped at a small café for lunch and then went home to await the Olsens who were to arrive around two p.m. Sophia had already started preparing a meal of tenderloin to be served with garlic mashed potatoes and white asparagus, which Jason avoided because it made his urine smell putrid. Jason smiled sadly to himself as he remembered how Philip would always tease him about his Jewish urine on the occasions that he did eat asparagus, and Jason would always retort that gentile urine was simply boring.

At precisely two p.m., the doorbell rang, and Jason greeted John and Evelyn Olsen along with Paul and Amy with long, warm, sad embraces. Jason took their coats, and Julia reluctantly put down her iPad at Jason's insistence, ran to each of them, and gave them hugs, after which she quickly ran back to her iPad. Jason noticed that Julia looked intently at Paul, who distinctly resembled Philip, and, at that moment, Jason knew that Julia understood Philip was not coming home. Sophia greeted everyone and continued preparing the meal, and Jason's father arrived a few minutes later to warm embraces by everyone. Jason served wine and cheese, and after an hour of small talk, Jonathan announced that Sophia and he were going to take a walk with Julia in the park. Julia jumped up immediately, said something in Spanish to Sophia, and the three departed.

"Jason, she is absolutely precious," Evelyn Olsen said, smiling. "Do you think she understands what has happened?"

"I just saw her look long and hard at Paul. She's so smart." Jason looked down. "I think she knows, but she hasn't said anything other than to ask me if I'm going on any long trips." Jason's eyes welled with tears. He hadn't cried in a while, and he was not going to start now. He took a deep breath. "I want you to know that I've found a nice condominium near here. I want to give this condominium back to you. It should remain in your family, and I think that would please Philip."

John Olsen interrupted. "Oh Jason, you are so wrong on so many levels. I guess very few people have ever said anything like that to you." John Olsen chuckled at that. "First of all, you *are* our family—every bit as much as Paul and Amy and Anna. Secondly, your moving out of this condominium would not please Phil at all. He would be furious. This is your condominium, free and clear. When you die, it will be Julia's. The furnishings and the art are yours to do with as you please. We've been through this before, and I don't want to hear any more about it. I've also paid off the mortgage on your condominium that Sophia lives in, so you own that free and clear as well."

Tears began trickling down Jason's face. "Dad, I can't let you do that. It's not right, and it certainly isn't fair to Paul and Anna. And I don't deserve all of this—"

John put his hand up to stop Jason. "Son, there is something you might not understand. I'm a very wealthy man. Paul and Anna will also be very wealthy one day, and they'll probably be wealthy on their own account before they inherit all of Evelyn's and my wealth. The cost of this condo and the one downstairs is nothing to me, and even the idea of you uprooting Julia and yourself and moving out of here is very upsetting to me." Jason tried to interrupt, but John put his hand up again.

"Also, you probably don't remember this, but in 2005, the first time Phil brought you home, I asked you where you would invest your money, and you replied that you would invest it in gold and gold mining stocks. Well, I did just that. Over the next five years, I turned a five-million-dollar investment into forty million dollars, and that was after I paid taxes, and all because of your good advice. And you probably don't remember, but in 2010 I asked you if it was time to get out of gold investments. You quoted Warren Buffet. I think he said 'get fearful when others are greedy,' and you said it seemed to you that the gold miners were getting greedy. So I sold, almost at the high. Jason, you made a lot of money for me. So just forget about this. I don't want to hear any more about it."

Jason couldn't control his tears and saw that Amy was crying as well. Paul scooted next to Jason and put his arms around him. John continued, "I just want to be certain you'll come and visit us with Julia frequently, and that you'll let us come to the city at least every other month so that we can spend time with you and Julia."

Jason wiped his tears. "Of course, I planned to come to Wilton every other weekend, just as before. I was hoping you would want that."

Evelyn said, "Thank God. We were worried that you wouldn't come as often—"

Paul interrupted. "Jason, we're here because we love you and want to be certain you're doing okay. But there is another reason we wanted to talk to you. We know how happy you and Phil were, and that happiness has been taken away from you. And a parent has been taken from Julia. None of us will ever get over this, particularly you. I can't imagine what it would be like if I lost Amy." Paul paused as Jason wiped his tears away. "When we were told about the circumstances of the accident, we immediately sent an investigator to San Francisco to get as much information as possible. We didn't want to give anyone time to plot some sort of cover up. What we know is that the truck driver was an insulin dependent diabetic, his blood glucose was below twenty, and he was basically unconscious when the accident occurred. The trucking company, which is a huge national firm, knew that the driver was on insulin. We also know they send all their drivers on the west coast to some quack doctor who is known to falsify medical records that are sent to the department of transportation in order for these drivers to get a commercial license. Who knows how many other truck drivers are out on the highways and on insulin?" Paul paused to give Jason time to assimilate the information. "The law is very clear on the issue of driving a commercial truck and taking insulin. I believe this doctor should be put out of business, and that there should be both a civil and criminal case against the doctor and the trucking company. We have a moral obligation to make sure this doesn't happen to anyone else. And to be blunt, you and Julia deserve to be heavily compensated for this. It's not going to bring Phil back, but at least you and Julia will never have any future financial concerns."

Jason sat stunned at the information. He had been told about the driver's hypoglycemia, but he had not given further thought to the circumstances surrounding the accident. He said in a soft voice, "I don't know what to say. In all honesty, I've been most worried about you two." Jason looked at John and Evelyn. "Losing Philip has been devastating for me, and, at the moment, I have a hard time envisioning a recovery from this. If something happened to Julia, I think I would have to kill myself. I cannot imagine what it would be like losing a child, even an adult child. I don't understand how you're so strong. If anyone deserves compensation, it is you both." Jason looked down as John took Evelyn's hand. "By the way, Philip had a two million dollar life insurance policy, and that money is going into a trust for Julia. So she will be well taken care of—"

John interrupted. "Son, Evelyn and I have each other to lean on, and we have you and Julia, and Paul and Amy and their kids, and Anna. We'll get through this, and we don't need any money. And, frankly, two million is nothing in terms of what you'll get from this company and doctor. Paul will represent you, and he'll be paid well for what he does, and if you want to give Anna something when it's all over, that's strictly your business. The gift you can give to Evelyn and me is to be our son, to regain your happiness, and to raise Julia to be a wonderful human being and part of our lives."

The only sound in the room was the sound air rushing from the heating vents and an occasional horn seventeen floors below. John and Paul Olsen looked at each other, and then Jason said, "What do I need to do?"

Paul quickly answered, "Nothing. Our people will continue their investigation, and, when they are through, we'll file a complaint against the trucking company and the doctor, and we'll ask the prosecuting attorney in San Francisco to look further into the case. The suit will be filed on your behalf and on Julia's behalf. I doubt that you will ever be deposed, and I doubt this will ever go to trial. The trucking company has already contacted us, and they're very worried, as they should be. We've told them that we would never settle for less than thirty million, and, even then, they would have to contend with the prosecuting attorney." Paul paused once again as his eyes moistened. "Jason, you know how I worshiped Phil. I'm devastated by all of this, but I'm also furious. This is something that we need to do, just to get some sense of closure."

Jason responded, "I doubt there'll ever be real closure for any of us, but I'll help you in any way I can."

John slapped his thigh. "Okay, enough of this morbid talk. I want to hear what is going on in that lab of yours, which I paid for. Am I getting my money's worth?" They all laughed, a welcome relief from the sadness.

Jason explained in simple detail the various projects going on in the lab. He explained the relationship of cancer and the immune system, mutations that occur in cancer cells that alter the immune response of humans, and the various projects in the lab that were trying to better define the mutations, how they cause cancer, and how some of the labs are creating proteins to counteract the mutations. He told them about the hundreds of articles that had been published and ended by saying, "So I hope that we're helping to give proper recognition to the Olsen name. We are certainly trying."

John laughed again. "Son, I've never met anyone so unnecessarily modest as you. I know about every honor you've received, and the Olsen Research Center has been written up in so many lay publications because of you, it's almost embarrassing. Harvey Glassman is somewhere smiling about the decision he made to put you in charge of his lab. And as you know, Harvey didn't smile very much. You've made everyone proud."

Jason turned characteristically red in the face, and the group continued talking about politics and the economy after Jason quickly changed the topic to current events. Sophia, Jonathan, and Julia returned, and Julia ran to Jason, sitting quietly on his lap punching her iPad. Occasionally, Jason would punch the iPad when Julia seemed stuck on the puzzle she was trying to solve. She would laugh, turn around, and hug Jason, and then resume punching her iPad, occasionally looking up and staring at Paul. Evelyn and Sophia served dinner, and the talk at the table was jovial and superficial despite the circumstances. Jason excused himself after dessert to give Julia a bath and tell her a bedtime story. He heard silence in the living room as he sang a song from *Frozen* with Julia. Julia loved singing with Jason, and she would typically laugh hysterically at the end of the song to Jason's delight. Jason tickled her neck with his nose and lips, kissed her, said his usual, "I love you, sweetheart," turned out the light, and returned to the living room where everyone had resumed discussing the recent presidential election.

"Well, Jason, if you ever get tired of research, you can become a professional singer." Paul chuckled as Jason rejoined the group. After another hour of conversation, which included Sophia who sat next to Jonathan, the Olsens left after warm embraces. Jonathan and Sophia left soon after, leaving Jason alone to digest all that had been said that evening. He took out his stationery and wrote a note to John and Evelyn Olsen:

*Dear Mom and Dad, I will be forever grateful for the short time I had with Philip. He was and will always be the love of my life. I never dreamed that I would have the good fortune to inherit another mother and father, and brother and sister. In addition to dear memories, Philip's legacy to me is that his family has become my family. Your generosity to me is overwhelming and unexpected, and I will do all in my power to repay you in love and devotion. Love, Jason*

# CHAPTER 4

O ver the next year, Jason Green-Olsen did indeed attest his love and devotion to the Olsen family. With rare exception, he went with Julia every other Saturday to Wilton, usually staying overnight at the Olsen mansion, returning home on Saturday night, only if there was an urgent need for him to be in his lab on Sunday. His considerable time spent with the Olsen family was striking, given the enormous demands resulting from his own work at the medical center and his labs. Sometimes Jason would bring his father, particularly on the holidays, and occasionally Sophia would join them as well. Jason called Evelyn most every day, and he avoided calling John every day, only because of his intense legal work. The relationship between the John and Evelyn and Jason was extraordinary and one that would rarely occur in the absence of common blood.

The relationship between Jason and Philip's brother and sister, Paul and Anna, also deepened over the year following Philip's death. Paul and Amy, and their two children, always had supper with Jason and Julia at the Olsen mansion the weekends that Jason would visit, and Paul would unexpectedly and frequently visit Jason at his office when he was in the city on business. If Jason were in a conference or in a lab meeting when Paul showed up, everyone knew that Paul was priority and that laboratory activities would have to wait. Paul's children, Ari and Zach, had become very attached to both Jason and Julia, and the three children played famously among themselves during their weekend visits.

And rarely did a week pass that Jason did not call Anna, who lived in Philadelphia and was next in line to run the University of Pennsylvania hospital system. Jason and Julia had also taken the train to Philadelphia to visit for a weekend several times over the year, and Anna would come to Wilton every six or eight weeks on a weekend that Jason and Julia visited. Anna had been in several failed relationships, at first, inexplicable to Jason because she was beautiful, vivacious, and brilliant. Jason had come to understand that Anna simply intimidated her significant others or did not devote enough time to the relationship because of her professional ambitions. She and Jason would go on long walks together in Wilton, reminiscing about Philip, and Anna would confide to Jason her struggles regarding her current love interest.

Jason startled Anna on one of their walks by making her understand that she was intimidating and perhaps not giving enough in her relationship. He was skillful in that regard because he never made statements, he simply asked questions—questions that made Anna realize that her priorities were, perhaps, not in the proper order.

After one of Jason's questions, Anna suddenly stopped, frowned for a moment, and then started laughing. "Jason, you are the smartest and wisest man I know." She hugged him, and they walked arm in arm back to the Olsen home.

Jason would go to Philip's grave on almost every visit, sometimes alone, sometimes with Anna or Paul, and stand silently for as long as an hour when he was by himself. When Paul or Anna was with him, they would usually have to take him by his arm and lead him away after ten or fifteen minutes. Tears had long been spent, but the emptiness that had initially consumed Jason persisted, and despite outward appearances of good humor and inspiring intellect, his sadness was evident to all of his family and close friends.

Julia turned five that first year after Philip's death and was happy and thriving. She was exceptionally smart and not only spoke English and Spanish fluently, but Jason had also begun teaching her Mandarin, which Julia practiced with two other Chinese Americans at her nursery school. She adored being with Jason, and they continued their weekend excursions to the museums and an occasional Broadway play—her favorite was *Matilda*. She loved the art museums and was able to start recognizing specific artists.

She only became angry when Jason wouldn't allow her to play with the iPad. On one occasion, she ran out of the living room, yelling, "I'm going to get a new daddy," only to return five minutes later to hug Jason and sit quietly in his lap while Jason finished reading a scientific paper. She had never mentioned Philip, but on visits to Wilton, she would frequently look at Uncle Paul for a long moment and, on occasion, would go to him and touch his face. The first time Julia did that, Jason began crying uncontrollably and had to quickly leave the room.

Jonathan Green had always been Jason's closest companion, from the time he was a small child, and that close relationship deepened even further after Philip's death. He would have dinner every Friday night with Jason, Julia, and Sophia, and he would frequently come for supper during the week. It also became clear to Jason that his father and Sophia had more than a casual relationship, and, finally six months after Philips death, on a Sunday afternoon, Jason said to him, "Dad, you know, you don't have to hide your relationship with Sophia any longer. I'm thrilled for you. I love Sophia. She is such an amazing person, and I couldn't imagine a better match for you." His father smiled and touched Jason on the face, and, after that, Jonathan and Sophia exposed their relationship to the delight of everyone. Sophia continued to live in the second floor condominium, and Jason suspected that his father frequently spent the night with Sophia, since it was not unusual for him to be with her in Jason's home at five-thirty a.m. to cook breakfast and take care of Julia.

Seven months after Philip's death, Paul and Jason went for their usual seven-mile run on a Saturday afternoon in Wilton. Paul had never been able to keep up with Jason, and Jason would run in place every few hundred yards to let Paul catch up. Midway during the run, Paul asked Jason to walk with him so they could talk. After catching his breath, Paul said, "Jason, we have to go to trial in San Francisco, and they are going to want you to testify. I'm not surprised. We're asking a lot. I know you don't want this, but it's necessary."

"They won't settle?" Jason asked.

"The company will settle for ten million, and the doctor for one million, and only with the proviso that we would not file a criminal complaint. I'm not willing to do either unless you insist." Paul stared at Jason as they continued their walk.

"I'm not concerned about the money, and I'm not worried about testifying, although I can't imagine what they could possibly want from me. And I will absolutely not expose Julia to any of this, under any circumstances." Jason stopped and looked at Paul as they continued their discussion.

"We have an order from the judge to excuse Julia from any involvement. However, if we don't settle, you would be required to testify. They don't even want your deposition. They feel they have enough information from the interrogatories that we answered."

They continued walking. Jason frowned, deep in thought. "What do you think they want from me?"

"We think they're going to try and sway the jury because of Philip's sexuality. I'm reluctant to mention this to you, but they apparently have some evidence of indiscretions on Philip's part. We're trying to find out details. This is an old-time firm, with old-time attorneys who apparently believe that being gay and having same-sex marriage is immoral and that a jury will feel the same. And, of all places, in San Francisco. They've threatened me that all of this will be brought out at trial if we don't settle." Paul continued to look at Jason for a reaction to this news.

After another hundred yards of silence, Jason stopped and looked at Paul. "I'll be happy to testify under a few conditions. First, I don't want you to object to any questions that they might ask me. There's nothing they could ask me that would embarrass me or denigrate Philip, and objections would simply make me look defensive. Secondly, I don't want to spend another minute on this prior to my testimony. Not a minute. I don't need or want to be prepared to testify by you or your team. And, finally, on direct examination, I want you to ask me only basic biographical questions—my age, what I do for a living, how long Philip and I were together and married, when we adopted Julia. I don't want to talk about my professional life. Nothing."

"Agreed," Paul answered immediately. "Just one question: Do you know anything about these so-called indiscretions?"

"Paul, I can handle that. Philip told me everything, and it meant nothing to me or to Philip. It had virtually no effect on our relationship, and I never gave it a second thought. Let's go."

Jason started running and ran the last three miles as fast as he could, leaving Paul far behind. He was incensed by the defense strategy. In fact, he thought, it was not a defense of their conduct at all but rather a separate prosecution of homosexuality and same-sex marriage. He quickly decided that he would do whatever he could to defeat those types of tactics.

Three months later, on a Wednesday, Jason, Jonathan, Sophia, and Julia flew to San Francisco so that Jason could testify on Thursday morning. Jason was insistent on bringing Julia. He wanted no thoughts entering her mind that he would be leaving her. Jason had arranged a private tour for Julia, his father, and Sophia while he was testifying.

Jason learned that he would be the last witness of the trial, which had already been ongoing for two weeks. Paul had explained to Jason that technically he was a witness for the defense, even though he was the plaintiff, and that Paul's decision not to call Jason as a witness had puzzled the plaintiff attorneys who were well aware of Jason's fame as a physician and researcher. The defense attorneys did agree to let Paul start the questions if, in turn, Paul agreed that he would only ask basic biographical information and would not ask any further questions after the defense finished their cross-examination. The defense attorneys were delighted with the arrangement, although Paul seemed confident that Jason's testimony would be devastating for the defense.

Paul related to Jason prior to his testimony what had transpired thus far. Paul had demonstrated unequivocal and overwhelming evidence that the doctor had falsified the records of, not only the truck driver who caused this accident, but also the medical records of numerous other truck drivers, thus allowing medically unqualified drivers to obtain commercial licenses. The defense's attempts to defend the doctor, using a highly compensated physician and an expert in trucking law, resulted in snickering among the jurors after Paul decimated their testimony on cross-examination. Documents from the trucking company confirmed that supervisors and executives, including the president of the company, knew that medical records of the involved driver had been falsified and that they did nothing to prevent him or numerous other unqualified individuals from driving their eighteen-wheeler trucks. Paul had an expert in trucking law testify that only under strict guidelines could an individual on insulin be issued a commercial license, and that the driver who caused this accident had not met any of those guidelines nor did the doctor or trucking company ask that the driver meet those guidelines. Paul had even obtained records that the driver had been taken to an emergency room on several occasions in the past because he had become unconscious as a result of low blood glucose levels and that the company had knowledge of those episodes. The evidence was devastating. Paul interrogated other experts, including an endocrinologist who explained what happened when an individual became hypoglycemic, and a financial expert who estimated the financial loss to Jason and Julia as a result of Philip's death.

Jason took the stand and was sworn in by the judge, a middle-aged man who was known for his intellect and patience. Jason looked at a packed courtroom and saw John Olsen sitting in the first row with a familiar looking young man. Paul began the questions.

"Please state your name for the jurors."

"My legal name is Jason Green-Olsen, with a hyphen

between Green and Olsen. I'm known in my professional world as Jason Green." Jason spoke clearly and with his typical deep southern accent.

"Please tell the jury where you were born and briefly your history up until your move to New York City." Paul was very direct and dispassionate.

"I was born in Mississippi, where I received my secondary education, my college education, and my medical school education."

"When did you graduate medical school?"

"In 2005."

"You have lived in New York City since that time?"

"Yes."

"I notice you have not lost your southern accent?"

"That's true, despite all attempts." Several jurors smiled at Jason.

"What degrees do you hold?"

Jason frowned at Paul, worried that he would go beyond basic biographical questions. "A bachelor's of science, a master's of Science, a PhD, and an MD."

"What is your occupation, Dr. Green?"

"I am a researcher and a teacher at Sinai Medical Center in New York City."

"You are gay?"

"Yes."

"When did you meet Philip Olsen?"

"The third week of my internship in Internal Medicine at Sinai Medical Center, the summer of 2005."

"And what were the circumstances of that meeting?"

"One of my hospital patients fell out of bed attempting to get up on her own, and I had to ask for an orthopedic consultant to operate on her fractured hip. The consultant was Philip Olsen."

"Please tell the jury briefly your subsequent relationship with Dr. Olsen."

"We began dating, we fell deeply in love, and, about a year later, we moved in together as domestic partners. Same sex marriage became legal in New York in June of 2011, and in August of that year we were married by Judge Lackland at Philip's home in Wilton, Connecticut." When Judge Lackland was mentioned, Jason saw that the trial judge sat up straight. Jason had discovered through an internet search that this judge was a classmate of Judge Lackland at Harvard Law School.

"You adopted a daughter?"

"Yes, a year after we married. We had the great fortune of being able to adopt a baby girl whom we named after my mother, who died of breast cancer during my second year of medical school."

"Was Dr. Olsen a good father?"

Tears welled in Jason's eyes, and he looked away from the jurors to gain control of his emotions and wipe the tears from his cheeks. After a moment, he turned back and quietly answered the unexpected question, "Yes, he was a wonderful father."

"Your honor, these are all the questions I have."

Jason saw that the defense attorneys and the judge appeared stunned at the brevity of the questioning, and there was complete silence in the courtroom as Paul turned around and walked toward his seat.

Suddenly, Paul turned back around. "Your honor, Dr. Green specifically demanded of me that I ask him only basic biographical questions. He will be angry with me for doing this, but the jury deserves to know a bit more about Dr. Green."

Jason held his hand up in a gesture to stop Paul, but Paul ignored him.

"Therefore, I would like to submit this *Time Magazine* as evidence to the jury of Dr. Green's character. The magazine has Dr. Green on the cover, which is entitled

'Research Pioneer.' I would ask the court to encourage the jury to read the article as part of their deliberations."

The defense attorney stood. "Your honor, I object. There is no evidence being presented as to the veracity of this article."

The judge looked at Paul. "Mr. Olsen?"

"Your honor, I submitted this magazine to the defense in response to some of their interrogatories several months ago. I specifically told them this magazine would be presented at trial. With all due respect, defense counsel has had more than enough time to find evidence that would disprove the veracity of this article. If they have such evidence, I would encourage defense counsel to ask Dr. Green about it during his cross-examination." Paul looked directly at the defense attorney who remained silent, frowning.

The judge looked at the defense counsel. "Will you be challenging the veracity of this *Time Magazine* article?"

"No, your honor," the attorney quietly answered.

The jurors were smiling, and the judge responded, "A copy of the article is to be given to each juror, and I would encourage each juror to read the article as part of their deliberations. Your witness, counsel."

The defense attorney stood at his table. "What should I call you during this questioning? Dr. Green or Dr. Olsen, or Dr. Green-Olsen?"

"Sir, call me by any name that pleases you. I would be pleased if you called me Jason." The jurors laughed audibly.

"And you are a homosexual?"

"Yes, sir, I am."

"And would you say that your marriage with Philip Olsen was a happy marriage?"

"Sir, I pray that the relationship you have with your wife is half as fulfilling and happy as the relationship that Philip and I had. We had what I would describe as a perfect marriage."

"Are you aware that Dr. Olsen had sexual encounters with other men on several occasions when he traveled?"

"Yes, Philip tried to tell me about those incidents. I was never—"

The attorney interrupted Jason. "I just wanted a yes or no answer, that's all."

Paul stood up to object, but Jason put his hand up again, and, this time, Paul sat back down.

"Sir, I traveled all the way from New York City to San Francisco to answer your questions. Please give me the courtesy of allowing me to answer your questions fully." Jason looked directly at the defense attorney who did not answer.

The judge intervened. "Dr. Green, please finish your answer."

"Philip tried to tell me about those encounters, but I stopped him each time. I knew he had certain needs that I could not provide, and those so-called indiscretions had no impact on our relationship, which, as I said, I considered perfect."

"He cheated on you, and you say you had the perfect marriage?" the attorney snickered.

"Sir, the definition of cheating is to deceive or break a rule. A third definition of cheating might be to be unfaithful. Philip never deceived me, he never broke a rule that we made, and he was the most faithful and loving partner and father one could hope for. I never thought twice about his so-called indiscretions."

The defense attorney began rummaging through his papers. After a pause, he continued, "Dr. Green, you are wealthy?"

"Sir, could you please define wealthy?"

"Well, you live in a very fancy condominium on Central Park."

"Yes, sir, Philip's father gave that condominium to Philip and me as a wedding gift. The condominium is worth a lot of money, I suspect, several million dollars."

"And what other assets do you have?

"I have several hundred thousand dollars in stocks and bonds as well as a pension plan through my employer that has several hundred thousand dollars."

"How much money do you need—strike that question. Just how much money do you think you deserve because of this tragic accident?"

Jason answered slowly, "Sir, I'm not certain what you mean by deserve. Furthermore, you and my attorney picked a jury to make that determination. Whatever that number is, I would pay a thousand times that to have just one more day with Philip." Jason paused and looked down as tears moistened his eyes. The defense counsel started to interrupt, but Jason put his hand up, and the defense counsel remained silent. "In the end, I would like to see a judgment that will make certain that doctors and trucking companies will not violate the laws that are meant to prevent tragedies like the one that took Philip from me and my daughter."

There was utter silence in the courtroom, and one of the jurors began to cry. The defense attorney sat down.

After a long moment, the judge said, "Mr. Olsen, redirect?"

"I have no questions, your honor."

"We'll recess for fifteen minutes and then hear closing arguments."

Everyone stood as the jury left the courtroom. As Jason stood down from the witness stand, the judge said, "Dr. Green, please give Judge Lackland my warm regards, and my deepest condolences to you and your daughter."

"Thank you, Judge." Jason nodded and walked down to where Paul was standing. Without saying anything, Paul hugged Jason as John Olsen and the young man sitting next to him walked to them.

John Olsen kissed Jason on the cheek. "Jason, you remember Kevin O'Malley?"

Jason frowned and looked closely at Mr. O'Malley. He looked to be in his early thirties, very handsome, tall with a square face, short blond hair, and deep blue eyes.

"You were the president's aide?" Jason asked.

Kevin smiled. "Yes, Dr. Green. It's been over ten years. It's a pleasure to see you again, although not under these circumstances. I was devastated to hear about Phil. My profound condolences to you and Julia."

"Thank you. But what brings you here?" Jason asked puzzled.

John Olsen interjected with a smile, "Jason, Kevin has been working for our firm for almost seven years. He retired from the marines in 2008 when the president left office and opened up an investigation and security firm in New York City. Kevin's people were the ones who found out all of the information regarding the doctor and the trucking firm."

"Well, thank you for that," Jason replied with a sad smile. "Paul, Dad, Mr. O'Malley, I'm going to leave you now and catch up with the others. I hope you don't mind if I don't stick around for closing arguments."

"Of course," Paul said. "A car is waiting for you outside. We'll see you at six-thirty at Parallel Thirty-Seven in the Ritz."

Jason got into the limousine that was waiting for him outside the courthouse. He met his father, Sophia, and Julia at the aquarium where Julia was delighting in the penguins. After lunch, they went to the Children's Crea-tivity Museum and then returned to Ritz at four-thirty p.m. to rest before supper at six-thirty.

At six-thirty p.m., the four went into Parallel 37, Ja-son carrying a happy but tired Julia with her iPad. Paul and John Olsen along with Kevin O'Malley were waiting as they walked in. The maître de opened a bottle of Dom Perignon, which he began pouring as the group greeted with hugs and kisses.

"We should all raise our glasses and give a toast to a bittersweet victory," Paul said with a smile. "Jason, I ex-pected that you would be on the stand for several hours, but the defense obviously realized that you did more harm to their defense than good. You were spectacular."

"There's a verdict already?" Jason asked surprised.

"The jury was out only two hours. An hour into their deliberation, they sent a note to the judge, asking if there was a limit to punitive damages. They came back with twenty million in lost wages and thirty-five million in punitive damages. The verdict was unanimous. Five mil-lion was assigned to the doctor, and fifty million was as-signed to the company."

Julia was playing with her iPad as Jason sat silently, stunned at the news. He saw everyone silently staring at him. He finally looked up and with a sad smile said, "Okay, let's drink to this success. Paul, Dad, Mr. O'Malley, I thank you for all that you've done. I'm sorry I was not more cooperative with your efforts. We can talk more specifics later." He pointed to Julia.

Jonathan Green looked at Sophia who nodded and smiled, and then he said, "Let's keep our glasses raised for just a moment. After losing my wife almost fourteen years ago, I never imagined that I would or could ever have another true love in my life. I did not believe that I was capable of loving two women, that I only had enough

love for one. But I was wrong. I will die still deeply loving my first wife, but I will die also loving as deeply my
second wife. Sophia and I are to be married."

Jason immediately started crying, and Julia quickly
climbed onto Jason's lap. "Why are you crying, Daddy?"

"Because your papa is going to marry Sophia, and I
am crying because I'm so happy for them," Jason smiled
through his tears.

Jonathan continued. "I want you to know, Jason, that
eventually you will also find happiness again. So here's a
toast to future happiness and second chances."

Jason handed Julia to Paul and stood up. He went to
Sophia, stood her up, and hugged her tightly, and then to
his father whom he held tightly and for a long moment.
He picked up his glass of champagne and said, "I'm so
happy for you both. I wish you a long and happy marriage. I just hope you don't plan on having children. Julia
and I are counting on your help." Everyone laughed and
congratulated the couple, and the remainder of the evening was filled with happy conversation and an intellectual
give and take between Jonathan and John regarding the
economy. John particularly enjoyed talking with Jonathan
about the economy, and Jason knew that many of John's
investment strategies had been based upon those discussions. Jason was mostly quiet, tending to Julia, sitting her
on his lap when she had finished eating and helping her
with a new iPad puzzle. Jason saw that everyone present
looked frequently at him, and he knew, in spite of the trial outcome, that he was unable to conceal his unrelenting
sadness. Jason also noticed that Kevin O'Malley sat silently the entire evening, eyes fixed upon him and Julia.

# CHAPTER 5

The entire group flew back to the East Coast in John Olsen's corporate jet on Friday morning. The Danbury airport was only twenty minutes from the Olsen mansion, and John convinced Jason, Jonathan, and Sophia to stay over Friday night. Kevin O'Malley hugged Paul and John goodbye at the Danbury airport. Jason was surprised at the affection. Obviously, there was a close relationship between the Olsens and Kevin to which Jason had not been privy. Kevin congratulated Jonathan and Sophia, tenderly patted Julia on the cheek, shook Jason's hand with a brief but inscrutable smile, and then left the group.

Evelyn and Amy prepared a large meal and insisted that Jason sing the Sabbath prayers and light the candles, a tradition which had always delighted John and Evelyn who were Presbyterian, and particularly Amy who continued to be an observant Jew and was raising their children Jewish with the blessing of the Olsen family. Jason continued to resist introducing any religion to Julia, despite continued protests from Jonathan. Jason was an atheist and simply didn't see the need for religion, but he had noticed that Julia had always been fascinated when

Jason sang the Sabbath prayers, and so he was starting to rethink the idea of letting Julia be exposed to religion and ultimately make her own decisions regarding her beliefs.

John asked Jason and Paul to join him in his study after the meal, leaving Jonathan to supervise the children and the women to clean the dishes. Jason thought that John and Paul probably wanted to discuss the monies awarded by the jury, and so he preempted the discussion by asserting that Paul, Anna, and he would get equal amounts after the legal fees and expenses were paid.

Paul immediately protested. "Jason, that's not going to happen. I'll be getting a hefty bonus for this case, so I'll be well taken care of. If you want to give Anna money, that's your business."

Jason replied in his southern accent, always unintentionally embellished when he was anxious, "Paul, any legal fees you get, you deserve. The monies after legal fees and expenses will be split three ways, period. It's not a point of further discussion. So do whatever is necessary to accomplish that. That's my desire, and I hope you'll respect that. So let's go back in and join the kids." Jason stood up.

"Wait." John motioned for Jason to sit back down. "We didn't want to talk to you about money tonight. That's not why we brought you in here. What we wanted to talk to you about is that it's been almost a year since Phil's been gone. We're all still, and will always be, sad. But life goes on. And it's time you move on as well. We really just wanted to assure you that, should you start seeing someone, it would not be offensive to us in the least. Quite the contrary. We want you to be happy, and Phil would want that as well. It's time you start having a social life, and nothing would make us happier than to see you develop a relationship. We were concerned that you might think we would be upset if you started seeing someone."

Jason sat quietly listening to John, trying not to cry. He had always cried so easily when emotional, and he hated that about himself. He thought it made those around him uncomfortable. "Well, I appreciate that. But, honestly, I have no interest at all in going out with strangers or developing a relationship. My life is full with Julia, and you, and my father and Sophia. And I'm so busy in the lab. You know, we are on the cusp of some major advances in cancer treatment." Jason paused, starting to stand, and then smiled at John and Paul. "Well, I appreciate your thoughtfulness, but I really just don't have the time or the desire, and I'm happy with my life as is."

"No, you're not. Sit down." Paul was uncharacteristically stern. "Having Phil to love and share is what made you happy. It wasn't your lab or even Julia. It was Phil, and you'll not be happy until there is another Phil. And don't insult me with the bullshit that there will never be another Phil. There are other wonderful people out there, and one of them is there for you." Paul paused and then continued, more controlled. "Now I'm not saying that Kevin O'Malley is the one, but it wouldn't hurt you to at least go and have coffee with him."

"So this is about setting me up with Kevin O'Malley?" Jason chuckled, shaking his head. "I was curious how y'all hooked up with him. I was surprised to see him at the trial."

John sighed. "Well, as I told you in San Francisco, he opened a security and investigation firm in New York City in 2008, and it has become the most respected firm of its kind anywhere. When he first opened up, it was just Kevin and one employee, and he contacted all of the legal firms in the area to announce his services. I immediately recognized him and invited him for an interview, and he has been doing all of our investigative work ever since. He now has over two hundred employees, he does work for the best legal firms, and his bodyguards protect many of the foreign dignitaries and celebrities who come into the city. He's an impressive guy."

Paul nodded. "He's always asked about you and Phil. He told us that he had become obsessed with you when you met with the president at Camp David. We tried many times to have him contact you and Phil, but he always declined. We thought that maybe you two could set him up with someone. He's never found anyone who has interested him. Anyway, he never contacted you and Phil because I think that he was worried about how he would react to being with you. In any case, a few months ago, he asked both of us whether we would be offended if he asked you to go out, and, of course, we told him we would be delighted. So if he happens to call you, it wouldn't hurt you to have some coffee with him."

Jason shook his head. "Well, I rarely drink coffee. Look, I'm grateful for your thoughtfulness and concern, but I really have no interest in going out with anyone at this time. When I'm ready, you'll be the first to know. Let's go see the kids." Jason got up and walked out, leaving Paul and John shaking their heads.

Jason went to the lower level family room where Paul's two children and Julia were playing, Jonathan sitting on the floor, characteristically involved in their activities. Jason sat admiring his father, recalling the entire episode with Chao Fang. Jason had discovered in 2005, when he was an intern working in Harvey Glassman's lab, that Chao Fang, one of Glassman's top research fellows, had been stealing data as part of a larger Chinese spy ring. Jason had been taken to Camp David to explain to the president and to the directors of the FBI and CIA what he had discovered, and while at Camp David had met Kevin O'Malley who was in the marines and an aide to the president. That entire day had remained a blur to Jason, but he remembered Kevin O'Malley because he spoke fluent Mandarin and was very attractive. That same evening after returning to New York City, Jason had been shot in the chest and barely survived. The shooting was an attempt to prevent Jason from divulging what he had discovered but which had, unbeknownst to the conspirators, already been disclosed to the highest authorities. While recovering in the hospital, Jason vividly remembered the president visiting him along with Kevin O'Malley. During that visit, Kevin had spoken to Jason in Mandarin and told him that if he and Philip ever ended their relationship, he would be very interested in seeing him. Jason had smiled and thanked him in Mandarin for the compliment. Philip had been jealous, Jason remembered, smiling to himself, but he quickly forgot about Kevin O'Malley. Jason had never even known his name.

☙❧☙

There was a bittersweet transition in Jason's personal life over the next three months. The upcoming marriage of his father to Sophia necessitated a frantic search to find a full time nanny for Julia. Jonathan and Sophia had protested that they would continue to serve in that role, but Jason would not consider that possibility. He wanted his father and Sophia to have a normal married life. Jonathan had a large condominium only a few blocks away, and Jason would keep Sophia's condominium for the new nanny. He knew and was relieved that his father and Sophia would continue to be very involved with Julia, but Jason insisted that they should have their own life together. Besides, money was no longer an issue. After legal fees and taxes were taken out, Jason's share of the trial

award was 8.25 million dollars. He no longer had to worry about supporting an expensive condominium or a full-
time nanny.

Jason wanted the new nanny to speak fluent Spanish
so that Julia would continue growing up bilingual. Sophia
had interviewed dozens of women with ages ranging
from the mid-twenties to the mid-fifties. She was meticu-
lous in her interviews, and with Jason's permission, John
had asked Kevin O'Malley to do background checks on
the three finalists. Jason laughed when John had made
that suggestion. "Still trying to fix me up?"

John smiled and responded, "No, son. Kevin is just
the best at this. But it still wouldn't hurt for you to see
him."

Alejandra Hernandez had emigrated from Argentina
to New York City with her husband and two year old
daughter twenty four years ago at the age of twenty-two.
Alejandra had worked as a hotel maid at the Algonquin
Hotel since arriving in New York City, and she had refused numerous offers to go into management because
she was unwilling to spend long hours away from her
husband, who had worked in construction and had died of
leukemia two years ago. Their daughter had graduated
from Cornell University and was teaching mathematics at
a private high school in Manhattan. Sophia had reported
that Alejandra had a wonderful personality, and an extensive background check by Kevin O'Malley's firm, after
interviews with her neighbors, workmates, friends, and
employer, revealed that she had a stellar work history and
no red flags in her personal life. Jason and Julia liked her
immediately, and, after several trial days with Sophia
looking on at a distance, Jason offered and Alejandra accepted the position, which Jason assured her would be
available at least until Julia went to college.

Alejandra was astonished at the annual salary of one

hundred thousand dollars and the free use of the second floor condominium, although much was expected from her. Sophia made clear that she was expected to prepare breakfast very early on weekdays while Jason did his six mile run. She would be responsible for walking Julia to and from school daily, staying with Julia until Jason came home in the evening, keeping Jason's home clean, and cooking supper on weekdays. She was also expected to be available on weekends should Jason need to work, and Jason had requested that she communicate with Julia in Spanish whenever possible. After three months, Julia had become very attached to Alejandra, and Jason was delighted with the arrangement. Alejandra was quickly becoming part of the family.

Jonathan and Sophia married in March of 2017 in a combined Jewish and Catholic wedding ceremony in the Terrace Room of the Plaza Hotel, officiated by Judge Lackland, the same Judge who had married Jason and Philip. Jason had maintained a close relationship with Judge Lackland, and it was at Jason's suggestion that he officiate the ceremony, even though everyone knew it would be emotional for Jason. The entire Olsen family was present, along with several of Jonathan's relatives and the few relatives of Sophia who lived in the New York City area. A number of Jason's close friends who had also maintained a close relationship with Jonathan were also present. In all, there were one hundred wedding guests.

Jason's sister, Susie, had been a great source of stress for Jason. She did come to the wedding with her two children, who were ten and twelve years of age, only after Jason threatened to sever his relationship with her if she did not attend. Susie had gone through a bitter divorce several years previously and had inexplicably distanced herself from Jonathan and Jason. She had not even attended Philip's funeral. Jonathan visited her often and gave her money. Her ex-husband had a failed business, and she and her children lived on her teacher's salary. Jason sent money to her frequently, as well, which she always accepted but without acknowledgment. Jason called her weekly but the conversations were short, and it was clear that she was bitter and resentful.

Jason had not visited Susie in New Orleans since he had married Philip, primarily because of his work demands and his unwillingness to leave Julia. But Jason had sent plane tickets for Susie and her children to come to New York, tickets that had never been used. After the financial award from the trial, Jason had funded 529 college savings plans for Susie's children with several hundred thousand dollars and had also sent Susie a gift of several hundred thousand dollars with barely a thank you. When Jason picked Susie and her children up at the airport for the wedding, he held her tightly and would not let her go until they both were crying. There was no discussion after that greeting about their past relationship, but following that visit, their relationship normalized, and they talked frequently. Susie and her children stayed weeks in New York City every summer after her father's wedding, and Jason became an important part of their lives.

Jason and Julia continued to go to Wilton every other weekend, and there was rarely a day that Jason did not talk to Evelyn, John, or Paul. There could not have been a closer family relationship. Three months after returning from San Francisco, the Olsens had a holiday party in early December. Jason knew most of the guests, including Judge Lackland and a number of physicians and administrators from Sinai Medical Center with whom John Olsen had formed close relationships. Also at the party was Kevin O'Malley, who came with another man. Jason had suspected that the Olsens had invited Kevin for obvious reasons, although it appeared that Kevin now had a companion.

Jason returned to the party after putting Julia to bed. Kevin and his companion were in conversation with a group and Jason joined a group of researchers from Sinai, including Seth Goldberg, his closest friend and confidant. Out of the corner of his eye, Jason saw Kevin break off from his group and approach him.

Kevin tapped Jason on the shoulder. "Dr. Green, can I speak with you?"

Jason turned, and the two moved a few feet away. Jason smiled. "Please don't call me Dr. Green. You're making me feel very old."

"I just wanted to see how you were doing," Kevin said with a tentative smile. Jason carefully studied Kevin's face. He was probably thirty-four or thirty-five, definitely younger than him, with a handsome face, short blond hair, and blue eyes. He was not quite as tall as Philip, but he clearly worked out in a gym, probably daily given his strong physique.

"I'm doing well, thanks for asking," Jason replied. "Life goes on as John Olsen likes to say."

After an uncomfortable pause, Kevin said, "I'll just be blunt." Another pause, as Kevin's face turned beet red. Jason liked that, since blushing was a trait that he himself had never been able to overcome. "I would really like to see you sometime. Perhaps you would have dinner with me."

"Kevin, I'm not sure I'm ready for any of that," Jason said, also starting to blush. "Besides, it appears that you have a friend."

Kevin smiled. "Mark is just a friend. He's just been through a bad divorce after a twelve year marriage, and I'm trying to divert his attention."

"Well, perhaps we could have coffee sometime." Jason looked down.

"Look, Jason, I'm not asking you to marry me." Kevin forced a smile. "But since Camp David, there hasn't been a day that I've not thought of you. That's been more than eleven years." Kevin paused, expecting a response. "At least give me the chance to get to know you. I know I'm being aggressive, and that's not my nature, but I also know I would have regrets the rest of my life had I not tried."

Jason laughed. "That you've thought of me every day for the past eleven years makes me question your sanity."

Kevin's eyebrows lifted. "Well, obviously, I saw something in you that Phil saw as well. I've become close friends with Paul and Amy. They told me how obsessed Phil was with you after he first met you. So I plead guilty to the same insanity." They both laughed.

"Well, let me call you next week, and we can set up dinner. I need to look at my schedule and make sure that Alejandra is available." Jason forced another smile, feeling very ambivalent about going out on a date.

"Thanks, Jason. I'll look forward to your call." Kevin handed Jason his business card on which he had written his cell phone number, looked at Jason and smiled, and turned to rejoin his group.

# CHAPTER 6

**B**ut Jason didn't call Kevin O'Malley. Jason found Kevin physically beautiful, intelligent, and affable, and there had been a history with Kevin going back twelve years. He had even fantasized about Kevin over the years, not knowing what had happened to him or even knowing his name. Instead, Jason wrote Kevin a note: *Kevin, I'm sorry I did not call. I'm just not ready. I hope that you understand. Jason.* Jason received a note from Kevin the following week, which said: *Jason, I am patient. When you are ready, I'll be waiting. Kevin.*

Kevin's note distressed Jason. He had no rational reason for his reluctance to have dinner with Kevin. Paul had confronted him on numerous occasions about going out with Kevin, and Jason would argue that he was too busy in the lab and that he would start an attending rotation on January first on the same unit that he had begun his internship in 2005. Jason knew that Paul understood the real reason he was reluctant to go out with Kevin was that he was not ready to let go of Philip and perhaps, more importantly, was not ready to bring another person into Julia's life.

Jason had a daily routine from which he rarely deviated. After his six-mile run at five a.m. each morning, he would eat breakfast prepared by Alejandra, shower, and dress, and then awaken Julia with whom he would snuggle before leaving for work. He would almost always walk the two miles to work and arrive by seven-thirty a.m. Most of the postdoctoral fellows and PhD students were already working when he arrived, and Eric Adelman, who had been promoted to a full professorship at Jason's insistence and designated as Associate Director of the Glassman Lab, arrived promptly at eight a.m.

For the first fifteen minutes after arriving, Jason went over inventory requests by each of the fellows. He then spent the next forty-five minutes visiting each lab. Each postdoc fellow expected Jason's visit and was prepared for a three-minute update from the prior day. Unexpected problems were discussed, and Jason routinely stunned the fellows by demonstrating complete command of the minutest of details in their ongoing experiments. At eight-thirty a.m., Jason met with Eric to discuss all of the ongoing experiments and, in particular, the lab that Eric was leading, the bioinformatics lab. Jason and Eric had developed computer programs that were capable of analyzing huge quantities of data, and this lab analyzed not only the data that accumulated from the other thirteen Glassman labs but also data from hundreds of labs across the US, Europe, and Asia. The monies that the Glassman lab received from these contractual relationships paid for the further development and maintenance of the bioinformatics lab as well as several other labs for which grant money was not adequate to meet costs.

In addition to the sophisticated programs used to analyze data, Jason and Eric had developed computer programs that were able to model proteins based upon genetic codes and proteins that would have binding affinity for other proteins of known structure. For example, if the structure of a protein unique for a tumor could be determined, the computer program could structure a protein that would have high binding affinity for that unique tumor protein, and then such a protein could in many cases be synthesized in a test tube. That synthesized protein could then be used in several ways. A chemotherapy agent could be attached to the protein and, after binding to the tumor protein, could, in theory, result in the death of the tumor cell. Or if that tumor protein were responsible in some way for tumor growth, binding the synthesized protein to the tumor protein could, in theory, block tumor growth.

As far as Jason and Eric knew, there were no other computer programs that were able to model proteins in this manner. Jason had been unwilling to sell this program to many enthusiastic pharmaceutical companies that had offered enormous amounts of money for use of that program, although he did partner with numerous labs in both academics and industry to help with their endeavors. As a result, Jason and Eric coauthored literally hundreds of papers published in all of the major journals.

Jason also knew that he was an enigmatic figure in the research community and was repeatedly reminded of that fact by his research colleagues at Sinai Medical Center. Jason would usually respond by smiling and shrugging his shoulder. Jason was probably the most prolific scientific investigator in the world, and yet he was never seen at research symposiums or scientific meetings. His postdoc fellows always attended and presented their findings at these meetings, frequently dominating the scientific sessions. The "Green Fellows" had the reputation of giving flawless presentations. The postdoc fellows routinely returned from these scientific meetings, reporting to Jason, among other more substantial information, that at evening social events the Green fellows were always surrounded by other investigators wanting to know all about Jason Green.

Furthermore, Jason never aspired to be part of the political structure of any of the medical or research organizations that virtually everyone in the academic community coveted. Cliques of the most successful and powerful researchers were always part of academia and had great influence in political circles and at the National Institutes Health. Such cliques literally determined where billions of research dollars were to be distributed. Jason's mentor, Harvey Glassman, had been an important part of those powerful research cliques, but Jason had no interest in partaking. Money seemed to flow to his research labs, both from National Institutes of Health and industrial grants, not to mention the contractual relationships he had developed from his bioinformatics lab, and Jason shunned the many attempts from other powerful academic figures to join these elite groups.

Instead, Jason's gratification was almost primal—it came simply from his research successes and, even more, from the successes of his fellows and students. To leave Julia and Philip, now just Julia, in order to attend a scientific meeting or to receive a prestigious award was out of the question, and the powers at Sinai Medical Center had long ceased trying to convince Jason to be more forthcoming in that regard. Jason had even refused to attend a White House dinner given by the president for the top American scientists. Jason received a handwritten note from the new President, which said that he was sorry he could not attend but looked forward to meeting him the next time he was in New York City.

Many of those elite and powerful researchers had visited Jason at his lab over the years, mostly because they were curious about Jason, but also because many of them partnered with Jason's bioinformatics lab. Jason was always courteous and made time for them, although he politely refused all social invitations other than having lunch at the faculty club in the hospital complex. Many of these very prominent researchers attempted to coerce him into accepting visiting professorships, but Jason had developed an exquisite manner of rejecting those offers without insulting these powerful men and women.

Two weeks before Philip's death, a Nobel-Prize-winning researcher from Harvard visited Jason to discuss a contractual relationship with the bioinformatics lab and to learn about his protein modeling computer program. Eric Adelman brought him to Jason's office after meeting him in the lobby of the building. "Dr. Green, it is certainly a pleasure meeting you after all this time."

Jason quickly stood up and went around his desk. "Dr. Ludmerer, it's such an honor to meet you. I've followed your research for many years, sir, and you have truly inspired me." Jason's southern accent was exaggerated, as usual, when he was excited, and in fact, Jason was genuinely excited to meet this famous scientist. At Dr. Ludmerer's suggestion the two had agreed to call each other by first names, although it was difficult for Jason to abide by that.

The two discussed their respective research efforts and came to an agreement regarding Dr. Ludmerer's use of the bioinformatics lab. At the end of the two-hour meeting, Dr. Ludmerer said something unexpected. "Jason, I've been authorized to offer you a fully endowed and distinguished professorship at Harvard. You can name your price, and you can have all the space you need and more. They will even give you your own building if need be. We want you there."

Jason was stunned at the unexpected offer but did not hesitate to respond. "Dr. Ludmerer, I mean Kenneth, I'm completely humbled by your offer and am dumbfounded.

To work in the same environment as you and the other amazing researchers at Harvard would be a dream come true for any scientist. But, sir, far more important to me is my husband and daughter, and the rest of my family and friends who live here. I'm completely at home here, and I could not, under any circumstances, uproot my family and leave my dear friends, even for the tremendous prestige that such a position would afford. I do hope you understand and also know how grateful I am."

Dr. Ludmerer smiled and after a long pause said, "I was told that would be your response. I'm close to a few of your fellow professors here, and when I talked to them about the offer, they simply laughed and said 'good luck.' I admire you, Jason, and look forward to getting to know you better." They shook hands, and Dr. Ludmerer left. Jason never told Philip or anyone else about that offer, nor did he ever have second thoughts about his response. Three weeks later, Dr. Ludmerer attended Philip's funeral, although Jason had only a vague memory of his presence.

The fourteen separate Glassman labs, what most referred to as the Green labs, continued to be highly productive without exception. Most of the labs concentrated on mechanisms of cell growth in various tumors, and the amount of information being gathered was enormous. Jason was particularly excited about one of his labs led by Dr. Marcus Blumenthal, a brilliant postdoc fellow in his third year with Jason. Dr. Blumenthal had received his MD and PhD from the University of Michigan, and, after a thirty-minute interview three years previous, Jason had accepted him for the position, recognizing immediately this young researcher's potential. Dr. Blumenthal had one PhD student working with him, Craig Henderson, who had graduated from Yale with a degree in biomedical engineering and who was ambitious and hardworking. The

Blumenthal lab, as Jason referred to it, also employed three research assistants.

The Blumenthal lab had discovered a peptide, a small protein, on the surface of human pancreas cancer cells that binds to a cell surface protein on T-lymphocytes, cells that have the ability to kill cancer cells. They discovered that when this peptide on the pancreas cancer cell binds to the surface protein on the lymphocyte, the lymphocyte self-destructs immediately. Ordinarily, the T-lymphocyte would destroy the cancer cell, but the pancreas cancer cell in a sense discovered a way of knocking out these protective T-lymphocytes, thus allowing the pancreas cancer cells to grow untethered. That discovery alone was exciting enough, and the lab made many attempts at isolating this cancer peptide in order to determine its exact structure. However, isolation of the peptide had eluded the team. At Jason's suggestion, the Blumenthal researchers successfully isolated the T-lymphocyte surface protein and determined its structure. Using Jason and Eric's sophisticated protein modeling computer program, a new protein, based on the structure of the isolated lymphocyte protein, was synthesized and shown to bind even more vigorously to the cancer peptide than the T-lymphocyte surface protein. Initial studies showed that, when this newly synthesized protein was added to the pancreas cancer cells, the T-lymphocytes maintained their ability to destroy the pancreas cancer cells. Everyone in the lab was excited about these discoveries and the potential this new kind of protein had in controlling or even curing pancreas cancer. Animal and ultimately human studies were in the offing. The excitement in Jason's lab was palpable.

# CHAPTER 7

On January 1, 2017, Jason began a six-week rotation on the general medicine unit as an attending physician. He would have ultimate responsibility for fifteen to twenty hospitalized patients taken care of by an intern who was in the first year of training after medical school graduation, a resident who was in the second or third year of training after medical school, and two third year medical students. Although attending on the medical unit was a major time commitment, requiring him to round with his team two hours daily, six days a week, he enjoyed this time immensely. Many of his own attending physicians had had a major impact on him during his medical school, intern, and residency years, and being able to have an impact on these young students and physicians was gratifying and fun for Jason. He gave little thought that he was considered the premier attending in Internal Medicine and that the medical students, interns, and residents all vied to be placed on his service.

On Monday, January second, at nine-fifty a.m., Jason walked slowly from his office to 10200, the floor at Sinai Medical Center where he started his own internship in 2005, remembering his own anxiety on that first day and his incredible journey during that internship year. A wave of sadness once again overwhelmed him as he recalled his initial confrontation with Philip.

Jason saw his team stand and face him as he approached and immediately put aside those thoughts, smiling at the young physicians.

The resident held out her hand. "Dr. Green, welcome. I'm Sarah Nash, your resident for the next six weeks. We're so excited to have you as our attending."

Jason shook Dr. Nash's hand. "I've heard great things about you, Dr. Nash, and I'm thrilled to be here with you. I know you came from the University of Chicago undergraduate, a wonderful place, and came here for your medical education." Jason turned to the intern. "And Dr. Clancy, I understand you did some research with a friend of mine at Southwestern, and he speaks very highly of you. It's a pleasure to meet you, and I look forward to working with you as well." Jason had a sudden flashback of introducing himself to Harvey Glassman the first day of his internship. He remembered Dr. Glassman saying that Jason's research mentor at the University of Mississippi, Franklin Deutsch, was a good friend and that he had said nice things about Jason, and that he hoped Jason didn't make a liar of him. Jason had been taken aback at the aloofness of Dr. Glassman.

"Thank you, Dr. Green. When I told Dr. Kaminsky you were going to be my attending, he asked me to give you his warm regards."

"Thank you for that." Jason turned to the two students. "And your names?"

"I'm Stephanie Summers, Dr. Green."

"Ms. Summers, it's a pleasure to meet you. I detect a bit of a Carolina accent."

"You're right, sir. I grew up in South Carolina and went to Duke undergraduate."

"Very good." Jason turned to the other student. "And your name?"

"I'm Jeffrey Allen, Dr. Green. I'm from Vermont and did my undergraduate work at MIT."

"Excellent," Jason replied. "Well, I'm looking forward to y'all teaching me a lot these next six weeks. I have a lot to learn." The four laughed at Jason's remark. "Shall we go see our patients?"

Dr. Nash took charge. "Dr. Green, I've been on this service for the past two weeks. Dr. Clancy and the students are new to the service today, so I'll present the patients to you." The intern, Seth Clancy, retrieved the portable chart rack and rolled it to the first patient room. The five walked into the patient room, and Dr. Nash said, "Mrs. Denkner, I want to introduce you to our boss, Dr. Green, and you've already met Dr. Clancy and the students."

Jason smiled, took Mrs. Denkner's hand, and said, "Mrs. Denkner, it's a pleasure to meet you. If you don't mind, Dr. Nash is going to tell us a bit about you." Mrs. Denkner appeared to be in her thirties. She smiled and nodded.

Dr. Nash continued. "Mrs. Denkner is a lovely thirty-six-year-old who has been in excellent health. She was admitted yesterday after having passed out at a New Year's Day party. She had only one glass of wine and was talking with a friend when she had the sudden onset of light-headedness, shortness of breath, followed by loss of consciousness. She fell onto the floor and struck her head, and you can see the stitches she required in the emergency room. Her friends called an ambulance, and the EMT noted that she had a rapid and irregular pulse with a blood pressure that was quite low at eighty over forty. They placed her in the ambulance, and an EKG confirmed that she was in atrial fibrillation with a rapid ventricular response of one hundred sixty. Her oxygen saturation in the ambulance was low at eighty-eight percent.

By the time she arrived in the emergency room, she had converted back to a normal sinus rhythm with a rate of ninety-six. Her systolic blood pressure remained in the nineties, and she was admitted for observation."

Dr. Nash looked at Jason who continued to intently listen, and then she continued. "Her past medical history is unremarkable. She has never been hospitalized and denies any chronic health problems. She has been on no medications, and she does not use tobacco. Her systems review is really unremarkable except for some hand stiffness when she awakens in the morning, and she has had occasional episodes in the past few years where she feels short of breath climbing up the stairs in her house. Her physical examination when she arrived yesterday on the floor was not remarkable and continues to be unremarkable. She is alert and oriented. Her cardiovascular examination was entirely normal, and her lungs are completely clear."

"Her labs were remarkable for being completely normal. Her oxygen saturations on nasal oxygen remain in the nineties, and her EKG was completely normal. We asked cardiology to see Mrs. Denkner. They performed an echocardiogram at the bedside, which demonstrated no obvious valve problems, no clots, and normal left ventricular function. It was their opinion that Mrs. Denkner had an isolated episode of atrial fibrillation, and they want to send her home with an event monitor so that her heart rhythm can be monitored for the next month. If she has recurrent episodes, she could be a candidate for surgical ablation or anticoagulation." Dr. Nash finished the presentation with an expectant look on her face.

Jason took Mrs. Denkner's hand once again. "So Mrs. Denkner, are you being well taken care of by these fine young physicians?"

Mrs. Denkner smiled. "Yes Dr. Green, they've been wonderful."

"Well, let me ask you a few more questions and do just a little examination. Do you work or do you stay at home with children?" Jason asked as he continued to hold her hand.

"I have two children, but I teach algebra to middle school students here in Manhattan," she answered.

"You are certainly busy then. Do you have time to exercise?" Jason continued.

"Oh, yes, my husband is very good about letting me exercise. I'm pretty obsessed with it. I run half marathons twice a year, and run almost every day." Mrs. Denkner smiled and looked over the entire group

Jason frowned. "Well, tell me more about these episodes of shortness of breath when you climb your stairs at home. For someone in such good shape that seems a bit odd."

"I thought so, too. It has happened only three or four times over the past year, and it lasts only a few minutes. I did see my family doctor about it, and he examined me. He didn't think too much of it and I just sort of forgot about it."

Jason nodded. "And tell me about the joint stiffness that you told Dr. Nash about."

"Well, my hands are usually quite stiff in the morning. That's been going on for many years. I can't even remember how long. Sometimes my knuckles will swell and become red. Occasionally, my knees will swell as well. I told my family doctor about that as well, and he said I should cut out my running because I was getting arthritis." Mrs. Denkner laughed. "Well, that's not going to happen, I have to run."

"I know exactly how you feel. I'm a runner myself. Two more question, Mrs. Denkner." Jason smiled again. "Did you have any problems during your pregnancies? And do you sunbathe a lot?" The students, intern, and resident looked at each other with blank stares, and Jeffrey Allen shrugged his shoulders.

"Not really. But I had two miscarriages before my first pregnancy was successful and then another miscarriage before my last pregnancy. It was very upsetting, and as far as sun bathing is concerned, no. I stay out of the sun. I burn very easily and break out in awful sun rashes."

"Thank you, Mrs. Denkner. Let me just take a quick listen to your lungs and heart." Jason listened and then asked the others to listen to her heart and, in particular, to take note of the second heart sound. After the others had listened, Jason took her hand once again. "Mrs. Denkner, it has been a pleasure meeting you. Dr. Nash and Dr. Clancy will be back later, and we'll get you out of here very soon."

The group walked out, standing in a circle. "So, anything to add to what the cardiology consultant advised?" Jason asked.

Dr. Nash turned a bit red in the face. "Dr. Green, I'm embarrassed, but what did you hear that I didn't hear with that second heart sound?"

"Well, y'all should go back after rounds and listen carefully. As you know, the second heart sound is normally split into two distinct parts: The first indicates aortic valve closure, and the second indicates pulmonary valve closure. During inspiration, that split widens because of increased right ventricular filling and delayed closure of the pulmonary valve." Jason looked at all four to sense whether or not they understood his explanation. "Understand so far?" The four nodded. "If there is increased pressure in the pulmonary artery, the right ventricle must work harder and longer for each contraction, delaying closure further. So that if there is increased pulmonary artery pressure, there will be an unusually wide split in the two parts of the second heart sound." All four nodded again. "Go back later and listen carefully. If you learn to hear and dissect that second heart sound, it will go a long way in helping you at bedside diagnosis. I believe you will find that her second heart sound is widely split."

"So what do you believe is going on?" Dr. Clancy asked.

"Dr. Clancy, that's not the right question." Dr. Clancy's face turned bright red. "What I'm going to tell you now is the most important lesson that I'm capable of giving to you or anyone in terms of clinical problem solving. I'm glad that this very first patient presented this way, and that she is such a great example of why this lesson is so important." Jason spoke very slowly and looked intently at Dr. Clancy. "This lesson is very simple, but I'm here to tell you that you will struggle to relearn it every time you see a patient. And I can tell you that most physicians forget this lesson and, as a result, practice, at best, mediocre medicine." Jason looked at the four, all now wide-eyed. After a long pause, Jason said, "You must learn to ask the right questions." The four looked at each other with a look of disappointment. Jason chuckled and continued, "I can see you're disappointed with this lesson, but I promise you, it is the most important lesson for you to learn. So, Dr. Clancy, what is the fundamental question regarding Mrs. Denkner's presentation?"

Dr. Clancy was reticent. "Why did she lose consciousness?"

"Well, that is a good question, but it is not the right question. It seems probable that the atrial fibrillation and hypotension at least contributed to her loss of consciousness. What is even more fundamental than that question?" Jason could see that Dr. Nash was understanding and knew where he was going, and she also knew to stay quiet so that Jason could continue teaching. "Ms. Summers, any idea what an even more fundamental question is?"

"Why did she go into atrial fibrillation in the first place?" Stephanie Summers replied.

"Exactly. Why would a young, healthy, physically active woman suddenly go into atrial fibrillation? Now the cardiology consultant basically told us 'just because,' but that's not a very satisfactory or sophisticated answer. I don't think they even asked the question." The group laughed at that. "Certainly, there are people who go into atrial fibrillation 'just because,' but there are also many more definable reasons for people to suddenly go into atrial fibrillation. Dr. Nash, will you tell us some of the many causes for atrial fibrillation. I'm not very good at remembering them."

Dr. Nash smiled. "Well, as you said there are many. Coronary artery disease, hyperthyroidism, pulmonary emboli, hypertension, cardiomyopathy, mitral valve disease, chronic lung disease, and a host of other less common conditions."

"Excellent, thank you, Dr. Nash," Jason continued. "So you can all go to Dr. Nash or any text and find out all of causes atrial fibrillation, in addition to the 'just because' reason, but the hard part is asking the question in the first place. So now, do any of y'all have further thoughts regarding Mrs. Denkner's presentation? Or better yet, any further questions regarding her presentation?"

Dr. Clancy spoke up, "Well, assuming she has pulmonary artery hypertension, why would she have that?"

"Excellent question. So let's assume I am correct about her physical exam, and she does have pulmonary artery hypertension. What are the causes of pulmonary artery hypertension? Again, y'all can ask Dr. Nash, and I guarantee you she can tell you all of the causes, or you can get out your cell phone and go to one of the medicine websites and have the answer in a minute." Jason looked at Dr. Clancy again, expecting an answer.

"Well, the major causes would be some sort of lung disease, pulmonary embolus, or primary pulmonary hypertension. I'm sure there are others but those come to mind."

Dr. Clancy's face continued to redden.

"That's excellent. Now I'm not very good at these things, so correct me if I'm wrong, but chronic lung disease and primary pulmonary hypertension are chronic and progressive disorders, which it seems to me would not fit her presentation."

"That's right." Jeffrey Allen spoke up for the first time. "But a pulmonary embolus could explain the pulmonary hypertension and the atrial fibrillation."

"Good job, Mr. Allen. And maybe even those episodes of shortness of breath going upstairs at home perhaps?" Jason queried.

"You mean, she is having repeated episodes of pulmonary emboli?" Sarah Summers asked.

"Well, another fundamental question is what is causing her episodes of shortness of breath. They seem episodic. She can run long distances without being short of breath, and yet she sometimes has difficulty climbing a flight of stairs? So that is a question that needs to be answered. So there are probably hundreds of reasons for someone having episodes of shortness of breath—again Dr. Nash can tell you all of them, or you can look them up. So let's assume that I am correct and that her physical exam does indicate pulmonary hypertension and that the most likely reason is that she threw a blood clot in her lung. What is the next fundamental question?"

Dr. Clancy immediately said, "Why should this young healthy woman be having blood clots?"

"That's excellent, and again Dr. Nash will give you a hundred reasons for people forming blood clots. Dr. Nash, what is the right question that would lead you to the correct answer in this patient?"

"The question is: Are there any history or clinical symptoms in this young otherwise healthy lady that would suggest a reason that she would be prone to forming blood clots?" Dr. Nash smiled at Jason.

"Exactly. Any ideas?" Jason looked at all four. "Well, this is a lady who had three of five pregnancies end in miscarriage. What is a common cause for miscarriage?"

"Blood clots, of course," Stephanie Summers shook her head. "My sister has had multiple miscarriages because of a clotting disorder and will have to take an anticoagulant when she becomes pregnant again."

"So," Jason continued. "Let's assume her miscarriages and her episodes of shortness of breath, as well as her current episode of atrial fibrillation, are all a result of blood clots. What is the question again?" Jason asked Dr. Clancy.

"What's causing her to be prone to blood clotting?"

"Correct. Any symptoms that she told us about that could suggest a cause?" Jason asked.

"I know," Ms. Summers said excitedly. "She has joint aches and swelling, and she is sun sensitive, and the question is what causes those symptoms. And the answer is, of course, lupus. Lupus can also cause a clotting disorder."

"Excellent." Jason smiled. "Of course, there are other diseases that cause joint swelling, sun sensitivity, and clotting disorders. Again you can ask Dr. Nash or Siri and complete your differential diagnosis. The point is, you must ask the right questions. So, good work, all of you. You have asked the right questions. Now you need to get to work and answer those questions." The four men and women looked at each other, stunned at Jason's lesson. "Okay, let's move on."

Dr. Nash presented the next patient who was a sixty-two-year-old man presenting with shortness of breath and pneumonia in the lower lobe of his right lung. He had been a long-term heavy smoker, and had a history of coronary artery disease, having had two stents placed two years previously. He also had high blood pressure. He was doing well until four days ago when he had the onset of shaking chills, fever to 102, cough, and shortness of breathe. He came to the emergency room where a chest X-ray confirmed the pneumonia, and he was admitted for further treatment. The four watched Jason as he asked a few questions and then performed a quick but thorough physical examination.

"Mr. Bradford, it has been a pleasure meeting you. Dr. Nash and Dr. Clancy are going to get you well and out of here as quickly as possible." Jason smiled and squeezed his shoulder, and the five walked out of the room.

Once again they stood in a circle. Jason looked at Dr. Clancy and asked, "Well, any discussion about this patient?"

Dr. Clancy frowned. "Well, Dr. Green, it just seems like a clear case of pneumonia in a smoker. I don't think there are any more questions to ask. I guess had I seen him when he first presented, before I had a chest X-ray, the question would have been what was causing his fever, cough, and shortness of breath. But by the time we saw him, the diagnosis was already made."

"Dr. Clancy, I'm not picking on you. I told you that this simple lesson is very difficult to learn. You didn't ask the right question. Dr. Nash?"

"Yes, Dr. Green. The question is: Why did this man get pneumonia. It is true that smokers have a higher risk for getting pneumonia because of the damage that tobacco smoke does to the bronchi and lung tissue. But there are other reasons that a smoker could get pneumonia as well, particularly a lung cancer that is blocking a bronchus." Dr. Nash looked at Dr. Clancy, who looked dejected.

"Dr. Clancy, there's nothing to be upset about it. I promise you that you will learn this lesson well before the six weeks are up. You might want to write on the front of that Washington University Manual of yours: 'ask the right question,' just to remind yourself." Jason took out his iPhone and showed his default screen to the four. On it was a picture of Julia, with the words *Ask the Right Question* below her picture. Everyone, including Dr. Clancy, laughed. "Now it's also important to do a very careful physical examination on your patients, and I will demand that of all of you. If I find something on examination that y'all miss, I'll not look kindly on that. So what I want you to do is this. After we finish rounding on all of our patients, I want you to go back in and do another physical examination on this nice man, and pay close attention to your lymph node examination. Then I want you to ask the right questions, and answer them before rounds tomorrow. Let's move on."

The team examined fourteen more patients and didn't finish until one p.m. After each patient, a discussion ensued and always focused on asking the important questions. In several cases, the discussion resulted in important changes in diagnosis or plans. Jason made clear that good clinical judgment did not come from knowing thousands of facts, but rather was the result of performing an excellent history and physical examination, and then on the basis of that information, asking the right questions. Answers to questions, Jason emphasized, could be looked up in minutes, but if the right questions were not asked, then the solutions to the clinical problems would be eluded.

When a discussion ensued regarding the possible answers to a good question, Jason would let Dr. Nash lead a discussion about the medical literature related to that question. When Dr. Clancy or one of the students was able to answer the question, Jason always complimented them. On occasion, Dr. Nash and the three others could not answer a question, and Dr. Nash would then ask Jason for the answer. Jason would reluctantly answer the question, citing a specific journal article, but he would always preface his answer by emphasizing that they could find the answer in minutes by searching in their computers.

By the end of rounds on that first day, the resident, intern, and two students were all smiling and enthusiastic.

"Good work today, ladies and gentlemen. I'll look forward to the answers to some of our questions tomorrow. Dr. Nash, walk with me to the elevators." The two walked away from the others.

"Dr. Green, that was the most amazing rounds that I've had since graduating medical school. Thank you so much."

"Thanks for that, Dr. Nash. And you too were excellent. It should be a wonderful six weeks together." Jason smiled. "Any issues with Dr. Clancy or the students?"

"Not really. There is a confidence issue with Seth, but I have a feeling that will be resolved by the end of this rotation. I don't know the students well, but I'll stay on top of them and let you know of any issues."

"Terrific. Then I'll see you tomorrow. We'll make quick rounds the first hour, and the second hour have the students present a patient." Jason shook Dr. Nash's hand and disappeared into the elevator. Rounds had taken an unusually long time, but Jason was pleased and now knew all of the patients. He also knew that Dr. Nash was excellent and had a good command of the team.

The following morning, Dr. Clancy reported on rounds that Mrs. Denkner had in fact been found to have multiple pulmonary emboli when a CT scan was done of her chest. Furthermore, her blood tests showed that she did probably have systemic lupus erythematosis and that she had a lupus specific protein in her blood that resulted in abnormal clotting. The students reported that they had listened to her second heart sound and now understood the significance of that sound. In addition, the team had re-examined the man who had pneumonia and discovered an abnormal lymph node above his right clavicle. A CT scan was done of the chest, which showed a tumor obstructing the right bronchus. Jason noticed that Dr. Clancy had written on the front of his Washington University Manual, a treatment manual commonly kept in the pockets of interns and residents worldwide, *Ask the Right Questions*.

Over the six weeks, Jason saw that the students, Dr. Clancy, and even Dr. Nash made huge strides in their clinical abilities, always asking questions before trying to spew facts. Jason always made clear that he was more impressed with questions than facts, and by the end of the six weeks, it was evident that Dr. Clancy had become much more confident in his clinical abilities.

The last day of the rotation, as was his and Philip's usual custom, Jason had the four members of his team for dinner at his home. Alejandra had prepared a wonderful supper and stayed to help serve the meal and clean. The group had arranged for one of the students on another team to take a picture of the team standing outside of a patient's room, and the group had a beautiful picture professionally framed, giving it to Jason when they arrived.

"Thanks so much for this. I'll treasure it. I had a great six weeks. I hope you had as much fun as I did," Jason said to the group.

"You have no idea how great it was for us, Dr. Green," Dr. Clancy responded immediately.

Everyone spent time with Julia, admired the view over Central Park, and at one point Dr. Nash said, "You know, Dr. Green, I was a student of Dr. Olsen during my third year of medical school. He was amazing, and when he passed away, I cried for days. I never said anything to you about it, but I want you to know how sorry I am."

෴

Two weeks later, Jason had a luncheon meeting with the new head of the Department of Medicine, Franklin Skor, who had been one of his attending physicians when he was an intern. Dr. Skor had a distinguished career as a researcher in hematology and at the age of fifty-six had taken over as the Chairman of the Department of Medicine after Henry Stern had retired. "You know, Jason, you're making all of the medicine professors look very bad. There were literally physical altercations among the students to be put on your service." Dr. Skor laughed as he said that.

Jason shook his head. "Well, that's ridiculous. I guess I'm going to have be tougher on them—they want me because I'm too easy."

"No, Jason, that's not the reason. Anyway, the reason I wanted to meet with you is that one of the board of trustees of the hospital would like to have a meeting with you, and he asked that I approach you. This is unusual, and I'm not certain why he couldn't just contact you himself. His name is Evan Thompson. He's CEO of a small biotech firm called Virtus Biotech. Anyway, I know little about the company, but he's been a big contributor to this institution, so I thought I would approach you."

"What does he want?" Jason asked.

"I really have no idea. He's been on the board of trustees of Sinai for years and seems to be well liked. I suspect he wants to pick your brain about some of the issues in their business. I don't know, but you would do a great favor for this institution if you would at least meet with him."

"Sure, happy to do it. You know I never travel, so I'm available at his convenience. Make it a luncheon meeting if you don't mind. I'm not taking any time away from Julia. So how are things going in your new job?" Jason asked.

"You know, I loved being a researcher and teaching," Franklin Skor said, smiling at Jason. "I remember well our time together when you were an intern—who could forget that amazing time?" Jason recalled that he had been Dr. Skor's intern when he was shot in the chest. "Anyway, I don't know if I'm suited for this job. Henry Stern was a master at fund raising. It's not my forte. But Henry is being very gracious and helping me master the job."

"Well, for what it's worth, I couldn't think of a better person to replace Henry Stern. You'll be a model for other chairmen." They shook hands and Jason returned to his lab.

# CHAPTER 8

It had been eighteen months since Philip's death, and Jason's personal life had been entirely limited to family. Julia and Jason had a bond that went beyond the usual father-daughter relationship. They had a palpable need for and understanding of one another, and that connection between the two was astonishing to the other family members. And yet Julia was an extremely social six-year-old who did not have separation anxieties and was usually the focus of attention among her peers. Jason and Julia continued their visits to the Olsen mansion every other weekend, and their relationship with the Olsen family also remained extraordinary.

One weekend in May, the Olsens had a dinner party for forty guests, and John and Evelyn had implored Jonathan, Sophia, Jason, and Julia to stay for the entire weekend instead of their usual twenty-four hours. After dinner on Friday evening, Paul and Jason went on their usual seven-mile run. Paul stopped Jason in the middle of the run, and, as they continued to walk, Paul said, "Jason, I want you to know that Kevin is coming to the dinner party tomorrow evening. There's no ulterior motive. It's just that I've become close friends with him, and we just won

another huge case because of his work. I know you refused to go out with him, and that's fine. I just wanted
you to know he's coming so that you wouldn't be surprised and uncomfortable."

"That's fine." Jason smiled. "I told Kevin that I just
wasn't ready to go out with anyone. I'm sure Philip made
clear to you that I'm not the easiest person to have a relationship with. I have a lot of baggage, and now with Julia,
I doubt there could ever be anyone who could handle my
mishigas." Jason chuckled. "Do you know what mishigas
is?"

"Jason, I'm married to a Jew." Paul paused. "In all
honesty, Phil never, ever hinted that you were the slight-
est bit crazy. I'd never seen anyone so in love in my life.
Anyway, let's run. I just didn't want you to be surprised
by Kevin. He'll be staying overnight at my place." They
ran the rest of the way back to the mansion.

Saturday was a beautiful late spring day. The huge
back yard of the Olsen mansion was filled with flowering
dogwoods and redbuds, and the Azaleas were in full
bloom. Jason and Julia played in the back while John and
Evelyn Olsen and Jonathan and Sophia Green sat in the
family room drinking coffee and eating bagels, watching
Jason and Julia in wonderment. At noon Anna Olsen arrived and as usual looked stunning, just like her mother.
Julia ran to her, and after a long and warm greeting, Anna
went to the rest of the family, giving a particularly warm
hug and kiss to Jason.

At two p.m., Paul, Amy, their two sons, and Kevin
arrived. The children played in the lower level family
room while all of the adults were engaged in a lively
conversation in the large living room. On several occasions, brief waves of sadness overwhelmed Jason when
vivid memories of Philip sitting next to him in this same
room entered his mind, and although the episodes were

brief, Jason knew that they did not go unnoticed. At three p.m., Jason announced he was going for his run.

"Do you mind if I join you?" Kevin asked.

Jason looked surprised. "Sure. Are you a runner? It's a seven-mile course."

Kevin smiled. "I know you're a great runner. I'll try and keep up."

"You can change in my old room, Kevin," Paul interjected. "I'll sit this one out, Jason. My plantar fasciitis is bothering me." Jason saw Paul's sly grin, which he was never good at disguising, and which was so similar to Philip's impish grins.

Jason had been running since high school and was an All-American long-distance runner at the University of Mississippi. Although at thirty-nine, he was not the runner he had been in his earlier years, he was still very fast, and few could match his skills. Jason intended to slow his pace in order not to offend Kevin, but his consideration was for naught. In fact, Jason had to muster his long-forgotten sense of competition to stay even with Kevin. At the end of the seven miles, Jason had been challenged in a way that had not occurred since his college years.

"Wow, Kevin, that was impressive. Where did you learn to run like that?" Jason asked, breathless.

"Oh, I ran in college, not as successfully as you, and I've been running since." Kevin smiled.

"Well, you certainly put me in my place," Jason said, still breathing hard.

"Well, you're still impressive for an old man." Kevin's smile turned into a laugh.

"Thanks for that!" Jason put his hands on his thighs, trying to catch his breath.

They walked into the mansion where everyone was still conversing in the living room. Paul started laughing. "So Jason, now you know why I sat this one out. I can't keep up with you, much less Kevin. You both are maniacs."

"Yeah." Jason smiled. "Had I known Kevin was so fast, my plantar fasciitis may have suddenly become a problem as well."

The dinner party was a formal and elegant affair, attended by forty guests and catered by a famous chef from the city. Sophia had bought Julia a beautiful dress, and Julia walked among the guests, enjoying the attention she was receiving, always keeping an eye on Jason. Jason knew most of the guests, several from John Olsen's law firm, Judge Lackland and his wife, and several from Sinai Medical Center, including Franklin Skor and Seth Goldberg.

Judge Lackland walked quickly to Jason when he arrived and hugged him tightly. "So how's the man who twice saved my life?"

Jason laughed. "Judge, I hope you're not as dramatic in the court room. I'm doing fine, and you look great. How much longer are you going to be writing those fantastic opinions of yours? I notice that you're becoming a bit more liberal as you age."

"Hold on, young man. I may hold you in contempt." The judge looked down at Julia, who was holding onto Jason's leg. "Jason, Julia is gorgeous. The word is out that you are doing a great job with her." Jason knew that Judge Lackland had deep affection for him. Jason had indeed twice saved him from certain death when he was an intern in 2005. He had also coerced the judge to cease using cigarettes, which, Jason was certain, accounted for his continued good health. Jason circulated among the guests, talking easily with everyone, occasionally looking at Kevin who was also engaged in animated conversation.

Jason and Sheri fed their children in the kitchen at seven-thirty. After a brief protest, Jason carried Julia upstairs to her bedroom, and after the usual reading and snuggling, Jason returned to the party as people were sitting down at the elegantly set tables. Jason had been placed next to Seth and Sheri Goldberg, and Kevin had been placed at a separate table with Paul and Amy.

Jason looked over at Kevin soon after everyone was seated and saw that Kevin was staring at him. Jason's face immediately flushed, and he quickly began a conversation with Seth and Sheri. He hated that he flushed so easily. Jason continued his conversation, but he was thinking about Kevin and the fact that he had been without a companion for almost two years. In fact, it had been almost two years since he had experienced any sexual arousal or had even thought of sex. He had recently begun to worry that his previously strong sexual appetite had vanished forever.

Jason chuckled, which was inappropriate for the conversation he was having with Seth. "Jason, your mind is somewhere else. What are you laughing about?" Seth laughed.

"Sorry, some thought just entered my mind, which made me laugh." Jason had, in fact, become aroused at the table while thinking about Kevin, realizing that his concern was needless. He smiled to himself, thankful that he was sitting at the table so that his arousal remained inconspicuous. Jason looked over at Kevin frequently during the dinner, and each time, their eyes met, evoking smiles from both men. The simultaneous looks and smiles continued throughout the dinner, and Jason suspected that their silent rapport was conspicuous to most everyone.

Jason awoke Sunday morning and looked at the clock—eight-thirty a.m. He couldn't remember the last time that he had slept so late. He quickly walked into Julia's bedroom and saw that she was already up. Probably Sophia and Jonathan were taking care of her. He showered and, as he dressed, looked at himself in the mirror.

He thought he still looked good for his thirty-nine years, thinking once again of Kevin who was four years his junior. He still had a perfect runner's build, his thick long curly brown hair now had a few hints of gray, but he saw that his face remained youthful. Jason remembered how Philip would lay with him in bed, stroking his face, telling him what beautiful eyes and lips he had. Jason wondered whether he would be attractive to Kevin.

He walked downstairs into the kitchen where Jonathan and Sophia, Paul and Amy, and John and Evelyn were having breakfast.

"Good morning. I'm sorry I slept so late. Where are the kids?" Jason asked.

"Out in back playing," Paul smiled.

Jason walked into the family room and watched Kevin outside gently throwing a Frisbee to the three children. After a few minutes, he opened the door and joined them. Julia ran to Jason who scooped her up and tickled her neck with his nose and lips. Kevin and Jason smiled at one another without saying a word, and they all started throwing the Frisbee to each other. Jason glimpsed at Kevin frequently, trying not to be too conspicuous. He was almost as tall as Jason, with full lips, perfect teeth, and a muscular body. At ten a.m., Kevin said goodbye to everyone, explaining that he had work that had to be completed that afternoon. Jason quietly got up and followed Kevin, noticing that everyone was staring as they walked outside together.

They stood next to Kevin's 5 Series BMW, saying nothing for an awkward moment. Then Jason said, "Kevin, perhaps you could come to my place Saturday night for dinner?"

Kevin smiled and said, "Well, my social schedule is awfully full. But sure, I'd love to. What time?"

"Seven-thirty?" Jason's heart was pounding. He had become aroused again and hoped that Kevin hadn't noticed.

Kevin opened the car door, and their eyes met one more time as Kevin got into his car and drove away.

ლადა

Jason's lab continued to be extraordinarily productive, and the amount of new information that was produced on an almost daily basis was astounding. All of the postdoc fellows and PhD students were continuously writing papers for publication in various scientific journals, and Jason reluctantly asked Eric Adelman for help reviewing and critiquing the papers since the numbers were too great for Jason to manage alone. Jason was particularly excited about the Blumenthal lab discoveries. Initial studies showed that their new protein resulted in cure of pancreas cancer in animal models, and negotiations were underway with one of the large pharmaceutical companies to begin first phase studies in humans. Jason thought of the irony should the Glassman lab discover a cure for pancreas cancer, a disease that had killed Harvey Glassman.

The week after the Olsen party was a typically busy week for Jason, but he was distracted by the thought of having Kevin over for dinner. Paul came by the lab on Wednesday for a brief visit and as he was leaving said, "I hope all goes well on Saturday," giving Jason that sly and exquisite smile that reminded him so much of Philip. Jason reminded himself almost hourly that he was a respected and successful scientist, a mature adult, a father, and that he shouldn't be so apprehensive about an insignificant dinner date. He remembered the exact same feeling prior to his first and second dates with Philip.

On Saturday morning, Jason and Julia went to the Museum of Modern Art. Julia now recognized all of the major artists. On the way home, Jason picked up preordered fresh tuna, tomatoes, mozzarella, potatoes, and a variety of vegetables. He had a cheesecake delivered from a nearby deli. Jason was not fond of cooking, finding it boring and not dissimilar to his chemistry courses in college. He preferred going to a good restaurant, but he didn't want to leave Julia, rationalizing that his leaving even for an evening would make her anxious. Jason knew that his reasoning was spurious. On the rare occasions that he went to an evening scientific event, Julia had been just fine staying with his father or Alejandra. Jason knew that the real issue was his own separation anxiety.

Kevin arrived promptly at seven-thirty with a bottle of cabernet. Jason had already fed and bathed Julia, and when Kevin arrived, Jason was surprised when she laid her iPad on the couch and ran to Kevin. Kevin picked her up and kissed her, and she wiggled her way down and ran back to her iPad.

"Julia, do you know this man's name?" Jason chuckled.

Without looking up, Julia answered, "Kevin."

Both Jason and Kevin laughed.

"It's good to see you, but I'm warning you now, I'm not a good cook, so I hope you don't have a delicate gastrointestinal tract," Jason announced.

Kevin smiled. "Do I have to remind you that I was in the marines? I can eat anything."

"Please sit. Have some wine and cheese while I put her to bed." Jason smiled at Kevin who was dressed in khakis and a cotton sweater and wore cologne that Jason didn't recognize but smelled subtle and expensive.

Jason returned after ten minutes, poured a glass of wine and joined Kevin who was looking out the window at the hundreds of people still walking in Central Park.

"This is quite a view. Cheers." Kevin clinked his glass with Jason's.

There was an uncomfortable silence. Jason then said, "You know, this is the first time I've had a date since Philip. I'm very nervous, so please forgive me."

Kevin put his wine glass on the coffee table, took Jason's glass, and placed it next to his glass. He then put his hand behind Jason's neck. "Jason, I've been dreaming about this day for twelve years. I know that sounds crazy. And don't get me wrong, I would have never wished ill for Phil, and I was truly devastated for you and the Olsen family when he died. But something happened to me when I met you at Camp David. I can't explain it." Kevin looked at Jason and then kissed him, at first lightly, and then passionately as Jason responded. It was a sweet kiss, not unlike Philip's kiss, perhaps not as gentle but sweet nonetheless.

"Whew, well, I guess the ice has been broken," Jason smiled. The two talked nonstop for the next hour, reminiscing about the Camp David experience and Jason insisting that he detail his two years as the President's aide. They moved over to the dining table, and the talk continued unabated. Jason answered Kevin's questions, quickly and briefly, and peppered Kevin with questions. Jason learned that he grew up in Omaha and after graduating from the University of Nebraska with honors went into the marines. His parents divorced when he was very young, and his father, with whom he lived, remarried a Chinese woman who taught him Mandarin. He applied for the presidential detail, and because of his academics and fluency in Mandarin, he was chosen. The president had apparently noticed him and chose him to be his personal aide. Kevin had two older sisters who were in Nebraska and with whom he spoke daily. He came out to his parents after he left the marines, and they had not spoken to him since. His sisters told him that they had always known he was gay and that they loved him all the same.

While in the marines, Kevin had learned many of the methods of covert investigations and how various technologies were used in gathering information. Because of his position, he had become good friends with various young FBI and CIA operatives, and they taught him various techniques used for tracking individuals as well as computer investigation, which basically was computer hacking.

"After I got out of the marines, I decided to start my own investigation firm, and so I moved here."

"Why New York?" Jason asked.

"Well, obviously, this is a huge financial center and an international city, but I think in large part because you were here."

Jason blushed. "Come on. You knew I was with Philip."

Kevin looked at Jason with a serious expression. "Of course, and I never had any intention of trying to come between the two of you. In fact, after I became close with the Olsens, I insisted that they not mention me to either of you. But I reasoned that you never know what happens in a relationship, and if you ever became single again, I would make my move." Kevin paused. "And then the unthinkable happened, and here we are."

"But there are a lot of great people out there waiting for someone like you. Didn't you go out over the past ten years?"

"Of course. I've got the same urges every young man has. But I never found anyone that I really liked, and no one that comes close to you."

Jason blushed again. "Kevin, you don't even know me. You know I'm a bit crazy."

"Aren't we all? I've followed your career, and I know you better than you think. Don't forget, I'm an investigator."

"You've been stalking me?" Jason laughed.

"Let's just say, I've been following you professionally by reading almost all of the papers you've authored, and personally by listening to the Olsens. I know you pretty well."

Jason asked Kevin about his work. When he arrived in New York City, Kevin opened a small office in the financial district and sent letters to the major law firms. John Olsen was the first to call and give him a job, and after several successes, he rapidly started building an investigative practice that brought him business from the most prestigious law firms in the New York City area. He soon had to hire other investigators, and then accountants who helped with financial fraud investigations. Embassies began calling him for help in protecting various diplomats who came to the city, and, finally, entertainment managers began calling for bodyguard protection of celebrities.

After seven years of working in the city, he had leased an entire floor and had almost three hundred full time employees.

"My God, Kevin. That's impressive. I guess you spend your time managing now."

"Believe it or not, I have great managers. I make certain they're doing their job, but I still love investigating and I oversee most of the projects."

"What a fascinating job you have. I guess you've met a lot of interesting people." Jason asked.

"A lot. I could start a gossip magazine if I were unethical. And the President still stays in contact with me.

We have dinner whenever he comes into town. He always asks about you, by the way."

The conversation continued unabated, and finally at one a.m. Jason said, "You know, it's really late, and Julia gets up early. I think we should call it a night. Shall I call a taxi for you."

Kevin laughed. "I live two buildings from here. I have the same view that you have."

"My God, how long have we been neighbors?" Jason asked surprised.

"About four years."

They both stood, and Kevin went to Jason. They began making out passionately, and then Jason pushed back after a few minutes. "Kevin, I have the three-date rule."

"Oh, yeah? When did you come up with that rule?" Kevin laughed.

"Just now." Jason smiled. "I'm not a prude, but let's go slow."

"I plan to ask you to marry me after the third date." Kevin blushed for the first time. He kissed Jason on the cheek. "Thanks for the dinner and the great night. I'll wait to hear from you. I have a feeling that my prayers are being answered."

"Kevin, you should know that I'm an atheist."

"That was a euphemism. If there's a God, I doubt he or she is concerned about my love life." They both laughed, and Kevin walked out the door.

Jason slept poorly, analyzing the night with Kevin. Jason also recalled their first meeting at Camp David. John had taken Jason, Philip, and Harvey Glassman to visit the president on a Sunday morning in 2006 after Jason had discovered the espionage by Chao Fang in Harvey Glassman's lab. Although Jason was shaken and disoriented that morning, he remembered that Kevin would not, or perhaps could not, quit staring at him. And then after he was recovering from the gunshot wound, the president and Kevin had visited him at the hospital. Kevin had spoken to him in Mandarin in front of Philip and the President making clear that he had feelings for him. Jason had thought of Kevin over the years and wondered what had happened to him. He had never dreamed that Kevin was in New York City and living only two buildings away.

Obviously, he was very bright and financially successful, not to mention physically beautiful. But how odd, Jason thought, that he would maintain those strong feelings for over a decade.

# CHAPTER 9

On Tuesday, Jason left his office at eleven-fifty a.m. and walked quickly to the luncheon meeting with Evan Thompson in the faculty club of the medical school. Dr. Skor was with Mr. Thompson as Jason entered the faculty club, which was an elegant restaurant on the top floor of the hospital overlooking the east side of Manhattan. The primary purpose of the faculty club was to have a place where hospital administrators and famous scientists could woo men and women of means to donate large sums of money to Sinai Medical Center.

Jason learned from various web sites that Evan Thompson's company, Virtus Biotech, was a nine-year-old biotech company that had specialized in developing new antiviral drugs and new treatments for osteoporosis. The company went public five years ago, and the stock had declined ninety-five percent from its initial public offering price, primarily because of failures for several of its potential drugs that had made it to various stages of clinical trials. The company had only one FDA approved drug, and the sales of that particular antiviral had been disappointing because of several superior antivirals used for the same purpose. There had even been recent reports of potential bankruptcy, which had resulted in further declines in stock price.

Dr. Skor made the introductions. "Evan, this is Jason Green. Jason, Evan Thompson who has been on our board of trustees for the past five years."

"Mr. Thompson, it's a pleasure to meet you." Jason smiled at both men. He was not happy to be at this meeting. He could not imagine how he could help Evan Thompson's failing company. After all, his expertise had nothing to do with antivirals or osteoporosis. Jason had a bad feeling about this meeting, but he couldn't refuse Franklin Skor, who had been an important mentor for him.

"I'm going to leave you two. Enjoy the lunch." Dr. Skor turned and walked away.

"Dr. Green, thank you for meeting with me. I've heard so many great things about you, and I'm grateful you've taken the time to talk with me."

"First of all, please call me Jason. And Franklin tells me you have been a great asset to our institution, so I thank you for that. Please sit." Jason noticed immediately that Evan Thompson seemed stressed. He didn't smile, and there was a strain in his voice. Jason thought he looked to be in his early to mid-fifties, balding, a bit overweight, and he had beads of sweat on his brow.

The two men talked superficially about family and politics, and after the waiter had taken their orders, Evan Thompson said, "Jason, I'll get to the point of why I wanted to meet with you. My company has had difficulties with the FDA, and, frankly, we've been unsuccessful at getting several of our drugs approved. Unfortunately, our pipeline has dried up. We've not invested enough in research, and we don't have the revenue or credit to acquire other companies. So bottom line: We need a new product pretty quickly, or we will likely not survive." He wiped the sweat from his forehead with his napkin.

"I'm truly sorry to hear you're having these problems," Jason said after an uncomfortable pause. Evan Thompson's distress was now overt. "But how can I be of help to you?"

Thompson looked at Jason, took a deep breath, looked around at the other tables, and continued in a more muted tone, "I've heard that you recently discovered a molecule that has great potential in curing pancreatic cancer. Apparently, your results in animal models were spectacular."

Jason flushed, and his heart began to pound.

"I would be grateful if you would let my company partner with you in developing and testing this molecule. We would do a great job for you, and, if successful, it would turn our company around. I have a check in my pocket for two hundred thousand dollars made out to you that I will give you in return for your cooperation."

Jason's heart continued to pound, and he knew that his face was now beet red. How could this man possibly know anything about their discovery? None of the in vitro or animal studies had been published. Jason had already contracted with a large pharmaceutical company and a firm specializing in clinical trials to begin human studies. There would be no way that Evan Thompson could know about this research unless someone in the Glassman lab or one of these two companies had leaked information, and the contractual relationship with these two companies strictly prohibited releasing any information to any unauthorized individuals.

"Mr. Thompson, I'm very sympathetic to your situation. And I wish that I could help you. But I'm afraid it would be impossible to help you in this instance." Jason wanted to get up and leave, but he also didn't want to offend this man who apparently was of some importance to Sinai Medical Center.

"Jason, I've given a lot to Sinai. I deserve some consideration from you, and I expect that you will come through for me." Thompson's tone had become aggressive in nature.

"Mr. Thompson, I'm *very* sorry, but what you are asking is impossible. I'm not certain where you're getting your information, but it's not accurate. In addition, we already have signed agreements with companies should any of our molecules make it to phase one studies. I'm sorry I can't be of help to you in this way." Jason put his napkin down as he saw Evan Thompson's facial expression turn into a fierce anger.

"You fucking Jew faggot. You'll cooperate with me or else. I have powerful connections here, and unless you cooperate, you'll regret it."

Jason stood up and said, "Mr. Thompson, I wish you the best, but this meeting is over." He turned and walked away. He was shaking inside, not because of the 'Jew faggot' comment, but because this man had knowledge of proprietary research to which he should not have been privy.

Jason returned to his lab and asked Eric Adelman to bring everyone from the Blumenthal lab to his office. Five minutes later, Dr. Blumenthal, Craig Henderson, and three research assistants walked into Jason's office with Eric.

Jason stood up and closed the door. "Thank y'all for coming. I'm sorry to interrupt your day, but it has come to my attention that data from your lab has been disclosed to one or more individuals who should not be privy your work. Y'all know that what goes on in this research lab is proprietary and should not, under any circumstances, be divulged to anyone outside of this lab. Everyone in this lab has signed agreements to that effect. It isn't because we don't want to share results with other scientists. Your research will be published and become known to the entire scientific and lay community. But y'all are doing the work. It is important that you see it through, publish the results, and get credit for all of your hard work. Your careers are, in large part, dependent on your work here, and I suspect that you don't want your career stolen from you." Jason looked at the five men and women, all of whom had serious looks on their faces. "That's all. Thanks for coming."

The Blumenthal researchers turned and left.

"What happened?" Eric Adelman asked.

"I just returned from a lunch meeting with one of the board of trustees of the hospital who happens to be CEO of a biotech firm that is in financial trouble. Franklin Skor asked that I talk with him. The man basically just tried to bribe me to partner with him in developing the Blumenthal protein. The meeting did not end cordially." Jason frowned. "I just don't understand how he would know about this research."

Eric turned white in the face. "Was it Evan Thompson?"

"Yes. You know him?" Jason asked.

"His wife and Fran have become very good friends. They work together on the Susan Komen projects. I think that his wife is on the national board. Anyway, they have had us to their house a number of times. They live in Great Neck. And they send us theater tickets all the time. I've never particularly liked him, but Fran and his wife are very tight."

"Have you mentioned anything to him about the research?" Jason asked.

"Absolutely nothing. He's always asking me about what goes on the lab, but I've never given him any details and have never mentioned anything about Blumenthal's project. And he has really never asked me anything about specific projects. I swear to you that's the truth." Eric was clearly distressed.

"I have complete trust in you, Eric. Do you think Fran could have mentioned something to his wife?" Jason persisted.

"You know, it's conceivable that I've mentioned to Fran that we have a protein that shows promise in treating pancreas cancer, but I cannot imagine that she would discuss this with his wife. She knows about the privacy issues, and she really is not particularly interested in what goes on here. But I'll talk to her. If it was Fran who mentioned it, I'm really sorry, and it will never happen again."

"Don't worry about it, Eric. Frankly, I hope that it was Fran. It would mean that there's not someone here divulging more detailed information." Jason smiled. Eric stood up, and Jason could see Eric's distress as he walked out of the office. Jason doubted that Fran was the informant. Evan Thompson had mentioned results in animal models, and it would not be likely that Fran would have that knowledge.

Eric returned a few minutes later. "Jason, I just talked with Fran. She swore that she has never discussed or mentioned any research that goes on here with Thompson's wife or with anyone else."

"Thanks, Eric. Thompson knew too much for it to come from Fran. The informant could be from anyone in the lab, not just the Blumenthal lab. You know we go over all of the data in detail at the Friday conferences."

Eric shook his head. "Do you want me to investigate?"

"I think a brief memo to everyone in the lab reminding them of their privacy obligations is enough. Hopefully, I've heard the last of Mr. Thompson. I made it clear to him that we would have nothing to do with him."

At three p.m., Franklin Skor knocked on Jason's office door. "Come in, Franklin." Jason stood up and shook his hand. "Please sit."

"Thanks, Jason. I just got off the phone with Evan Thompson. I gather your meeting did not go well. He was furious and would not talk with me. He actually hung up on me."

Jason recounted the entire conversation. "My real concern is how he got the information about our research. It must have come from someone in our lab. I can't imagine my commercial partners divulging any information, but I will certainly talk with them about this."

"Jason, I'm very sorry that I put you in that position. I had no idea. Sean Whitaker called me and asked me to arrange that meeting with you. He said that Thompson was a major donor and on the board of the hospital, so I thought I was just doing a favor for the institution. I had no idea." Jason knew Sean Whitaker only superficially. Whitaker was the president and chief administrator for the hospital and, at the young age of forty-three years, was already considered one of the brightest and most successful hospital administrators in the country.

Jason smiled, trying to put Franklin at ease. "Don't think twice about it. Mr. Thompson is obviously under a lot of stress, and he's desperate. I simply couldn't help him. Besides, we are further in development than he knew and, in fact, have already signed contracts with clinical investigators."

"I'll relate what happened to Sean Whitaker." Franklin shook his head. "I question whether this man should be on the board of trustees."

"Oh, Franklin, just drop it. I wish no ill for Mr. Thompson. I doubt we'll hear anything more about this."

"The slander and bribery, I think, precludes his being on our board," Franklin insisted.

"Well, again, I think he is simply desperate. I really don't want to be the cause of any further pain for Mr. Thompson, so why don't we just let it be for now." Jason made it clear he wanted no further action.

❧❧❧

Jason quickly forgot about the meeting with Evan Thompson. He was consumed with managing the fourteen labs, all of which continued to be extraordinarily productive. Jason was also consumed by thoughts of Kevin O'Malley. On Wednesday, he called Kevin after arranging for his father and Sophia to stay with Julia after they returned from visiting the Olsens in Wilton on Saturday afternoon.

Kevin was obviously pleased. "I was hoping you would call."

"Hey, I was wondering if you could have dinner with me on Saturday. Not at my place, but at a restaurant. My daddy is going to stay with Julia after we return from Wilton." Jason frowned as he listened to Kevin chuckle. After a pause, Jason asked, "What's so funny?"

"Oh, Paul has mentioned to me several times how he gets a kick from you referring to your father as 'daddy.' I know it's a southern thing. It's cute," Kevin said reassuringly. Jason was glad Kevin could not see him blushing. "So, of course, but I'm taking you this time. We're going to Bouley, a French restaurant. What time shall I pick you up?"

"Is seven-thirty okay? Is it casual dress?" Jason asked.

"See you at seven-thirty. Khakis and no jacket. Can't wait to see you."

"Me, too." Jason answered, and then he heard a click as Kevin disconnected.

Jason and Julia drove to Wilton Friday afternoon. Julia was particularly excited to go because she had become very close to her two cousins, Ari and Zach. Julia had already announced that she was going to marry Ari, Paul and Amy's oldest son, but Jason hadn't mustered the courage to let her know that a marriage to Ari would not be possible. Paul, Amy, and their two sons were at the Olsen mansion when they arrived, and Anna arrived shortly thereafter.

Jason had continued to call Anna weekly, and they remained close confidantes. Anna had developed a deepening relationship with a genetics researcher but had not yet consented to marry him despite his numerous appeals. Anna had told Jason that she was not yet certain that he really wanted to marry, and when she was certain, she was going to say "yes."

The children played outside, and at supper, Jason sang the Sabbath prayers. Jason had continued to resist this tradition, but after Philip died, Evelyn Olsen prevailed in convincing Jason to sing the prayers for Julia, who always looked adoringly at Jason as he sang. She had recently started to sing along to the delight of everyone.

After the children were asleep, everyone congregated in the living room to chat. Paul and John Olsen prodded Anna to give updates on her professional and personal life, and Anna reluctantly obliged.

Jason had always been amazed at how different Philip and Anna were. Philip had always confided every detail of his personal life to his parents, whereas Anna had always been more enigmatic, except with Jason who knew virtually every detail of her professional and personal life.

"Say, Anna, what do you know about Sean Whitaker?" Jason asked.

"Who's Sean Whitaker?" Paul immediately interjected.

"He's president of your Sinai Medical Center," Anna said with a frown. "He was a few years ahead of me at Penn and was not particularly well-liked but supposedly brilliant. And he's gay by the way."

"That's not right. I understand he's married with children." Jason looked surprised.

"Yeah, well, Dr. Naive, in case you haven't heard, there are a lot of married men with children out there who like having sex with men. It was common knowledge at Penn that your president liked having sex with men when he was in school. Maybe a miracle has occurred. Anyway, why do you ask?" Anna asked.

"I just wondered. He set up a meeting between a CEO of a failing biopharmaceutical firm and me, and it was an unpleasant meeting. I'm sure that Mr. Whitaker must have known that this man was having financial problems, and it's just curious why he would have put me in such an unpleasant situation. It's not worth talking about. Just wondering."

After another thirty minutes of chat about family and business, Anna looked at Jason and said, "Jason, you've been unusually quiet, and you look nervous. So tell us what's on your mind. You can tell us. We're your family."

Jason could see that everyone was staring at him and waiting for him to answer. "Well, Anna, as usual, you're very perceptive. So, yes, I am nervous. Y'all know that I will love Philip till my last breath, and y'all also know that Kevin O'Malley has contacted me several times. Well, I did finally have dinner with him, and there is a connection. I just have to be certain that none of you have any problems with me going out with him." Jason saw everyone staring at him, and then, in unison, they all smiled.

"Jason, nothing would make us happier than to see you with Kevin." Evelyn Olsen was animated, clasping her hands and her eyes moistening. "Well, maybe seeing Anna finally getting married would make us as happy. But we consider Kevin part of our family, primarily because of you, and we have been praying that something would happen between the two of you."

"Good job, Jason," Paul clapped his hands. "So has it gotten physical yet?" Amy slapped Paul on the shoulder.

Jason blushed, as usual, and everyone laughed. "No, Paul, I'm not that easy. Well, I'm relieved. I just didn't want y'all thinking that my love for Philip would in any way be diminished."

# CHAPTER 10

Jonathan and Sophia walked into Jason's home promptly at seven p.m. on Saturday. Jason kissed them both and thanked them for giving up their Saturday night.

"We're not giving up anything," Sophia said. "You don't let us take Julia enough. And it's about time you get a little bit of a social life." Julia ran to Jonathan and Sophia and kissed them.

"I'll get her in her pajamas for you," Jason said.

"Forget it. Go finish getting ready. We're perfectly capable of taking care of Julia. And don't be so nervous. You look like you're ready to jump out of your skin," Sophia said, laughing and waving Jason on to his room.

Jason picked Julia up. "Do you mind if Daddy goes out for dinner tonight. Papa and Nana are going to stay with you."

"You're going with Kevin?" Julia asked. Jason nodded, and Julia continued. "I like Kevin. Is he going to be my daddy too?"

"You're silly." Jason tickled Julia's neck with his nose and lips, making Julia scream with laughter. Jason knew that Julia was extraordinarily smart and intuitive, and he also had the feeling that she had some remote memory of Philip, even though she was only four at the time Philip died and it was two years hence. Jason had been stunned that somehow Julia understood that a significant other for Jason would be male and not female—that somehow her daddy was different than other daddies. She never directly asked Jason about that issue other than to occasionally ask if she would ever have another daddy, never a mommy like her friends, only a daddy.

Jason dressed in khaki pants and a blue cotton pullover sweater. He wore the same Calvin Klein Obsession cologne he had used since high school. Despite attempts by his father, Philip, and Sophia to interest him in more stylish clothing, Jason had never bothered and rather bought almost all of his clothing on the web from LL Bean or Eddie Bauer.

He had one nice suit and one sports coat that he had bought at Bloomingdales for the unusual occasions that he was required to dress more formally, but, otherwise, his wardrobe was drab and a frequent topic of discussion and ridicule with family and friends.

On such occasions at which Anna was present, she would always openly embarrass Jason by exclaiming, "Don't listen to them, Jason. With that beautiful face and body, and that long dark Shirley Temple hair, no one looks at your clothes anyway."

Jason rode the elevator seventeen floors down to the street level ten minutes early, feeling very nervous. The concierge, Mr. Gregory, with whom Jason was very friendly, said his usual good evening and, after watching Jason pace the floor for several minutes, said "Dr. Green, don't be so nervous. You've got it all, man."

Jason laughed nervously and thanked him, and at that moment Kevin drove up in his BMW. Jason waved at Mr. Gregory and exited the building.

Jason got into the car and looked at Kevin. He noticed that Kevin had let his hair grow out a bit, and, as Kevin looked at him and smiled, Jason knew immediately that there was a connection between them that he had heretofore been unwilling to acknowledge. They looked at each other without saying anything until Jason broke the silence with a simple "Hey."

"Hey," Kevin answered, and again there was comfortable silence as they continued to look at each other. And then Kevin leaned over and kissed Jason. Jason put his hand on Kevin's face and responded, and after a minute or so, Kevin silently drove off.

"You know, I think we should go Dutch, or let me pay for dinner tonight. I called you, after all."

"It's my turn, and it's my restaurant. And don't worry about my finances. I can afford it." Jason had gathered from Paul that Kevin had become very wealthy from his business and had more money than he would ever need for several lifetimes. Still, Jason had never been comfortable with having his dinners—or anything else, for that matter—paid for by others.

The restaurant was intimate and quiet, and Kevin and Jason were given a corner table that was relatively secluded. The waiter brought bubbly water and a Chardonnay, which had obviously been preordered. Kevin tasted the wine and nodded, and the waiter poured both glasses. Kevin lifted his glass and looked at Jason with a serious expression. "This is a toast to you, with the hope that you fall in love with me as I have with you." Jason blushed, Kevin smiled, and they clinked glasses together.

"How do you know that I'm not already in love with you?" Jason asked.

"I could only hope. But I'm obviously a patient man. I've been waiting a long time."

"Kevin, what in God's name would have happened

had Philip and I been together until we were old men?"

Kevin looked down. "I don't know. I would have eventually found someone. I had resigned myself to that probability. I've dated over the years and have even had a couple of relationships that lasted for a year or two. I was actually in a relationship when Phil passed away, and I broke it off very soon after. I knew what I had to do."

"I don't know what to say. I'm flattered, puzzled. You didn't know me except for a superficial meeting at Camp David, and even now you really don't know me. I'm a little off center, you know."

At that moment, the chef came to their table. "Mr. O'Malley, it's good to see you again, and this is the young man you have mentioned so often." The chef had a deep French accent and introduced himself to Jason. He then asked each what they would like, suggesting that the lobster looked particularly good. Jason suggested that he simply prepare what he thought were his best dishes, and that would please him very much.

When the chef left, Jason said, "Last time we talked, I learned all about your family and your business. So tell me about you. What do you like doing?"

"I like to dance," Kevin said.

"Hmmm. You know, I've never been dancing. I had never even been to a gay club until I moved to New York, and really then only one time. And Philip and I never went dancing. But I'm open to it. What kind of music do you like?"

"I like rock and roll and rap." Kevin looked at Jason expectantly.

"We do have a problem. I think I'm four or five years older, and maybe that's the difference. I can't stand rap. Maybe it's a kind of poetry, but it's not music."

Kevin laughed. "So what do you like?"

Jason began to blush. "Barbra Streisand, Brian

McKnight, Dave Brubeck, David Sanborn, Beethoven, Brahms, Prokofiev, Stravinsky. Shall I go on?"

Kevin laughed. "My, we do have a problem. Well, I tell you what, I'm open to all of those people, if you're open to going dancing with me."

"Deal," Jason agreed.

The banter continued throughout the meal, which was exquisite, starting with a delicate quiche. The main course was duck, followed by a *salade nicoise* and finally a plate of fine cheeses from Normandy. The wine was a rich Cabernet from the Bordeaux region. Jason hadn't experienced such a fine meal since his fifth year anniversary dinner with Philip over two years ago. It was obvious to Jason that, although Kevin had not been raised in a sophisticated environment, he had certainly developed sophisticated tastes.

"Favorite movie?" Jason asked.

"The Godfather movies, all three," Kevin quickly answered. "Yours?"

"Schindler's list." Jason looked for a reaction from Kevin. "Do you know I'm Jewish?"

"Of course, I do. Amy is Jewish, and Paul might as well be Jewish now. When I first met Paul and we became friends, he told me all about Amy. He continues to be absolutely crazy in love with her. He always says she is gorgeous, brilliant, and Jewish, that she is basically Jason Green without the penis." They both laughed.

"I know. I've heard him say that. What would your family say if they knew you were going out with a Jew?"

"Honestly, I don't think I knew any Jewish people growing up in Omaha. I never knew anything about Jews, and my parents never mentioned anything to me about Jews. I heard the usual slurs, but it never meant very much to me, and I never gave it much thought. As far as I know, you're the first Jew that I've kissed. I don't know.

I've kissed more than a few people in my life, so maybe I have kissed a Jewish boy. But I know you are the first Jew that I've kissed in which the kiss was meaningful. In fact, you're the only person that I've kissed in which the kiss was truly with deep meaning." Kevin paused, looked at Jason, smiled, and said, "And what a nice kiss it was." Both men blushed at that.

"The other thing you should know about me, I think I told you, is that I am an atheist and anti religion." Again Jason looked at Kevin, expecting to get some sort of reaction from him.

"No argument from me on that score," Kevin said. "I think the various bibles are poorly written books of fiction."

At ten p.m., the two left the restaurant without having received a check. Kevin had obviously made prior arrangements to pay. "Thank you, Kevin. That was a special meal, and I had a great time." After the valet brought Kevin's car, Jason asked, "Would you like to come to my place for a nightcap?"

"I was actually hoping you would come to my place for the same," Kevin answered with a coy grin.

"I can't. My father and Sophia are babysitting. I have to let them get home," Jason said, determined.

"Of course, I'm sorry, I should have known. Do you think your father and Sophia would mind or be embarrassed if I came up?"

Jason laughed. "Of course not. I'm a big boy now. I'd like to see your place sometime, though. I know the building, and it's very nice."

"Well, maybe if you're lucky, I'll invite you up sometime." Kevin smiled. "Actually, I can't believe I'm sitting here in the car next to one of the most prominent and brilliant scientists in the world." Kevin looked at Jason with his piercing blue eyes.

"Kevin, you really don't know me. Being a scientist is relatively far down the list for me in terms of import."

"So, where am I on the list?"

Jason laughed. "Movin on up."

A few minutes into the ride back to Jason's home Kevin took Jason's hand, and Jason did not resist. They smiled at one another, and the remainder of the ride was in silence, Kevin occasionally rubbing Jason's hand with his thumb, causing Jason to become aroused.

They entered Jason's home, and Jonathan and Sophia stood. "We're going to have a nightcap. Please stay and have a drink with us," Jason said, as he kissed his father and Sophia.

"No, we're going home. Julia was a joy, as usual, and she didn't miss you one bit," Sophia informed them. "And her Spanish is almost perfect now." Jonathan hugged Kevin, and Sophia kissed Kevin and patted him on the cheek. "It's good to see you, Kevin, and thanks for getting this guy to go out for a change."

"It's good to see you both again," Kevin said. Jason thought their greeting was more familiar than it should have been. It suddenly dawned on him that probably the Olsens had talked to his father and Sophia about Kevin, although as far as he knew they had met at the Olsens on only a few occasions.

"What would you like to drink? I'm rather limited. The only hard liquor I have is scotch, but I have a nice sweet Riesling." Jason was visibly nervous.

"The Riesling is perfect," Kevin said, not taking his eyes off Jason. They sat on the couch facing Central Park. They clinked glasses.

"So, Kevin, what you didn't quite answer at dinner was what would have happened had Philip and I been together until we were old."

"I don't know. As I said, I would have probably

found someone, but I would have never been truly happy. There would have always been a void. I fell in love with you at Camp David. I can't explain it. From what Paul told me, the same happened to Phil. I never want to compare myself or compete with Phil. I couldn't. He was obviously an amazing and talented person, not to mention gorgeous." Kevin paused and looked down. "I don't want to sound disingenuous, but I really was devastated when he died. Actually, his death continues to be a source of great angst for me. I love Phil's family as if they're my family, and their torment after his accident sent me reeling. But on the other hand, well, here we are."

Jason set his wine glass down on the cocktail table and took Kevin's wine glass from him, setting it beside his. He moved close to Kevin, remembering his first kiss with Philip in this very room. He put his hand behind Kevin's neck and drew him close to him, and then they kissed passionately, each surrendering to the other. After a few minutes, Jason stood up and took Kevin's hand, leading him into his bedroom.

"I thought you had a three-date rule," Kevin whispered.

Jason did not respond. For the next hour, they made love passionately, naturally, with great joy, each exploring and pleasing the other. When it was over, they both lay in each other's arms, breathing deeply, both with faint smiles on their faces.

"How was it for you?" Jason asked after several minutes.

"Better than I had even fantasized." Kevin smiled, kissing Jason's neck. "And you?"

"I was nervous. You know, you're only second person I've ever had sex with, and you are only the second person I've ever made love to." Jason kissed Kevin tenderly on the lips.

"You're kidding? When you were a teenager, and in college, you didn't experiment?" Kevin asked, surprised. "Or you just don't have a high sex drive?"

"Oh, Kevin, I doubt you've met anyone who has a higher sex drive than the person you're looking at. But I grew up in a small town, and even in college, I just never met anyone who interested me. So I did a lot of fantasizing."

"Well, I can't say I was the good boy you were. But what I can say is that you've met your match in terms of sex drive." Kevin began kissing Jason passionately, and they made love a second time. Afterward, they showered together, washing and exploring each other's body.

"You know, I'm four or five years older than you. Maybe I'm too old for you." Kevin did not answer and continued washing Jason. They dried off, and Jason continued. "You didn't answer me. Maybe I'm too old for you."

"You are beautiful, Jason Green. I want to grow old with you."

They kissed again. "As much as I want you to stay over and sleep with me, I'm not ready to explain that to Julia yet, and she gets up early."

Kevin smiled. "I understand. You know I'm patient."

# CHAPTER 11

After that night, Jason and Kevin talked daily. Kevin worked late most nights, and the two rarely saw each other during the weekdays, although on an occasional Wednesday or Thursday, Mr. Gregory would call Jason around nine p.m. to announce that Mr. O'Malley was in the lobby. On those occasions, they would make love with little talk, and, usually, Kevin would want to have a second go-around. Jason discovered, to his amazement, that Kevin's sex drive surpassed that of Philip's and his own, which suited him fine. By the fourth week of their relationship, Jason told Mr. Gregory that it was no longer necessary that he be called when Kevin arrived and that he had given Kevin a key to his home, resulting in what Jason thought was a bittersweet but genuine smile. Mr. Gregory had been very close to Philip and the Olsen family.

Jason was usually sleeping by ten p.m. since he arose each morning by four forty-five in order to be ready for his six-mile run when Alejandra arrived at five. Jason would always awaken and snuggle with Julia before he left for work at seven, and he would rarely return home after five p.m. so that he could have dinner and spend

time reading and playing with her. Eric Adelman and all
of the postdoc fellows knew not to approach Jason after
four-thirty, and on the rare occasion that someone needed
to talk with him in the late afternoon, Jason would simply
say, "Follow me. We can talk on my way home." Eric or
the postdoc fellow would then walk quickly with him,
sometimes the entire two miles to his home discussing
the problem.

Kevin gradually became more involved in Julia's
life. He delegated more responsibility to his managers
and worked only on the Saturdays that Jason and Julia
went to Wilton. Otherwise, his managers knew that he
was not to be disturbed on the weekends, except for
emergencies. Kevin would show up at Jason's home on
Saturday mornings, and, usually, Kevin, Jason, and Julia
would go to Central Park or a museum, have lunch at a
small ethnic restaurant, and then spend the afternoon at
Jason's home reading and listening to music. On Saturday nights, Jason and Kevin would usually eat out at a
nice restaurant, frequently with Seth and Sheri Goldberg
or one of Kevin's friends, and either Jonathan and Sophia
or Alejandra would stay with Julia. On Sundays, Kevin
would usually spend the entire day with Jason and Julia.
Occasionally when Jason had pressing work that needed
to be done on Sunday, Kevin would take Julia to the zoo
or to a museum. Julia was becoming very attached to
Kevin and Kevin to Julia, and after four months, she
would frequently ask Jason whether Kevin was going to
be her daddy. Jason would always answer, "We'll see."

Jason had been grateful that Kevin had not pressured
him regarding his every-other-Saturday visits to Wilton,
and, in fact, Kevin had never mentioned the trips other
than to tell Jason and Julia that he would miss them and
see them Saturday evening. Six months into the relationship, Paul visited Jason in his office, as he often did. "Ja-

son, you have no idea how thrilled Mom and Dad are that you and Kevin are together. I talk to Kevin all the time, we confide in each other. It's time you bring him to Wilton with you. I know he wants to come and feels lonely when you're away. I doubt he has mentioned anything to you about it because he doesn't want to pressure you."

"You don't think it would make your parents uncomfortable? Or make you uncomfortable?" Jason asked with a serious tone.

"Frankly, we're uncomfortable that you're not bringing him. He's part of our family too." Tears welled in Jason's eyes when Paul said that, and from that time forward Kevin completely stopped working on weekends and drove to Wilton with Jason and Julia every other weekend.

Jason and Kevin's visits seemed as natural as when he had visited with Philip, although there were times when a sudden wave of sadness overwhelmed Jason, particularly when he and Kevin sat together in the oversized leather chair in the living room chatting with the rest of the Olsen family. It was the same leather chair that Jason and Philip had sat in many times during their visits now so long ago. Jason would always attempt to hide his sudden emotion, but his tears were always out of context to the conversation, and his sadness was obvious to everyone. Kevin would simply take Jason's hand and occasionally kiss him on the cheek when that occurred. No one ever commented when those episodes occurred, and the only noticeable reaction from any of the Olsens was that John would take Evelyn's hand.

The first time Jason shed tears in that leather chair, Jason said to Kevin later that evening as they were readying for bed, "Kevin, I'm sorry about earlier." Jason knew that Kevin understood what he was referring to.

Kevin went to Jason and kissed him tenderly. "I know you have enough love for two people. I don't expect you ever to stop loving Phil or thinking about him. I just hope you finally love me as you do Phil."

Jason looked at Kevin and smiled. "Have I not told you yet how much I love you?" Kevin didn't answer, and Jason held him, whispering in his ear, "I love you as much as anyone can love another person. I can't live without you, and we have to start thinking about living together." They made love and fell asleep in each other's arm. Ironically, it was only at the Olsen house that they slept together, since Julia did not seem to notice that they stayed in the same room. That misconception was put to rest about two months later when Julia crawled into their bed during the middle of the night after having had an apparent nightmare. She separated Jason and Kevin, who were entwined as usual, and crawled between them where she slept the rest of the night. Jason, who was a deep sleeper, had no recollection and was stunned when he awoke and saw Julia fast asleep between him and Kevin. Kevin was awake, looking and smiling as Jason opened his eyes.

෫ඁ෫ඁ

Shortly after the New Year, 2018, about eight months after Kevin and Jason had begun spending time together, Jason was in his office intently reviewing the final versions of two articles that were to be simultaneously submitted to the New England Journal of Medicine. Jason had already discussed the importance of these articles with the editors of the prestigious medical journal and was assured they would be published quickly after an immediate review. Jason's submissions had the reputation of being flawless, and it was rare they were not given priority. In addition, the editors of the New England Journal were particularly eager to have the honor of publishing what appeared to be extraordinarily important research.

The first paper described the isolation, structure, and mechanism of action of the Blumenthal protein and discussed the theory of how it would result in the destruction of pancreas cancer cells. The second article described the mouse studies, which demonstrated high cure rates in mouse pancreas cancer, and discussed how this research related to a potential cure for human pancreas cancer. Jason's concentration was suddenly interrupted by a soft knock at his door, and without looking up he motioned the intruder to come in. Everyone in the lab knew that Jason was hard at work editing these papers, and Jason was annoyed at the interruption. It was already two p.m., and he was determined to finish the revisions before going home. He looked up and was surprised to see Sean Whitaker, the President of Sinai Medical Center, standing at his door.

Jason stood up and went around his desk. "Mr. Whitaker, to what do I owe the pleasure of this visit?" Jason shook his hand and motioned for him to sit down. Jason thought it strange that the President of Sinai Medical center would show up in his office without first calling. He was annoyed at the interruption. He didn't let his annoyance show, but whatever the purpose of Whitaker's visit, his priority was to finish editing these two articles before the end of the day.

Jason had met Sean Whitaker at several different Sinai events over the years, but he had never talked with him other than very superficial greetings. He appeared to be in his mid-forties, was trim and handsome, and was dressed as if he were going to a formal affair.

"Dr. Green, I'm terribly sorry to barge in on you without calling first. But I thought it important, so I hope you don't mind."

"Not at all. What can I do for you?" Jason suddenly had a sinking feeling it involved Evan Thompson and Virtus Biotech, and, if that were the case, he was determined to quickly put an end to any such discussion. Jason sensed that Mr. Whitaker was tense, and he did nothing to ease that tension, continuing to stare silently at him.

"I know that I put you in a bad position several months ago with Evan Thompson. You probably know that he has been a substantial donor to the medical center and has been on our board of trustees for the past five years." Sean paused, waiting for a response, but Jason sat silently, continuing to stare at him. "I know that he asked for your help, and that you declined. Dr. Skor told me of the very unpleasant conversation, and I'm really disgusted and sorry about that." Another pause, and again there was no response from Jason. Mr. Whitaker leaned forward. "Here is the bottom line. Evan Thompson has informed me that his scientists have isolated what he believes is the same protein that you have isolated, and they have begun their animal studies to determine efficacy in treating pancreatic cancer. He has, apparently, already submitted a patent application for this protein and expects expedited approval at any time. He intends to proceed with legal action should you publish anything having to do with this protein."

Jason's heart was pounding, and his face was flushed. He couldn't stop the flushing, but other than that there was no reaction from Jason as he continued to stare at Sean Whitaker.

After an uncomfortable pause, Sean continued. "Mr. Thompson is willing to work with you. He understands that you have the knowledge and expertise to move this protein further and more quickly to market. And he is offering that, if you partner with his company, he will sign the patent over to you." Sean Whitaker sat back in his chair, and Jason sensed that he would stay silent until Jason responded. However, Jason sat silently, continuing to stare at Mr. Whitaker. The silence continued for several minutes, and Mr. Whitaker finally broke the silence. "Dr. Green, Sinai doesn't want to enter a legal battle with Evan Thompson. It would be terrible publicity for Sinai and would potentially tarnish your reputation and the reputation of our medical center. I would be very grateful if you give some consideration to what Mr. Thompson proposes."

Jason sat silently, trying to analyze all that he had just been told by Sean Whitaker. He quickly concluded that further discussion with Mr. Whitaker would not be beneficial in terms of either learning more about Evan Thompson's intentions or how Evan Thompson was able to garner information about the protein. He decided to end the conversation and then try to understand what had occurred. He stood, walked around his desk, and opened his office door. "Mr. Whitaker, thank you for your visit. Have a nice day."

Sean Whitaker stood, and after a moment's pause and with a frown on his face he walked silently out of Jason's office.

Jason closed the door and sat down at his desk, his heart still pounding from the revelations. Jason was certain that there was no possibility that the scientists at Virtus could have isolated, determined the structure, and synthesized this protein on their own. Their scientists had no experience with cancer proteins. From the research that he had done after his prior conversation with Evan Thompson, Virtus simply did not have the expertise to accomplish such a complicated scientific feat.

Jason concluded that Thompson must have stolen the structure of the protein from his lab—either from someone in his lab or from one of the groups that were contracted to perform human studies. Once they had knowledge of the structure, any second rate lab could synthesize the protein. Someone must have given Thompson the structure, and then his scientists quickly synthesized the protein and performed some animal studies while at the same time applying for a patent. Jason also knew that Virtus did not have the expertise to perform adequate animal or human studies to determine the efficacy of the Blumenthal protein and was using the patent as a means for forcing Jason to partner with Virtus. Evan Thompson's previous blackmail attempt, offering two hundred thousand dollars to Jason, hadn't worked. Now Thompson increased the stakes: If Thompson were successful in his patent application, years of important research by Jason's lab would have been nullified, and an important breakthrough in cancer treatment would be suppressed for years.

Jason also realized that he would have to delay submission of the two articles to the New England Journal of Medicine. All authors were required to sign an affidavit that there were no conflicts regarding any contents of the article to be published. Jason was becoming angrier by the moment. He felt obligated to inform the head of the Department of Medicine regarding the matter, but he would not use the medical center's legal counsel to help resolve the problem. Jason believed that in some way Sean Whitaker must have a vested interest in Evan Thompson's theft and was not to be trusted. Why would Sean Whitaker become beholden to this uncouth man with a failing business? The fact that Thompson had been a big donor and on the board of trustees of the medical center didn't change the fact that he twice tried blackmailing one of the medical center's scientists into entering an inappropriate relationship.

Jason called Franklin Skor who invited Jason over for an immediate conference. Jason explained the situation to Dr. Skor who was clearly shocked and angry at the developments. Skor immediately suggested a meeting with the medical center attorneys, but after explaining that he believed that Sean Whitaker was somehow involved, Jason convinced Skor to allow him to use his own sources and attorneys before involving the power structure of the medical center. Dr. Skor agreed and concluded the meeting by saying, "Jason, keep me informed. You know there is no one that I trust or respect more than you."

Jason returned to his office, closed the door, and began to perform the task that he, more than anyone, knew best—ask the right questions. There were several facts that Jason knew regarding this matter. First, Virtus had stolen the structure of the Blumenthal protein. Second, Evan Thompson instigated this theft because of a failing business and most certainly imminent personal financial ruin. Third, it was probable that someone in Jason's lab had cooperated with the theft, and it was certain that either someone in his lab or the contracted entities cooperated with the theft. Fourth, Virtus would be unable to proceed with development of the protein without Jason's cooperation. Finally, Jason was certain that Sean Whitaker was somehow involved with the theft.

The questions that needed to be answered were several. First, what would motivate someone from his lab or the contracted entities to cooperate with such a theft? Money was the obvious answer. Evan Thompson had tried to bribe him with two hundred thousand dollars, and for a research technician or a PhD student, and even for a postdoc fellow, that sum of money could seem astronomical. In terms of the contracted companies, only a few of the scientists knew anything about the structure of the protein. After all, the structure of the protein was unimportant to these companies. How that structure affected the progression of pancreas cancer was their real interest. In addition, the few scientists in these companies who did have access to the structure made a good living, and a few hundred thousand dollars would unlikely be enough incentive to commit a felony.

Of course, there could be motivations other than money. Evan Thompson was clearly prone to bribery, and there could be other underlying reasons that bribery would result in cooperation.

Another question was what would prompt Sean Whitaker to cooperate with Evan Thompson? Jason was certain that money would not be his motivation, since Mr. Whitaker's annual salary was over a million dollars. Jason had long ago learned, mostly through voracious reading since his childhood years, that there was usually one of two factors that resulted in a man's ruin—money and sex.

A third question was what Sean Whitaker's involvement was in the theft. Was he responsible for obtaining cooperation from someone in his lab or from one of the contracted entities? If so, it would seem more likely that it would be someone from his lab, since by virtue of location the chances of a connection between Whitaker and someone in lab would be relatively very high compared to a connection with a scientist at one of the contracted entities whose headquarters were in Princeton, New Jersey.

The final questions regarded the legal aspects of this matter. If he was unable to prove a theft, and Evan Thompson was successful in his patent application, did Jason have any legal recourse? And was there something he could do immediately to stop the Virtus Biotech's patent application?

Jason had finished his mental analysis at four-thirty p.m. and wrote down his questions on a note pad. He was agitated and angry. He packed his briefcase, deep in thought, and walked quickly to the elevators.

Eric Adelman called after him as the elevator door opened, "Jason, is everything okay?"

The elevator door closed without Jason acknowledging Eric. Jason had not even heard his question.

Jason walked quickly the two miles to his home, barely acknowledging Mr. Gregory as he entered the lobby of his building. Jason typically stopped and talked with Mr. Gregory for a few minutes before going up to his home. Going up the elevator, Jason thought he needed to let this matter go for the evening. He wanted to read and play with Julia. He took several deep breaths as the elevator door opened to his home. As he walked into the living room, Julia was sitting on Kevin's lap, and, they were playing a game on Julia's iPad. Julia jumped up and ran to Jason who scooped her up and tickled her neck with his nose and lips, causing the usual laughter.

Kevin stood up, and Jason said, "Hey, what a nice surprise."

"I was worried. I tried calling you all afternoon, and you didn't answer. I thought maybe something was wrong." Kevin look concerned.

"I'm sorry. I turned my phone on silence during a meeting and forgot to turn it back on." Jason smiled and hugged Kevin. He never kissed Kevin in front of Julia, and their greetings in Julia's presence were limited to hugs.

"Daddy, you can kiss Kevin. It's okay," Julia said with a smile, sitting on the couch with her iPad looking at Kevin and Jason.

"You're silly," Jason said, lifting her again and kissing her cheeks.

Julia frowned. "You always say that. I'm not silly."

"You don't look so good," Kevin said. "What's wrong?"

"Can you stay for dinner? I hope you didn't cancel anything important because of my absentmindedness." Jason went into the kitchen and hugged Alejandra, who was finishing dinner preparation.

"Of course. Can we talk later?" Kevin asked.

Jason nodded. He knew that Kevin was worried. Jason took out his phone and saw that Kevin had called ten times that afternoon. "I'm really sorry, Kevin. I'll explain why after Julia's asleep. Can you stay?"

"Absolutely."

Kevin went back to Julia, and they continued playing their iPad game. Jason watched as the two interacted and laughed. He looked at Kevin, his anger dissipating as he became aroused. He couldn't believe how lucky he was, falling deeply in love with another person whom he considered, like Philip, complete perfection.

Jason thought that had lived a near perfect life, which he attributed entirely to luck. He had two parents who had nurtured him flawlessly. He was born with an unusual intelligence that his father had optimally fostered. He was born with his mother's beauty. He was mentored by some of the great scientific and medical minds. And he had the luck of having two perfect partners. Not to mention having his father, Sophia and the entire Olsen family close to him. Of course, not all had been perfect for him. Vivid nightmares had plagued him since childhood, and although they had disappeared after moving in with Philip, they had returned after Philip's death. He had almost been killed by an assassination attempt. And the loss of Philip and his mother had been, and remained, heartbreaking. Nevertheless, on the whole, he had lived a charmed life. Jason continued looking at Kevin, deep in reflection.

After dinner, Jason bathed Julia. She was now six and a half, and Jason thought that soon she should be taking her own baths. After the bath, he took her into her bedroom, and they read together for a half hour. Julia talked Jason into singing to her. He sang her favorite song from *Frozen*, which caused her to squeal in delight. After the song, he kissed her and tickled her neck with his nose and lips, turned out the light, and Julia was asleep within a few minutes.

Kevin was in the living room and had poured two glasses of Riesling. Jason took the glass from Kevin and started kissing him passionately. "Hey," Kevin pushed Jason back. "Don't you want to talk?"

"No, I want to make love. Is that okay? I need to make love to you."

Kevin laughed. "Have you ever known me to refuse that kind of offer?"

"Get into bed. I need to make a quick call."

Kevin disappeared into the bedroom while Jason called Paul. "Paul, a bit of an emergency has come up. Is there a possibility that you could meet with me at your office in the morning."

"Of course," Paul said with concern. "I have a deposition I can easily postpone. Is everything okay with you?"

"It's regarding work, nothing personal. I'll explain tomorrow. Do you happen to know a patent attorney who could come to the meeting?"

"Shouldn't be a problem."

"I'm going to ask Kevin to come along. I think his expertise will be needed."

"Okay, come anytime. I'll be waiting."

Jason went into his bedroom. Kevin had undressed and was lying on the bed, exposed and aroused. Jason immediately forgot about his troubles, quickly undressed, and they made love eagerly and passionately. Afterward, they lay breathing heavily, Kevin touching Jason's face and looking into his eyes. "Should we talk now? I'm worried about you."

"There's nothing to worry about. Kevin, I want you to move in with me. It's time. I want to marry you, and I want to spend the rest of my life with you."

Kevin rolled onto Jason, and they made love a second time.

Afterward, Jason said, "Stay tonight. I have clothes for you here."

"What about Julia?" Kevin asked while running his hands through Jason's hair.

"Julia knows we're a couple. She's asked me several times why you weren't staying here. She'll be happy you're here."

"I've been dreaming this would happen." Kevin kissed Jason tenderly.

"What is your schedule tomorrow?" Jason asked.

"Just the usual work. We have a lot going on. Why?"

"I'm going to Wilton to meet with Paul tomorrow morning. I need your help. I'll explain everything tomorrow if you can come. I completely understand if you can't. It's last minute. I'll explain everything to you tomorrow afternoon if you can't come. It's late, and we should sleep now."

"Of course, I'll come with you. I just need to make a few calls on the way in the morning." They fell asleep in each other's arms. Jason awoke during the night, shuddering and sweating after a vivid recurrent dream of a murder scene from *A Farewell to Arms*, the Hemingway novel he that had read when he was thirteen. The victim in his nightmare was Philip. Kevin knew about his nightmares and held him tightly until he fell back into a deep sleep.

Kevin got up at four forty-five with Jason, and they ran the six-mile path around Central Park together. They showered and dressed together, and Jason woke and dressed Julia at seven a.m. Kevin was at the dining table as they came in for breakfast, and Julia broke out into a big smile, running to Kevin and hugging him.

"Is Kevin staying with us now?" Julia asked excitedly.

"Do you want Kevin to stay with us?" Jason asked.

"Yes, yes!" Julia yelled.

# CHAPTER 12

On the way to Wilton, Kevin made a few calls, and Jason called Eric Adelman to let him know he would be in late. After the calls had been made, Kevin asked, "Do you want to tell me what's going on?"

"I'd rather talk about us. I'll explain everything about my problem when we get there. There's no sense in repeating everything twice."

"Okay, what about us?"

"Well, you didn't answer me last night. Will you marry me, and will you move in with Julia and me? Not necessarily in that order." Jason smiled, and Kevin laughed.

"As if you don't know my answer to those questions," Kevin snickered. "Yes and yes, emphatically."

By the time they arrived at Wilton, they had decided that Kevin would sell his home and would start moving his belongings immediately. They would retitle Jason's home in both names. Kevin's home was a spacious twenty-eight hundred square foot condominium on the sixteenth floor overlooking Central Park, and he thought that the market value was probably around eight to ten million dollars.

Kevin insisted that he purchase half of Jason's condominium, an offer that Jason immediately rebuffed as being unnecessary. Kevin and Jason had never talked finances previously, and Kevin spoke emphatically, "Jason, I'll never feel like it is my home unless I pay for half of it, so you have to let me do this."

"It's a lot of money," Jason replied. "What kind of mortgage do you have on your place?"

Kevin chuckled. "Jason, I know from the trial and from what you've told me about your investments that you don't need my money. But you don't have to worry about me. I have over twenty million dollars in investments, and there is no debt on my home. I've made a fortune from my business. So money is not an issue. In fact, if you want to buy a bigger place together, I'm okay with that."

"Wow, I'm proud of you! I guess you're not after me for my money." Jason laughed. "Honestly, I think my place is perfect for us, and you never know what the future holds. I prefer to keep overhead as low as possible and stay out of debt. But if a bigger place is important to you...well, I'm fine with that."

"No, I love your place, and I know it has special meaning for you, and so it does for me. I just wanted you to know I'm open to anything and that money isn't an issue. But I want to pay you half the market price so I can feel it is my home as well."

They continued discussing how they would work out their financial affairs together and then decided they would soon have a dinner with the Olsens, Jonathan, and Sophia to make the announcement. They held hands in silence for the remaining twenty minute ride to the Olsen law firm in downtown Wilton.

The Olsen law firm was housed in its own building overlooking the Norwalk River. The law firm had been founded by Henry Olsen, John Olsen's great grandfather, over one hundred years ago, and despite its relatively rural location, the firm had developed a national reputation in corporate fraud defense as well as plaintiff product liability. The firm consisted of twelve partners headed by John Olsen and twenty associate attorneys who performed much of the research for the various cases.

John Olsen had made a fortune in various class action suits involving a variety of toxic pharmaceuticals as well as asbestos claims, and Paul had already developed a reputation as a brilliant corporate fraud attorney, having defended a number of high profile CEOs and CFOs for several Fortune 500 companies.

Paul came out to meet Jason and Kevin as they arrived, hugging both of them. He brought them into his spacious office where John Olsen was standing with another distinguished looking man.

John went to Jason with a worried look on his face and kissed him on the cheek, and then hugged Kevin. "Herc, this is my son, Jason Green, the brilliant scientist I've been telling you about. Jason, this is Herc Newman, one of the nation's foremost patent attorneys."

"Mr. Newman, it's a pleasure to meet you, and thank you for coming on such short notice. Dad, Paul, thank you for arranging this. I hope I didn't disrupt your schedules too much. Mr. Newman, this is Kevin O'Malley. He is the principal of O'Malley and Associates, an investigative firm."

Mr. Newman smiled. "John, you needn't have told me anything about these two young men. I've read all about both of them. It's my pleasure to meet you both."

The five men walked to the conference room next to Paul's office and sat at a Mahogany table that was identical to the conference table in Jason's conference room.

"Dad, this conference table is identical to the one in my lab. Is that a coincidence?"

John Olsen laughed. "No, I gave that table to Harvey Glassman as a gift. The same man who made ours made yours. You're very observant. So, Jason, what is this about? Paul told me there was a problem and neither of us slept much last night."

Jason took a deep breath. "I'll try to make this as concise as possible to give you an overview, and then we can go into more specifics. I have fourteen separate research laboratories that I oversee, each of which is directed by a postdoctoral fellow who supervises one or two PhD students and two or three research technicians. One of my labs has discovered a protein that cures pancreas cancer in animal models and has the potential to do the same in humans. It's an exciting discovery, and I had just finalized two papers which I was going to submit to the *New England Journal of Medicine*, literally today, for expedited publication." Jason paused for a moment and looked at everyone. "About three months ago, Franklin Skor, who is chairman of our department of medicine and who is an outstanding individual in every respect, called me and asked that I meet with a man named Evan Thompson. He is the CEO of Virtus Biotech and has been on the board of trustees of Sinai Medical Center for the past five years. Dr. Skor didn't know what Mr. Thompson wanted to meet about, but because it was Franklin Skor, I agreed to have a lunch meeting with him. It turns out the President of Sinai, Sean Whitaker, called Franklin to set up the meeting, which I didn't know at the time. Any questions?"

Jason looked at the four men again and, when they remained silent, he continued. "I met with Mr. Thompson about two or three months ago. I can get the exact date if that is important. Mr. Thompson related that his company was in financial trouble, which I had already known from a little investigation that I did prior to the meeting. The firm had gone public about five years ago and has had a number of failed drugs. The stock has plummeted nine-five percent, and there has been a lot of talk in the financial news of bankruptcy. In any case, Mr. Thompson told me that he had learned of this protein that we had discovered in our lab and the success it had in animal models, and he proposed that I partner with his company to further develop and market the protein. He said that it would turn his company around. He took a check out of his pocket, made out to me for two hundred thousand dollars, and handed it to me. I gave the check back to him and told him that I was sorry about his financial problems, but that I was unable to help him in that regard because other arrangements had already been made. He became very angry and verbally abusive."

"What did he say, exactly?" Paul asked.

"I don't think it's necessary to go into that, but—"

"It is indeed necessary. What did he say?" Paul persisted.

"He said that he had powerful friends at the medical center and that I had better cooperate or there would be repercussions. When I made it clear that it wouldn't be possible, he called me a Jew faggot." John Olsen looked down, and Jason thought that he saw tears well up in his eyes. "I just stood and told him the meeting was over, and I walked away." Kevin squeezed Jason's arm, and Jason smiled sadly at him.

"So, obviously there is more to this," Paul said with a frown.

"Yes, this is just the background. I returned to the lab, and Franklin Skor came over later that afternoon after a brusque conversation that he apparently had with Thompson. I explained what had happened, and it was then that he told me it was Sean Whitaker, the President of Sinai, who asked him to set up the meeting. Franklin was very upset and wanted to talk to the medical center's legal counsel, but I asked him to forget about it. But I was very upset about the incident, not because of Thompson's comments, but because Thompson had garnered proprietary information about important research. Everyone who works in our laboratory has signed a confidentiality agreement and is strictly forbidden to discuss research outside of the lab. Please understand, it's not because we don't want to share this information. It's because I'm responsible for developing the careers of these young scientists, and I'm responsible for making certain that the millions of dollars we spend yearly on these projects are dollars spent productively. To give this information away before it is published would be a major disservice to these young scientists and to the grantors of this research money—"

John Olsen interrupted, "Jason, you don't have to justify the secrecy issue. It's a given."

"Thank you for that. Well, at that point, I had no idea how Evan Thompson could have learned about this protein, other than through one of the people in our lab. I had also already contracted with a firm who organizes human clinical studies and a major pharmaceutical house to help with the human studies. Only a couple of scientists in these two companies have knowledge of the protein, its structure, and mechanism of action, and these scientists are in Princeton, New Jersey, so I assumed someone in my lab had talked. In any case, I sent a memo to everyone in my lab, reminding everyone of the privacy issue. I did speak directly to the men and women who work in the pertinent lab, and all denied talking to anyone outside the laboratory. But virtually everyone in the fourteen labs knows details of this discovery. In any case, I forgot about it after that day. Probably a mistake, but we were extremely busy, and I just thought my lunch meeting with Thompson ended the whole affair."

All four men continued to stare at Jason, and there was utter silence in the conference room. Jason continued, "Yesterday, Sean Whitaker came to my office unannounced. He said that Thompson had called him, told him that his scientists had discovered and synthesized what Thompson believes is the same protein that we had discovered, and that they were in the process of performing animal studies. In addition, Thompson had already applied for a patent. He said that Thompson had threatened legal action if I were to pursue any further use of this protein. Whitaker then said that Thompson was willing to sign over the patent to me if I were willing to partner with him in further developing the protein."

Jason took a deep breath. Paul interrupted, "What did you say?"

"I said nothing. I just stared at him, trying to digest what he was telling me. Then Whitaker said that I should reconsider, that Sinai did not want a legal battle with one of their board members, and that such a legal battle would tarnish my reputation and the reputation of the medical center."

"And what did you say?" John Olsen asked.

"I stood up, thanked him for coming over, and opened my office door. He reluctantly stood up and left. I didn't see any purpose in talking further with him."

The four men looked at each other, and Jason could sense that they understood the implications of what they had just heard. "So here are the facts of which I'm certain. First, Evan Thompson somehow obtained the structure of this protein, and his scientists have probably synthesized it, which is relatively easy to do. He stole it because he is in financial trouble. Someone probably from my lab has been involved in the theft. It is conceivable but doubtful that someone from the two contracted companies was involved in the theft rather than someone in my lab. In addition, I'm certain that Sean Whitaker is somehow involved in this whole affair. I have no evidence for that, except that his intervention in such a matter is entirely inappropriate. For a president of a hospital to pressure a scientist to become involved in unethical activities would be extraordinary unless he had a vested interest. It seems that Evan Thompson is prone to bribery, and I suspect that there is something going on between Thompson and Whitaker. Finally, there is no possibility that the Virtus scientists would have the knowledge to proceed with development of the protein without my help or the help of other sophisticated laboratories who have a lot of experience in cancer research. So those are the facts. This theft, if successful, would essentially be the theft of several years of intense research by multiple scientists who have spent millions of dollars, and it would likely destroy the careers of one my postdoc fellows and a PhD student." Jason sat back, took a deep breath, and waited for questions.

"Jason, isn't it possible that Thompson's scientists discovered this protein on their own?" Paul asked.

"Not a chance," Jason said immediately. "This is not a naturally occurring protein. It is man made, and we were able to create it only because we have a very sophisticated computer program that is able to model proteins to have very specific mechanisms of action. No one else on this planet has such a program with this capability. I can assure you that he stole the structure."

Paul persisted. "So if I asked him in a deposition how he was able to come up with the structure of this protein, he wouldn't have an answer?"

"I suppose that he could say that his scientists stumbled upon it. But the crazy thing is that Virtus has never been involved in cancer research, and in particular pancreas cancer research. I don't know how he could possibly make that argument, or if they had somehow magically created this protein how they would have known it would relate to pancreas cancer cells," Jason said with a frown.

John shook his head, looking dour. "Jason, this sounds like Nobel Prize winning research." He looked at Jason expecting a response. "Is it?" John persisted.

Jason shrugged. "I've never given that any thought. I suppose that if the protein does result in a pancreas cancer cure, that discovery along with the computer program might be worthy of consideration. I'm not worried about a Nobel Prize. My motivation is strictly related to my students and grantors."

"I know, I know. I know you well," John said with a smile. "I was just trying to understand the importance of this research, and it sounds more than impressive. Here's my take," he said, pausing for a moment. "I believe that Evan Thompson is a criminal and that we need to take the offensive. Herc, are you able to intervene regarding the patent application?"

"I know the people at the patent office. We'll contest the Virtus application and present your own application. Dr. Green, I'll need some information from you. I'll have my secretary email you a detailed questionnaire, and if you would attach the two articles that you are going to submit for publication, that would be very helpful. Time is of the essence, but the patent office doesn't move quickly, so I doubt that Thompson's application has been acted on. As soon as you get the information to me, I'll go down to DC and present the legal papers to the head of the patent office. I have a good relationship with him, and

I'll explain the situation. I can't guarantee they will cooperate, and we may have to fight this in a civil action."

"Thanks, Herc. Kevin, I understand why Jason wanted you at this meeting. What are your thoughts?" Paul asked.

"Well, I certainly agree with John that Thompson is a criminal, and I suspect Jason is correct that Whitaker is somehow involved. I've worked on very similar cases, and they are all pretty much the same. The motivation is almost always money, and, usually, sex is somehow involved as well."

Jason chuckled. "It's funny you should say that. Based on a lot of reading, fiction and nonfiction, I came up with the same conclusion: money and sex. And regarding Whitaker, he makes over a million dollars a year, so I would doubt that a bribe involving money would be his motivation. However, Anna happens to know him from Penn. She told me last time she was here that it was well known that Whitaker was gay. He's now married with three children. So just a situation that may be of no import."

John looked at Paul. "Do you think we should start a civil action, just to annoy Thompson and let him know we're on this? Maybe he would back off?"

Paul paused in thought and then said, "I think we should let Kevin do his thing first, and in the meantime, hopefully, Herc can prevent Thompson's patent application. I'm afraid if we start a civil action such as a restraining order or even a damage claim, Thompson and Whitaker will cover their tracks, and we may never get to the bottom of this. I don't think it's enough that we simply stop Thompson from this thievery. I think we need to put Thompson out of business. Do you agree, Jason?"

Jason looked at Paul and hesitated. A sudden wave of sadness overwhelmed him. Paul looked so much like

Philip, and some of his mannerisms were similar. Tears welled in Jason's eyes, and he softly said, "Paul, I'm not certain what you mean by putting him out of business." Kevin noticed Jason's sadness and grabbed his hand.

"Jason, are you okay?" Paul asked, concerned. Jason nodded and waved him on. "What I mean is that Thompson should never be in a position that he can bribe someone or steal someone else's work in the future. I just think we have that moral obligation. This guy is obviously a sociopath, and although our primary obligation is to make you whole, I just believe that we need to be certain he doesn't try this again."

The four men looked at Jason who had now composed himself. "I can't disagree with that. If Kevin can find out how this all happened, I think it will put an end to all of it. Mr. Newman, we will have to involve the Sinai legal staff in the patent application since Sinai is my employer. I assume that you have no problems communicating with them, and I can assure you that they will allow you to take the lead, particularly since I'm footing the bill." Mr. Newman nodded.

John looked at Kevin. "Kevin, how do you propose to go about finding out what happened?"

"John, I don't think you want or need to know the answer to that question. But I'll find out, and I predict Mr. Thompson will soon be busy trying to defend himself in a court of law, in order to prevent doing prison time in upstate New York."

The five men sat in silence for a moment. Jason took a deep breath. "I cannot thank y'all enough for your help. Mr. Newman, bill me directly. I have been very frugal with my laboratory money, and I have plenty to pay y'all for your work. Paul, I expect to be billed. I know we are family, but this is business, and my business has plenty of money to pay. And the same goes for you, Kevin. Money is no issue, and I will not sleep unless I get reasonable bills from all of you." All four men began laughing, and Jason flushed in his face, as usual. "I'm not trying to be funny."

John Olsen went to Jason and hugged him. "You're coming this weekend?"

"Of course, I am, with my first payment to your firm."

Paul took Jason aside. "Are you okay? You seemed to choke up a bit."

"I'm fine. When you were talking, I just saw Philip and got a little weepy. I'm sorry."

"See you this weekend," Paul smiled sadly and hugged Jason.

As Kevin and Jason walked to the car, Kevin asked, "Are you okay?"

Jason nodded with a sad smile as they continued to walk silently to the car.

"I know how much Paul reminds you of Phil." Kevin took Jason and held him for a minute before they got into the car. Jason didn't resist. He knew that Kevin understood his sadness and Jason loved him all the more for enduring his emotional lapses.

# CHAPTER 13

On the drive back to the city, Kevin began grilling Jason with questions. "Do we have to talk about this already?" Jason asked, suddenly feeling fatigued.

"Yes. I know you seem overwhelmed by all of this, but time is of the essence. One or more of these players are going to find out that we are on to them, and as soon as he or she does, it's going to make my job more difficult." Kevin seemed insistent and very business-like.

Jason frowned. "So what do you need to know?"

"So you oversee fourteen different labs. How many of those labs would have access to the data and structure of your protein on their computers?"

Jason quickly answered, "Only two: The Blumenthal lab and the Bioinformatics lab under Eric Adelman. Why?"

"Do the people in the other twelve labs have access to those computers?"

"Only the postdoc fellows and PhD students in those two labs have passwords to those computers, and they are strictly forbidden to give those passwords to anyone else, including other postdoc fellows or PhD students. The lab technicians are unable to access the computers." Jason answered, yawning.

"Is there any chance that the fellows or students gave their passwords to technicians or fellows or students in one of the other labs?" Kevin had taken his notepad out and was writing as Jason continued to focus on driving.

"You know, anything's possible. But everyone knows that I consider it a serious problem if that happens and that if there's a breach in protocol, there had better be a good reason or that individual could be let go. After our experience with the espionage in 2005, Eric and I developed ways to detect breaches in protocol."

"How's that?" Kevin asked.

"Well, for example, we know when every computer in every lab is accessed, what time the password is put in, and whose password it is. In other words, everyone has his or her own individual password. I get a printout daily and if there were unusual times for access, say two in the morning, I would usually ask the fellow or student what brought them back at that time."

"How often does that happen?" Kevin persisted.

"It's not uncommon. These are very driven young men and women, and if they have intense experiments going on, sometimes they don't sleep well and end up coming to the lab at all hours of the night and on the weekends. But I will usually mention something to them, usually in the context of telling them to get enough rest or just take it a bit easier."

"I'd like to see that log that you keep of computer access for those two labs. So then it seems to me that it would be unlikely that passwords would be given out by any of the fellows or students, in which case, I would suspect that the person we are looking for is either in the Blumenthal lab or the Bioinformatics lab. Wouldn't you agree?"

"We do have Friday conferences, and everyone would know what was going on in the Blumenthal lab at that conference. And in terms of the structure of the protein, everyone would be able to see the structure on a slide that would be shown by Blumenthal."

Kevin persisted. "Would someone be able to copy the structure from that slide, or was there ever a handout of the structure given to everyone?"

"No, never a handout. Someone could I suppose take a picture of the slide, but I would have noticed that."

"So I believe that we're dealing with someone in one of those two labs. Could it be one of the research technicians?" Kevin asked, looking at Jason who was pursing his lips in thought.

"They don't have a password to the computers. It's unlikely. I suppose that, when the computers are on, a research technician—or, for that matter, someone from another lab—could surreptitiously print out data regarding the protein, including the structure. But when both the fellow and students are out of the lab, the computers are supposed to be shut down. For example, at the Friday conferences, all of the computers are shut down." Jason paused again in thought. "I think that it would be very difficult for someone from a different lab to come into the Blumenthal or Bioinformatics lab, know where the specific data is for the protein on the computer, and print it out. So I think you're right. Most likely it would have to be a fellow or PhD student in one of those two labs. Can we stop talking about this now?"

"I need the names and cell phone numbers of the fellows, PhD students, and research technicians in those two labs." Kevin continued, ignoring Jason's plea.

Jason reached into his pocket and took out his iPhone. "Look under contacts." Jason proceeded to give the names of the two postdoc fellows, three PhD students, and three research technicians in those two labs. "Why do you need their phone numbers and how are how are you going to look into this?"

"You don't need to know that. Anything unusual about any of these people you have mentioned?"

"No. They are all fine individuals. They are all ambitious, driven, very smart, even brilliant, and I have no memory for anything unusual regarding their behavior." Jason paused and frowned. "You know, Craig Henderson, one of the PhD students in the Blumenthal lab, did suggest that he and I go out to dinner. That was probably a year or more ago. And it was out of context. He came to my office about a problem he was having with some statistics."

"What did you say?" Kevin laughed. "I'm getting jealous."

"I ignored the comment and continued discussing the statistics. He never made the suggestion again, and I forgot about it until now."

"Do you know if he's gay?"

"No idea. I know little about these people's personal lives, except when one has a baby. Then everyone celebrates. I try to have each lab group to my place for dinner once a year, and they're allowed to bring their husband or wife, but not girlfriend or boyfriend. I believe Craig came by himself when his group was invited. That would have been four or five months ago. So I assume he's not married."

"What do you know about him?"

"Very nice young man. Graduated from Yale summa cum laude. He had a perfect academic record, extremely smart, maybe even brilliant. He writes very well, he gets along with others, seems very considerate of others. No ego problems that I can see."

"How do you remember all of this? Do you know all of your people this well?"

"I have a pretty good memory," Jason said.

"How well I know. Anything regarding any of the others in those two labs that stands out? What about Eric Adelman?"

"He and I have been best friends forever. He would never do anything unethical. I would bet my reputation on that."

"What is his salary?"

"I've managed to get it up to two hundred and twenty-five thousand. He is the highest paid PhD at Sinai, and I had to fight the system to get that." Jason took his eyes off the road for an instant to look at Kevin writing. "Eric is frugal. His wife is from a wealthy family. They're not hurting for money."

"Okay. Sorry. I'm just trying to be thorough," Kevin said as he continued writing. "And what else do you know about Sean Whitaker?"

"Only what I said this morning. Anna knew of him at Penn, he was three or four years ahead of her. He was apparently a whiz kid, was hired as a vice president at Sinai right out of school, and quickly became president after the previous president retired. Anna said it was well known at Penn that he was gay. But I know that he married soon after moving to the city, and he has two children. That's all I know about him personally. His salary is public knowledge. I know it's well over a million. When he came to my office, I sensed that he was pretty desperate to get me to cooperate. He knew what he was asking was inappropriate, and he knew that I knew. Can we stop now? I'd rather talk about you and me."

Kevin persisted. "What else can you tell me about Thompson?"

"Again, just what I told you this morning. Maybe I didn't give you a sense of how desperate he was at the lunch meeting. He was sweating, and his face was flushed. He looked *really* desperate. And when I refused, I thought he was going reach across the table and choke me. He was really angry. I got the sense that he has no morals and would do anything to get my help. But I know nothing of his personal life. Can we stop now? We're almost home."

"What about Franklin Skor?"

Jason frowned. "Forget him. He's a brilliant, wonderful human being, not an unethical bone in his body."

"Why did Whitaker ask him to call you? Why didn't Whitaker just call you?"

"Whitaker meets regularly with all of the departmental chairmen, and I'm sure they know each other well. I've never spoken to Whitaker other than to say hello at a hospital function. I have a reputation of resisting unnecessary meetings or getting involved in hospital or medical school politics, and I'm sure Whitaker knew that Franklin would have a better chance of success at setting up the meeting. Now can we stop?" Jason pleaded once again as they were pulling up to the valet in front of their building. It was already approaching noon.

"I have what I need. Jason, please say nothing to anyone about any of this, including Adelman and Skor. You can tell Skor that you're trying to stop Thompson's patent application, but absolutely mention none of this to Adelman. People can slip up and talk when they don't mean to."

The valet took Jason's car. "Do you want to have a quick lunch?" Jason asked, suddenly becoming aroused.

Kevin laughed. "I see you want more than lunch. As tempting as it is, I've got work to do. I'll see you this evening."

"See you this evening." Jason kissed Kevin tenderly, turned, and began his two miles walk to his office. He was deep in thought, recounting all that had transpired that morning, completely unaware of the frenetic movement of people passing him on the sidewalk or the streets jammed with frustrated drivers trying unsuccessfully to move at a speed that would get them to their destinations on time. Jason recalled the theft of data when he was a medical intern in Dr. Glassman's lab twelve years previous and how it almost resulted in his own death. At least, Jason reasoned, that theft was by a government that was trying to advance itself in the scientific world. At least one could rationalize that such a theft, however unethical, was done for noble purposes, however ignoble the means used. There was nothing noble about Thompson's theft. Thompson's only motivation was greed. Jason wondered how far Thompson would go to get his way.

"Hey, mister." Someone tapped Jason on the shoulders while standing at a corner, waiting for the light to turn green. Jason turned to see a very young man smiling at him.

"Do you have five dollars to spare?" The young man looked to be in his teens and had the appearance of a highly paid Fifth Avenue model.

Jason took five dollars from his wallet and gave it to the young man as the light turned green. Jason smiled and started walking across the street.

"Wait, mister." The young man continued to walk with him. "For just a little more, we can have some fun."

"Young man," Jason answered, "you need to get off these streets and stop this kind of behavior. If you need help, you can wait in my office at Sinai Medical Center. I'll call our social service department, and they'll come over to help you."

The young man turned around and quickly walked away. Jason watched him disappear around the corner and then continued his own walk, feeling sad for the young man and his uncertain future. But Jason thought it strange that such an attractive, well-dressed young man would be asking for money or soliciting for sex. He was physically beautiful and could have easily obtained a job with a modeling agency.

# CHAPTER 14

Over the following two weeks, work returned to normal for Jason. He called the editors of the *New England Journal of Medicine* to inform them there would be a delay in submission of the two articles. Jason explained to them that the articles were finalized and ready for submission but that there were some legal details that needed to be finalized before he was allowed to submit. The editors seemed to be satisfied with that explanation and said that they looked forward to receiving the articles in the near future.

When Eric Adelman questioned Jason regarding the submission, Jason explained that he was delaying the submission because of "the Thompson affair." Jason knew that Eric was not satisfied with that explanation and was grateful that Eric did not press him further. Eric was his close friend and partner, and he wanted to tell him all that was happening, but Kevin had been adamant that Jason not disclose any details to Eric or to anyone else. He knew Eric would ultimately understand after the whole affair was resolved.

Jason had asked the two contracted companies to proceed as quickly as possible with developing a plan for the human studies of the protein. He felt certain that the Thompson problem would be resolved by the time a plan was developed and finalized. Furthermore, additional animal studies of the protein showed a ninety-five percent cure rate of pancreas cancer, a remarkable development since cure rates in the animal models using other therapies was no different than in humans. If this protein could cure ninety-five percent of human pancreas cancers, this discovery would be a momentous development in cancer research and would propel Sinai Medical Center to the forefront of all research institutions.

Jason wanted the Thompson affair resolved, and, although he was usually a patient individual, he pressed Kevin every day to reveal any new information that may have been garnered. Kevin's response was always the same. He would go to Jason, kiss him tenderly on the lips, and say, "Jason, be patient. We're making progress, and I don't want you involved in the intricacies and details of our investigation. It wouldn't be good for you, and it wouldn't be good for me. It's going to take several more weeks, maybe a few months, before we solve this. But as sure as I love you, we will solve this."

After a week of daily pressure, Jason gave up and said nothing further to Kevin.

Jason and Kevin's relationship became more intense by the day. They talked to each other three or four times daily, and after work hours the two were inseparable. Kevin had moved all of his clothing and personal items into Jason's home, and they made love and slept together every night. Jason was stunned that his love for Kevin was as intense as it had been for Philip. Feelings of guilt or betrayal—he couldn't decide which—frequently invaded his thoughts, but he learned to compartmentalize those thoughts, believing that Philip would want his happiness.

Julia was ecstatic with the union and asked Jason several times whether Kevin was going to be her new daddy. Jason would always answer: "We'll see." It was clear to Jason that, like Philip, Kevin adored Julia. The two would be in their own play world, reading or playing on Julia's iPad. Nothing could divert their attention. Jason would occasionally attempt to interrupt them with a question and would be completely ignored, making him silently laugh in relief. It was as if he didn't exist when they were playing together.

Jason could see the joy in his father and Sophia after Kevin had moved in. It was as if a huge weight had been lifted from Jonathan Green's soul. He was once again gregarious, laughing and telling jokes, discussing economics and politics with Jason and Kevin. The change in his father's demeanor had greatly relieved Jason since he knew that it had been his own sadness that had burdened his father since Philip's death.

One month after the meeting at the Olsen law office, Jason, Kevin, and Julia went to Wilton and, as usual, spent Friday night with the Olsen family. Nothing was said of the Thompson affair, and the weekend was typical, with Jason, Paul, and Kevin running the seven-mile route, Paul and Amy's children playing with Julia, and a lively dinner discussion of politics and economics. During supper, Jason invited the entire Olsen family to a dinner the following weekend that he would host at Trattoria del'Arte. He saw the immediate surprise on the faces of all of the Olsens as they all gazed at each other, wide-eyed. He knew their surprise resulted from Jason's refusal to go to that restaurant after Philip's death. Trattoria del'Arte had been Philip's favorite restaurant, the place that he had taken Jason on their first date, the place that Jason, Philip, the Olsens, and his father and Sophia had eaten and celebrated so often over the five years of

Jason and Philip's marriage, the place that Jason and Philip had celebrated their fifth wedding anniversary only two months before Philip's death.

❦❧

Jason had reserved the upper section of the Trattoria del'Arte for the dinner. Everyone dear to Jason and Kevin was present: John and Evelyn Olsen, his father and Sophia, Jason's sister who had flown in from New Orleans, Anna Olsen, Paul and Amy with their children, Seth and Sheri Goldberg, Eric and Fran Adelman, and Alejandra. Kevin's two sisters had also flown in from Omaha for the dinner, the first time they had visited Kevin in New York since he had moved there in 2008. After the wine was served, Jason clinked his glass and stood up, the lively chatter ceased, Julia crawled onto Kevin's lap, and everyone stared at Jason.

Jason took a deep breath and then spoke slowly. "There is a Hebrew proverb which says 'Say not in grief that he is no more, but live in thankfulness that he was.' I wrote that proverb on the back of my iPhone after Philip died, and I read it many times every day. It didn't help very much. Many of you here told me, in kindness, that time would heal. But time can be an eternity, and grief is not bound by finite schedules. It was only because of your love and support, and because of my love for Julia, that I've been able to bear this terrible grief.

"I wanted to have our meal here tonight because, on so many levels, this restaurant has meaning for me. Here was my first date with Philip, and here Philip and I celebrated each anniversary after we married." Jason paused to wipe his tears. "It was here that Philip went frequently with his family growing up, and here was the center of many fond memories that Philip would frequently talk about with me. In the end, the grief resulting from Philip's death cannot be extinguished, nor should it be. But in the end, Philip's love for me, for all of us, has left memories that also cannot be extinguished, and because of those memories, this grief has become tolerable."

Julia sat in Kevin's lap, transfixed on Jason. Most everyone at the table had moist eyes or was shedding quiet tears. Jonathan Green's tears were flowing. Jason had never seen Kevin shed a tear, but he was wiping his eyes with a napkin.

"I promise, the rest of tonight will not be gloomy, because we're here to celebrate not only good memories, but also a new beginning. I met Kevin in 2005 at Camp David. We spoke Mandarin to each other that day and, although, I would occasionally think of him over the years, I never dreamed that he would one day become part of my life. When my daddy announced his engagement to Sophia in San Francisco, he said he would love my mom till his dying day, but he discovered that he had enough love for two. I envied and admired him for that and thought such could never be possible for me. But I was wrong. Over the last eight months, I have fallen deeply in love with Kevin O'Malley. My love for him is as profound a love as any one person can hold for another. As it was with Philip, Kevin is whom I first think of when I awake, and the last person I think of before falling asleep. Every day I say to myself that I could not possibly love Kevin more, but the next day I find that I am wrong. What good luck I've had to find perfection once again.

"I am so grateful for all of you, I am so grateful that Kevin is so understanding and tolerant, and I'm so grateful that in my eternal grief I have once again found happiness and contentment. Kevin and I wanted to be with all of you tonight to announce our engagement to be married."

Julia immediately shouted, "Can Kevin be my daddy now?"

Everyone laughed and clapped as Kevin, whose tears were drying on his cheeks, stood, holding Julia who could not take her eyes off of Jason. Kevin walked next to Jason, and Julia reached over for Jason to take her. As Jason kissed Julia, Kevin began to speak.

"I want to say just a few brief words. I inexplicably fell in love with Jason Green on that day at Camp David. That love has endured for almost twelve years, as strange as that may seem. I never dreamed or expected that my love for Jason would ever be returned. But because of horrific circumstances, here we stand. Phil leaves fond memories, but, more importantly, he literally lives on in everyone here whom he loved and who loved him. I can never replace Phil, but I will always honor him by being Jason's loving husband until my last breath and by being a loving father, uncle, brother, and son to all of you sitting here."

Julia whispered into Jason's ear as everyone stood up to congratulate the two, "Is Kevin my daddy now?"

"Yes, sweetheart, you can call him Daddy now. Now you have two daddies." Jason tickled her neck with his nose and kissed her, and then she squirmed down. She sat on a chair, and Jason looked over at her frequently as she sat quietly watching everyone kissing and congratulating Kevin and him. He wondered if Julia had some instinct that she once had another daddy, and perhaps that daddy was a man named Philip. Julia had never asked him about the other man in the picture that sat on the buffet table in their living room. But Julia was so smart, Jason thought, she might even be brilliant. He suspected that she knew. One day he would tell her everything.

The rest of the evening was jovial. Kevin and Jason sat close, holding hands under the table, pressing their legs against one another, much like Jason and Philip had routinely done. Jason had never told Kevin that pressing legs under the table had been a ritual between Philip and Jason that started on their second date and would frequently result in what seemed to others inappropriate laughter. Jason avoided talking about Philip with Kevin, although Kevin frequently asked questions about their relationship. Kevin had made it clear that he admired Jason's deep love for Philip and that his mission would be to make Jason love him the same. When Jason would occasionally become weepy after a vivid memory of Philip entered his thoughts, Kevin would quietly hug and kiss Jason. Jason would always smile sadly and thank Kevin for understanding.

Jason had suffered frequent night terrors from the time he was a small child up until his relationship with Philip. After he and Philip had moved in together, the night terrors gradually disappeared, but they returned with intensity after Philip died. They were becoming less frequent since he and Kevin were sleeping together, but each time one did occur, Kevin would hold him, just as Philip had, until he fell back into a dreamless sleep. Jason often thought of the dichotomy between his professional and personal life. In his professional life, he was strong, bold, determined, ambitious, rock solid, even powerful. And yet, in matters of the heart, he was emotional, neurotic, at the edge of a cliff. He often wondered why Philip, and now Kevin, could be attracted to someone who was so emotionally vulnerable.

Kevin's sisters traveled to New York without their spouses in order to spend time with Kevin and Jason alone. Like Kevin, they were physically beautiful, and the older sister was outgoing, jovial, and obviously adored Kevin. The younger sister was more reserved and had never accepted Kevin's homosexuality. Nevertheless,

Kevin, Jason, and Julia spent all day Saturday prior to the dinner showing them New York City, and, by dinner that Saturday evening, both had become comfortable with Kevin and Jason together.

John took Jason aside at the dinner between the hors d'oeuvres and entrée. "Jason, I want you to know how much your words meant to Evelyn and me, and I want you to know how much we love you and Kevin, and how happy we are that you two are marrying. We would also like you to have the wedding at our house, maybe not the lavish affair that you and Phil had, but—"

Jason interrupted, "Dad, I don't have to tell you what y'all mean to me, and I appreciate your offer. But, in all honesty, I don't believe I could emotionally handle a wedding at your home. And I don't think that would be fair to Kevin. I also know it would have to be terribly emotional for you and Mom, and Paul and Anna. So I've thought about this. I really think it best that Kevin and I get married alone, and just not make a big deal of it."

John smiled and nodded. "You're the most considerate person I've ever known. I was hoping you would say that, because you're right, I'm not sure Evelyn and Anna could handle it, even though they are genuinely thrilled for you two." John hugged Jason, kissed him on the cheek, and returned to his seat.

☙❧

The following Friday, Jason had his weekly conference with his postdoc fellows and PhD students from ten a.m. to noon, rather than the usual two-thirty to four-thirty p.m. There was considerable speculation among the fourteen labs regarding the schedule change. Everyone knew that the Friday afternoon conference was sacrosanct for Jason Green. In all the years that he had been head of the Glassman laboratories, since 2010, there had never been a Friday afternoon conference that had been cancelled or changed to a different time. The major rumor that had spread through the labs was that Jason was ill and had to have a surgical procedure Friday afternoon.

Everyone gathered in the conference room at ten a.m. and when Jason entered everyone was unusually quiet. Jason looked at everyone and sensed that many were anxious. "Okay." Jason smiled. "Eric tells me there are all sorts of rumors about the schedule change. I'm not sick, I'm running six miles everyday, I don't have cancer, and I'm not having surgery. I'm getting married this afternoon." Everyone stood up and applauded, and someone yelled out, "Who is he?"

"Y'all will meet him soon. We've been seeing each other for the past year, and he's amazing. So relax, your research efforts are not at risk." Everyone laughed and sat down, and the conference went on as usual until noon. Jason left hurriedly, everyone attempting to congratulate him as he ran to the elevator.

At two p.m., Judge Lackland entered Jason and Kevin's home. Jason and Kevin were both dressed in beautiful designer suits. Julia did not go to school that day and wore her favorite beautiful white frilly dress that Jason had bought at Saks. Jonathan and Sophia were also present and dressed in the same clothes they wore to their own wedding. Jason hired a photographer who inconspicuously photographed the affair.

In a brief ceremony, in which Julia handed two beautiful Tiffany gold rings to Judge Lackland and stood holding Jason's hand, Jason and Kevin were married. Although Philip's presence was conspicuous, the ceremony was joyful, and for those brief minutes, Jason thought only of Kevin, how much he loved him, and how lucky he was to have been given a second chance with such an amazing and beautiful person.

# CHAPTER 15

Following the wedding ceremony, Jason, Kevin, and Julia drove to Wilton, and that evening Kevin announced that they had been married. Jason had not told the Olsen family when the wedding would occur. He simply wanted everyone's lives to continue seamlessly without emotional upheaval. Jason had asked John to explain to the family the rationale for a simple and private ceremony, and Jason could see that Evelyn, Paul, and Amy were not surprised when they made the announcement. Everyone was genuinely happy, and after hugs and kisses, John served expensive champagne, and Evelyn brought a present that she had obviously planned for whenever the wedding occurred.

Evelyn handed the gift to Kevin and kissed them both on the cheek. Kevin opened the beautifully wrapped very large box, and in it was a stunning oil painting of John, Evelyn, Anna, Paul, Amy, Kevin, Jason, and the three children that had been painted by a well-known artist based on photos given to him by Evelyn. Jason fought back tears unsuccessfully, and, after taking Jason's hand, Kevin said, "We will always treasure this painting. Thank you so much." Jason smiled sadly and nodded. Everyone knew that Jason's tears were because there was one person missing.

After supper, Julia and her two cousins played downstairs, and Paul, John, Jason, and Kevin sat in the living room. Jason sat with Kevin in the oversized leather chair as he had with Philip so many times. "It's good to see you two in that chair together," Paul said as he sat on the couch next to his father. "Jason, Herc Newman called me late this afternoon after getting back from DC. He tried to call you in your office, but you apparently had better things to do." Paul laughed at his own humor. "Anyway, he asked me to give you the news. He went to DC and met with the head of the patent office. He explained the situation, showed him the *New England Journal* articles, and the man apparently became furious. He's apparently had run-ins with Thompson and Virtus in the past and is going to send Thompson a denial, stating that the patent office needs to review all of his scientific data before considering his application."

"That's good news," Jason said with a crooked smile. "Do you think it would be okay to go ahead and submit my articles to the *New England Journal*? Did you discuss that with Mr. Newman by chance?"

"I did, and he agrees you should submit the articles," Paul answered with obvious satisfaction. "Kevin, are you making any headway?"

"Paul, we are, but I'd rather not discuss it now. I'll have this whole thing solved pretty soon. I've not discussed anything we've found with Jason, and I just don't want him involved right now. He's got enough on his mind—"

Jason frowned and interrupted. "Kevin, I'm a big boy. I've quit bugging you about it, but I can handle it."

"Trust me on this. It's a nasty business. Right now, I have a lot of inconclusive information, and all it would do is distract you from what you do best." Kevin put his hand on Jason's arm.

"And what is it that I do best?" Jason looked puzzled.

"Your research, teaching, being a father, being my husband. Forget it for now. Soon I'll be able to tell you everything. I know you, Jason. It will all just upset you unnecessarily."

Paul quickly said, "Okay, lets change the subject."

John had been listening quietly but sat up straight. "You know, I've been listening to you three young men. You three are so smart and wise. I think it's time for me to retire. Tell me, Jason. Was Julia at your wedding."

"She was," Jason said, smiling.

"What do you think is going on in her head?" John continued.

"You know, I think she's smarter than any of us. She loves Kevin and is already calling him daddy. I'm sure she knows who Philip was, but she never mentions him. She looks at his picture frequently and stares at Paul when we're together. I'm sure she doesn't mention Philip because she's figured out that it would make me sad. She notices everything. She's amazing." Jason smiled.

∞

The following Tuesday Jason catered a lunch for the entire lab. Jason's marriage was the talk of the lab, and everyone wanted to meet his new husband. Eric had mentioned that he thought everyone's curiosity was actually interfering with laboratory activities, and so Jason arranged the lunch, asking Kevin to come so that he could introduce him to everyone in his lab. Jason watched as Kevin mingled easily among all of the postdoc fellows, PhD students, and research assistants. Jason had always admired Kevin's outgoing personality and his ability to engage anyone in conversation. Jason could not stop looking at his new husband. Kevin was not only physically beautiful but had a bit of an amusing swagger that Jason had not previously noticed. Jason thought he must have received a lot of attention from other men and women over the years. As with Philip, Jason had learned to disengage from those thoughts—it was unimportant.

After lunch, Jason took Kevin on a tour of the fourteen labs and then to his office. "I wondered when you were going to invite me to your lab. Wow, this is an impressive operation." Kevin closed the door and went to Jason, kissing him tenderly.

"Careful there, you're going to make me do something inappropriate in my office." Jason laughed and walked to his desk, his expression turning serious. "So I received these photographs in the mail today." Jason handed Kevin two photographs. One was a picture of a stunning looking young man who looked like a model. The second was a photograph of Jason standing on a street corner handing the same young man money.

"Was there any note with the pictures?" Kevin asked, staring at the photographs.

"No, just the pictures," Jason answered, looking at Kevin to see his reaction.

"What do you know about this?" Kevin asked, still studying the photos.

"This was taken on the day we went to Wilton to meet with Paul and Mr. Newman. I was walking back to my office after we returned, and this boy tapped me on the shoulder a few blocks from here. He asked me if I could spare some money, so I gave him five dollars. I started walking again, he continued walking next to me, and then he propositioned me in exchange for some more money. I told him that he shouldn't be out on the streets like this and that if he were having problems, I could have our social service department work with him. He took off after I said that."

"Have you received any phone calls about the pictures?" Kevin asked.

"No, I just got them this morning. It never occurred to me to tell you about this kid. It was sad, and I forgot about it until today." Kevin kept staring at the pictures without answering. Jason persisted, "Hey, you don't think I had anything to do with this boy, do you?"

After a moment Kevin looked up. "Sorry, I was just thinking. Of course, I don't. You're being set up for a bribe. You're going to receive a call or a note from someone soon to set up a meeting about these pictures. If you do get a call, go ahead and arrange a meeting, but not today or tomorrow. Okay?"

Jason was stunned. *Set up for what?* It must have something to do with the Thompson affair. "That's fine. But what do you think this is all about?"

"We'll talk this evening. No meetings with anyone today, understand?" Kevin looked concerned.

"Okay," Jason answered.

"I'll take the pictures. See you this evening. I love you." Kevin kissed Jason, put his hand on Jason's face and looked at him for a moment, turned and walked quickly to the elevators. Jason could sense the deep love Kevin had for him.

The remainder of the afternoon, Jason finalized the two articles for the *New England Journal* and had them sent to the editors in Boston after reassuring them that the conflicts had been satisfactorily resolved. He then made his rounds to the fourteen labs to get updates and help with problems. In every lab, he was greeted with the same sentiments—what a great husband you have!

Jason arrived at his home at five p.m. to the pleasant

aroma of spices from the meal being prepared by Alejandra. In the living room, Julia was sitting on Kevin's lap reading a book written in Mandarin, which Kevin was teaching her. She was beginning to speak Mandarin proficiently and, according to her teachers, was starting to speak in Mandarin to some of the other Chinese children in her class. Julia jumped up and ran to Jason who scooped her up and tickled her neck with his nose and lips, resulting in her usual squeals and laughter. After dinner and after putting Julia to bed, Kevin and Jason sat in the living room on the couch facing Central Park, close to each other. Kevin leaned over and kissed Jason.

"Everyone loved you in the lab. I think all the women were jealous of me." Jason laughed. "So tell me what's going on. You've kept me in the dark long enough."

"First of all, did anyone call you today to set up some meeting or talk about those pictures?"

"No calls."

Okay, I'll tell you what I know so far. Some of this will be upsetting to you, but I think we'll put an end to this soon. First of all, the boy in that picture was found dead in an alley not far from Sinai three days ago. He had two gunshots to the head."

"Oh my God!" Jason almost shouted. "So do you think this kid had something to do with Thompson?"

"I think so. Here is what I know. Your PhD student, Craig Henderson, has been having an affair with Sean Whitaker for the past eighteen months."

Jason was stunned. "Jesus, you know that Craig is the Blumenthal fellow. He has been an integral part of the research."

"How well I know. That's not all. Henderson has been seeing the kid who was shot as well. They met in a gay bar about a year ago, and Henderson had a number of sexual encounters with him at his apartment. What's more, the kid was only seventeen years of age when he was shot. He was sixteen when Henderson started having sex with him."

"I can't believe all of this," Jason said, shaking his head. "How did you find out about Henderson and the kid?"

"I can't tell you. It's illegal. But I can also tell you that Thompson was primarily responsible for getting Whitaker promoted from vice-president to president of Sinai two years ago. He meets with Whitaker frequently, and there is some bad blood between them. They usually meet at a family restaurant on the West side, and they have been seen arguing frequently."

"So you think that Whitaker somehow talked Henderson into stealing the data?"

"I'm sure that's the case," Kevin answered.

"But why would Whitaker do that? He doesn't need money, and why would Henderson cooperate?" Jason said with a puzzled look.

"That's what I'm working on. I need access to Blumenthal's computers one night this week when everyone is gone. Does everyone in the lab have their own password, or is there a list?"

"Everyone has their own private password."

"That's no problem. My computer guy needs to sit down for few hours on that computer. Saturday or Sunday would be fine—just sometime when no one else is there. If you wouldn't mind, we can go together, let him in and show him the computer."

"Just let me know when. Most everyone is gone by seven p.m., certainly by ten p.m. Have you found out anything about Thompson?" Jason asked, scooting closer to Kevin.

"A lot, but not now. Be patient. We'll have this wrapped up soon," Kevin said, aware that Jason was becoming aroused.

"You're amazing," Jason said, leaning over and kissing Kevin passionately. They made love as they did most evenings, but this night Jason felt a contentment that he had not known since his last year with Philip.

# CHAPTER 16

The following morning a FedEx letter envelope was delivered to Jason's office. In it was an unsigned typed note that said he was to be at Carmine's at six p.m. Jason was familiar with Carmine's. He and Philip had eaten there several times over the years. The note instructed him to come alone, and the reservation for two would be under his name. He was to go directly to the bathroom before sitting down. The last sentence was a warning that if he did not comply, the pictures would be turned over to the police, resulting in serious repercussions.

Jason called Kevin immediately and read the letter to him. "Okay. How do you feel about going through with this?" Kevin asked.

"Do you think I would be in danger? Even the thought of leaving Julia is dreadful, not to mention you."

"Well, these are dangerous people. But I'm certain there'll be no danger to you this evening. They need you, and they need you to cooperate. He wants you to come into the bathroom to make certain that you have no recording devices on you. But look, we don't need to do this. I can finish this up without involving you."

"No, of course, I trust you. I'll do it," Jason quickly replied. "Do you know who sent the letter?"

"I'm certain I do. Again, you don't have to do this. But I would never let anything happen to you."

"No, it's fine. Let's do it." Jason was adamant.

"Okay. I'll call Alejandra. She'll stay with Julia till we get home. Don't bring your briefcase into the restaurant with you, and don't be nervous. Nothing is going to happen to you. I'll be at another table with a beautiful woman who is one of my employees. We'll have a microphone hidden at your table. He is going to threaten you and ask for your cooperation with Thompson in return for disposing of the pictures. Don't let him know that you know about the murder. Tell him you'll need to speak with Thompson, and that Thompson will need to come up with the same offer that he previously made. If he asks what that was, just tell him that Thompson will know. I'll be right there. I won't let anything happen to you."

The rest of the afternoon, Jason reviewed papers that were to be submitted to various scientific journals, but he had difficulty concentrating. He knew these people were dangerous. After all, a young kid had been murdered. There had already been an attempt on his life back in 2005 after he discovered the Chinese espionage, and those memories continued to haunt him. Now he had Julia. The thought of leaving her was unbearable and brought tears to his eyes. But he completely trusted Kevin. Everything would be okay.

At five-thirty p.m. Jason got into a taxi and headed towards Carmine's. The traffic was extremely heavy, and Jason arrived five minutes late.

He entered the restaurant and told the maître de that he had reservations for two. He was led to a corner table that was isolated and empty.

"I'll just go the men's room before I sit down," Jason told the maître de.

"Of course, sir. I think perhaps your guest is in the men's room as well," the maître de responded.

Jason walked into the men's room, and a tall, husky man with a moustache and goatee was washing his hands. He was dressed in an expensive gray suit, and Jason could see a bulge in his suit jacket at the belt line. He turned around and continued to dry his hands, staring at Jason.

"You're late. Pull your shirt up," he said abruptly.

Jason said nothing, pulled his shirt up, and the man approached him. He inspected Jason's chest and back, and then he said, "Pull your pants down." Jason complied, and he looked at Jason's legs and felt around Jason's underpants. "Now go sit down. I'll be there in a minute."

Jason tucked his shirt in and went back to the table. He saw Kevin two tables away drinking a glass of wine with a beautiful woman. Kevin wore fake glasses, his hair was dyed dark brown, and he had a fake moustache. Jason stifled a smile. Kevin was engaged in a lively conversation with the woman and appeared not to notice Jason or the large man who had exited the bathroom and was approaching the table.

The restaurant was dark, and most of the tables were filled with couples. The man looked around and sat down, staring at Jason.

"Why are you blackmailing me?" Jason asked.

"Shut up," the man responded.

"What is your name, and what do you want of me?" Jason persisted.

"I said shut up. You know my client, Mr. Thompson. He asked for your cooperation, and you refused. He is asking one more time for your cooperation. If you refuse again, those pictures will be turned in to the police."

"You know full well that I have never had anything to do with that boy. He asked me for money on the street, and you or one of your people took that picture. I'll take my chances. He'll tell the truth."

"He won't tell anything. He's dead, and we'll provide evidence that you killed him. We'll provide notes that he tried to blackmail you for having sex with a minor, and we'll provide a gun that has your fingerprints on it and that was used for killing him."

Jason sat still, silent, appearing stunned at the revelations. "You killed that poor boy?" Jason asked.

"Collateral damage. This can all go away. All you need to do is cooperate with Mr. Thompson. If you don't, your career is ruined, and you'll spend the rest of your life in prison. And if you try and tell anyone about this meeting, you'll be putting your daughter in jeopardy. Do you understand what I'm telling you?"

Jason sat silently for a moment, seething at the threat of harm to his daughter. "I need to meet with Mr. Thompson. I want the same deal he offered me at our first meeting."

"What deal is that?" the man asked.

"He'll know," Jason answered.

The man stared at Jason for a moment, took out his iPhone, and texted a message. A minute later, there was the vibration that indicated a response. "Wait here," the man said as he got up, and then he walked out of the restaurant. Jason glanced over at Kevin, who was still in conversation with the woman and did not look at Jason. A waiter approached and asked if he would like something to drink. "I'll wait just a moment for my guest to arrive," Jason responded.

A few minutes later, Evan Thompson entered the restaurant and walked directly to the table. He sat down without saying anything and stared at Jason.

Jason stared back and finally said, "So you're blackmailing me to get my cooperation. And you would commit murder to get what you want?" Evan Thompson did not answer and continued staring at Jason. "How did you get the structure of that protein, and how did you get Sean Whitaker to cooperate with you?" Jason continued. "He must have somehow gotten the information for you."

"You faggots are all the same. A stiff prick has no conscience is the old saying. I used that to get his cooperation, and now I had better have yours."

"I want the same deal as before," Jason said.

"You're getting no money this time around. You had your chance. I want your cooperation, or you're going to jail," Thompson said, not taking his eyes off of Jason.

"I'll take my chances. I want a check, or no deal," Jason said with no emotion. When there was no response from Thompson, Jason started to get up.

"Sit down," Thompson ordered, and he took a check from his pocket. The check was made out to Jason for two hundred thousand dollars.

"I want your complete cooperation. I'll have a contract over to you tomorrow, giving Virtus fifty percent ownership of the drug and giving us complete control of production and marketing. I'll be at your office at four p.m. to pick it up. If you don't sign, the pictures and all of the other evidence will be turned over to the police. Do you understand what I'm telling you?"

"How do I know that you'll not use all this so-called evidence against me in the future?" Jason asked.

"Because I know the faggot who killed the kid, and after you sign the contract, the police will know who he is as well," Thompson answered with a smirk.

Jason nodded. "Okay."

Evan Thompson stood, staring condescendingly at Jason. He then looked around the restaurant and walked out to a waiting limousine. Jason sat shaking inside. He was furious with Evan Thompson, and the threat against Julia enraged him. The waiter came over and asked if Jason's guest was not staying. Jason pulled out a fifty-dollar bill and gave it to him, explaining that he and his guest had to leave unexpectedly.

Jason looked around the restaurant and then at Kevin. Kevin mouthed and gestured for him to leave and go home. Jason went outside, flagged a taxi, and was home by six-fifteen p.m. The entire experience had taken less than thirty minutes. When he walked into his home, Julia jumped up and ran to Jason, yelling, "Daddy." Jason scooped her up and kissed her, tickling her neck as usual with his nose and lips. Alejandra was just serving dinner and put an extra plate down for Jason.

"Where's Daddy Kevin?" Julia asked. Julia always referred to "Daddy Kevin" when talking to Jason, although she always called Kevin Daddy when talking to Kevin directly.

"He won't be home till later, sweetheart. He has a meeting." That answered satisfied Julia. After dinner, Alejandra cleaned while Jason bathed Julia. Jason thanked and kissed Alejandra goodnight, and, as was routine, Julia crawled into her bed and read to Jason for thirty minutes. Julia then asked Jason to sing her a song from *Frozen*, which made her squeal in delight. Jason showered, dressed in his underclothes, and sat in the living room, reading a medical journal while waiting for Kevin to return. He was still shaking inside from the whole experience and was anxious to get reassurance from Kevin that Julia would not be harmed.

At eleven forty-five p.m., Kevin walked in. His hair was still brown, but the moustache and glasses were gone. Jason got up and went to him. "I like your blond hair better." Jason kissed him tenderly. "You look tired."

"I am." Kevin smiled. "Let me shower and then I'll fill you in." Kevin returned fifteen minutes later. His hair was blond again, and he wore a tired smile. He sat down next to Jason.

"You were terrific this evening." Kevin put his hand on Jason's face. "I mean it. You saved me another week of work to put this away."

"What happened after I left?" Jason asked.

"First of all, three of the other tables were filled with undercover detectives and FBI agents. Your conversations in the bathroom and at the table were recorded, and everyone was listening real time."

"Jesus, how did you arrange that?" Jason looked stunned.

"I've been working with the FBI and local police for the past ten days. They know me and understand that I would never lead them on a wild goose chase. I was able to get the FBI involved because of your research, which is funded by the NIH. So anytime federal monies are involved in a crime, it's a federal offense, and the FBI becomes involved. Plus, I have a lot of contacts." Jason sat silently but obviously stunned. "To make a long story short," Kevin continued, "Thompson and his thug personal assistant are in jail on charges of bribery and murder. His assistant's name is Harold Brown. He's been on Thompson's payroll for four years, but has a long history of violent behavior prior to that."

"Who killed the boy?" Jason asked.

"Brown did. I tapped into their phones and have it all documented. They were in the process of framing another poor married guy who had been seeing this boy on the side. The boy was seventeen years old. Thompson was giving him thousands of dollars to do their bidding. Apparently, the kid threatened to expose Thompson unless he gave him a large amount of money, and so Thompson had Brown kill him."

"My God, both are cold-hearted killers," Jason said as tears welled in his eyes. "What about Whitaker and Henderson?"

"As I told you before, Whitaker and Henderson have been seeing each other since shortly after Whitaker arrived here. Somehow Thompson found out about the relationship and threatened Whitaker that he would expose the relationship unless Whitaker arranged the data theft. Whitaker obviously believed that exposing that relationship would ruin his marriage and threaten his professional status. What I still don't know is how Whitaker got Henderson to cooperate, but I suspect it was because of the boy, who was only seventeen. I know that Henderson had several encounters with him."

"What will happen to them?" Jason asked with concern.

"Whitaker will have to be prosecuted and will likely go to jail. He was directly responsible for the theft. You and I need to talk with Henderson tomorrow. The police are going to arrest Whitaker tomorrow, but I have asked them to hold off on Henderson until we talk to him. They've agreed."

Jason shook his head. "I just don't understand how Thompson could think he could get away with all of this."

"Jason, he's the classic sociopath. I don't have to tell you."

"I know, I know. I just can't believe that I'm in the middle of this nasty business. One time in my life was enough, and now this." Jason began having vivid flashbacks of the events surrounding his discovery of the Chinese espionage, his near-death experience, Philip at his bedside, never leaving him. Tears began streaming down his cheek, and he began to visibly tremble. Kevin held him and, after a few minutes, led him to bed. Kevin held him until he was fast asleep.

# CHAPTER 17

At eight a.m. the following morning, Jason went to the Blumenthal lab and asked Craig Henderson to follow him back to his office. Jason sat at his desk. Kevin and another man dressed in tie and sports coat sat in two of three chairs arranged in front of Jason's desk. Henderson stood staring at the three men, obviously frightened.

"Mr. Henderson, please sit down." Jason gestured for Craig to sit in the available chair. "As you know, Mr. O'Malley is my husband, but he is also one of the most respected security analysts in the country. This is FBI agent Jim Henson. I'm going to let Mr. O'Malley discuss the issues with you."

Kevin turned his chair slightly to face Craig. "Mr. Henderson, if you feel the need to get an attorney and stop this meeting now, I understand. But we are here to help you. Jason, Dr. Green, believes you were forced into an untenable position, and so he wants to make certain that you suffer the least possible consequences of what is a very nasty affair."

Craig turned pale and began sweating.

The FBI agent cleared his throat. "Mr. Henderson,

I'm an FBI agent. I'm required to tell you that anything you say today can be used against you in a court of law. I'm not here to arrest you. There may or may not be legal action, including criminal action, taken against you. You have the right to get an attorney and stop this meeting right now. Dr. Green has made it clear to us that he wants you treated, as Mr. O'Malley has stated, so that you suffer the least possible legal consequences."

Mr. Henderson put his head into his hands and wiped the sweat from his forehead. "Mr. Henderson," Kevin continued, "do you want to talk or would you like to get an attorney?"

"I'll talk," Henderson answered quietly.

Kevin continued, "Let me briefly tell you some of what we know. We know that you have had a relationship with Sean Whitaker for at least the past eighteen months. We also know that you have had sexual encounters with a young boy, Steven Kemp, over the past year. Steven Kemp was murdered a little over a week ago. The people responsible for that murder are in jail." Craig looked up at that news, wide-eyed, and began sobbing. Jason reached over and handed him Kleenex. After Craig composed himself, Kevin continued, "We also know that you were responsible for giving Sean Whitaker data from the experiments that have been performed in your lab over the past four years. We know exactly what data was copied, and when it was turned over." Kevin stopped talking, and there was complete silence for over a minute. "So Mr. Henderson, tell us the circumstances around all of this."

Craig raised his head and looked at all three men with a frightened and sad demeanor. "Sean and I have been seeing each other since he arrived here. We met at a hospital function, and there was an immediate connection. I knew he was married, and I should have cut it off.

But our relationship became much more than sexual. He always made it clear to me that he would never divorce his wife. There were times I would get angry and go to the bars. That's where I met Steven. He approached me and wanted to go home with me. He looked very young, and I made him show me his driver's license which confirmed he was nineteen—"

Jim Henson interrupted. "We have several of his fake IDs, including a driver's license which indicates he's nineteen."

Craig grimaced. "We did have a sexual relationship. I've brought him to my place at least four or five times over the past year. About four or five months ago, Sean told me that the CEO of a pharmaceutical company wanted information from my lab, and that if he didn't get the information, both Sean and I would be arrested for having sex with a minor. Apparently, he was only sixteen when I first saw him. Sean never told me who the CEO was. Sean told me that Steve had approached him in his parking lot about a year ago and that he had been having sex with him as well. I can't give you any details about that relationship, but according to Sean this CEO had hired Steve to seduce both of us. Sean put a lot of pressure on me. He said his marriage and his career would be destroyed if I didn't help him. I didn't know what to do." Henderson wiped the tears that were trickling down his cheeks away with his hands. "I almost came to you, Dr. Green, but Sean pleaded with me. I love him, and I knowingly did the wrong thing. I printed out a lot of the data from our studies and gave it to Sean. He told me the CEO's company was working on the same molecule and he just wanted to see if his data matched our data. I knew that was a lie, but I did it anyway. I stopped seeing Steve after that. I still see Sean, and he has not talked about any of this since I gave him the data." Craig looked at the three men and paused for a moment. "That's it. I don't know who this CEO is. I don't know what he has done with the data. I've just tried to forget about it, hoping it would all go away."

"Did Whitaker ever tell you about any meetings that he had with Dr. Green?" The FBI agent asked.

"Never," Craig said, shaking his head.

"What did he tell you about this CEO?" Kevin asked.

"Only that he was mean, and that he had powerful connections and would make sure we both went to jail if we didn't cooperate."

There was a pause. Jason had been staring at Henderson the entire time and finally asked, "Mr. Henderson, did you know you could be committing a federal crime when you did this?"

"I knew what I was doing and that I was breaking a contract that I had entered into when joining this lab. I knew that what I was doing was highly unethical. I honestly had not given thought to whether or not what I was doing was a crime. Is it?" Sweat continued to trickle down Henderson's brow.

"I don't know," Jason responded. "You'll have to talk with the prosecutors and see what your options are. What is your background?"

"What do you mean?" Craig asked.

"I mean, where did you grow up, give us a little of your history," Jason said in a stern voice.

"I grew up in Nashville. I told my parents I was gay at age seventeen. They kicked me out of their house. They're strict Southern Baptists. They told me I was going to hell and wanted nothing more to do with me. They've not spoken to me since."

"Go on," Jason said.

"A friend's family took me in until I graduated high school. I got a full scholarship to Yale, and I did well there. And then I was fortunate enough to get into your PhD program."

"What about the relationship with your parents?" Jason persisted.

Tears welled in Craig's eyes. "I understand where they're coming from. Their religion is all-important to them. I've tried to communicate with them, but they're still unwilling to talk to me. But I understand and still love them. I'm hoping that one day they'll come around."

Jason thought, as he often did, how lucky he had been. When he told his parents that he was gay, they were completely supportive and loving. There had never been a negative comment from either parent, and all they wanted from him was to be happy. Had his parents reacted like Henderson's parents, Jason thought he would likely have not overcome that rejection and that his life would have been drastically different. Jason was dumbfounded that Henderson had been able to overcome such a fundamental rejection and impressed that he was not resentful of his parents' behavior.

"What happens now?" Henderson asked.

The FBI agent responded, "My suggestion would be that you meet with the prosecutors and see what your options are. You can hire an attorney to be with you, or you can hire an attorney and refuse to meet with the prosecutors, in which case the proceedings will likely become more difficult. But again you have the right to legal counsel."

"Dr. Green, do you have any advice for me?" Craig asked.

"I would suggest you talk with the prosecutors, and after your situation is resolved, we can meet and discuss your future here."

Henderson began sobbing. Jason wanted to console him but sat silently.

"I'm so sorry, Dr. Green. I am so ashamed of myself." Craig looked at the FBI agent. "Where do I go? I'd like to get this started."

The agent stood and led Craig out, leaving Jason and Kevin looking at each other.

"He was telling the truth about his background," Kevin said. "His parents did kick him out of their house, and he has lived on his own since. He was being modest. He was an all-state basketball player in high school and a straight A student in both high school and college. He has never been in any trouble and, by all accounts, was an outstanding college student, president of his fraternity, and liked by everyone. He worked throughout college and even sent money to his parents when he got extra. It's sad. What are you going to do with him?"

"I don't know. But I don't want him charged with a criminal offense."

ᚱᚢᚱᚢ

Over the next two months, there was complete resolution of the case. Evan Thompson hired a high-powered criminal defense attorney, but the evidence that Kevin had accumulated was so overwhelming that the defense had no choice but to bargain with the federal prosecutors. Kevin had discovered several prior bribery attempts, some successful and others unsuccessful. In fact, Thompson had obtained his CEO position at Virtus after arranging a relationship between the prior CEO and a sixteen-year-old girl. The prior CEO was prosecuted, and Thompson manipulated himself into the CEO position. The day after the murder of Steven Kemp, there was a twenty-five thousand dollar transfer of money from Thompson to Harold Brown's disguised bank account, which Kevin had uncovered through several wiretaps.

Kevin had broken into Thompson and Brown's Smart-phones and had downloaded numerous incriminating texts, which confirmed Thompson's complicity in the murder. The texts made clear that the young boy wanted twenty thousand dollars, or he would tell the police what he had been hired to do. Thompson ordered Brown to "get rid of him."

Harold Brown confessed to the murder after the gun that killed the boy was found in a disguised safe deposit box, which Kevin had also discovered. Brown admitted that Thompson gave him twenty-five thousand dollars, but initially stated that it was not for the murder. When threatened with the death penalty versus life imprison-ment, he confessed that the twenty-five thousand dollars was payment for the murder.

Evan Thompson was given a thirty-year sentence without the possibility of parole, and Harold Brown was sentenced to life-imprisonment without the possibility of parole.

Sean Whitaker was arrested and charged with bribery involving a program funded by federal monies. He pled guilty and was sentenced to five years' probation and a two-hundred-and-fifty-thousand-dollar fine. His position at Sinai was terminated the day following his arrest after the chairman of the board of trustees met with Jason to confirm Whitaker's complicity.

Craig Henderson was charged with a misdemeanor and released. Jason discussed the affair with Dr. Blumen-thal who knew Craig Henderson better than anyone else in the lab. Blumenthal was stunned by the news. He told Jason that Craig was a hard worker, extremely bright, even brilliant, humble and even-tempered, and that he would have bet his pension plan that Craig would have never been involved with data theft or any other unethical activity.

Jason asked Dr. Blumenthal to tell Henderson to stay away until Jason made a decision regarding his future in the laboratory. Jason was torn. Normally, a PhD student who had been involved in such activity would be immediately dismissed from the program. It would be unlikely that the student would ever be accepted to another PhD program, and, in effect, the student's career as a scientist would be ruined. Henderson admitted that he knew exactly what he was doing, but his actions were the result of pressure from someone he loved and under the threat of going to prison for having sex with a minor. By all accounts, this was the first unethical act that he had ever committed. In addition, Jason reasoned, he overcame rejection by his own parents without any apparent bitterness.

One week after Craig's admission, Jason called him to his office. Jason observed that he had lost a significant amount of weight and had dark circles under his eyes. "Sit down, Mr. Henderson."

"Dr. Green, I—"

Jason interrupted him, and in his usual deep Southern accent, said, "Mr. Henderson, I have struggled with your situation more than one can imagine. I've been under tremendous pressure from the PhD committee to dismiss you from this program. But I've concluded that it would be a waste of a good mind and would destroy the career of someone whom I believe is innately good and ethical. I have told the PhD committee exactly what I have just told you, and they have agreed to let you continue your research and studies here." Tears were already trickling down Craig's cheeks. "At our Friday conference, the day after tomorrow, I want you to give a concise explanation regarding this whole affair. Everyone in the lab, including the research assistants, will be there. I want everyone to know the truth. I don't want you to be the focus of quiet talk and rumors. After that talk, I expect you to get back to work, and I expect that work to be stellar. I expect in two or three years to read a PhD thesis that is superior to any thesis that I've ever read."

Jason stared at the young man for a moment and then waved him out, quietly mumbling, "Now get to work." Craig stood up, still crying, and started to speak, but again Jason interrupted him and said in a louder tone, "Get out!"

That evening Jason and Kevin sat on their couch looking out over Central Park after Jason's usual routine of reading and singing with Julia. They sat together holding hands silently for what seemed a long while. Kevin stared at Jason and after another few minutes said, "You look exhausted, and sad."

"I'm tired. I don't know why I struggled so much with Henderson. The PhD committee called a special meeting and asked me to attend, which I hate doing because they waste so much time. Anyway, it seems they voted unanimously that Henderson should be fired. I told them that I disagreed, that he was brilliant, had tremendous potential, and was pressured into turning the data over to Whitaker. We went back and forth, and then one of the new members of the committee, a young PhD from Texas, told me that I was defending him only because Henderson is a homosexual."

"Jesus, what did you say?" Kevin asked.

"I'm sure I turned bright red. I told him that it was apparent he wanted to change the topic of the meeting to a discussion about my own character and not Henderson's. So I invited him to begin the discussion."

Kevin chuckled. "And what did he say?"

"The chairman of the committee intervened, apologized for the remark, and asked the eight members of the committee if anyone had an objection to following my recommendation. There was complete silence, I thanked them, and then I left. I think I did the right thing."

"You did," Kevin quickly said. "I have so much information on Henderson. If you ever want to look at his file you can. Suffice it to say, that young man is pretty amazing. He could be the next Jason Green, if that's possible."

Jason smiled sadly at Kevin and kissed him tenderly. "Speaking of amazing, how in the world did you put all of this together and get all of this information? I've tried not to pry, but the amount of information you gathered on all of these players was astounding."

"Oh, I had a good teacher."

"You never mentioned your teacher. Who was it?" Jason asked surprised.

"You," Kevin said with a serious expression.

"What are you talking about?" Jason asked with a puzzled look.

"I learned early on from discussions with John and Paul that you'd always attributed your successes to one major lesson—learning to ask the right questions. I learned it was no different in my business. If you ask the right questions, the answers will always lead you to a solution. I learned your lesson well."

❦❦❦

On Friday, a memo was passed to all fourteen labs that everyone, including research assistants, was to attend the Friday afternoon conference. Everyone knew that there had been problems with Craig Henderson and rumors were rampant, mostly speculating about some sort of sexual scandal. Jason had not discussed what had happened with anyone in the lab, other than Dr. Blumenthal and Eric Adelman.

At two-thirty p.m., Jason walked into the jammed conference room, and the chatter ceased. After Jason sat down, Craig, who was standing silently against a wall, walked to the front of the conference room and stood to the side of Jason.

The only sound was air rushing through the air conditioning outlets. Craig had a sad demeanor with dark circles under his eyes.

Craig spoke slowly, with palpable sadness in his voice. "Albert Einstein, one of my heroes, wrote: 'Most people say that it's intellect which makes a great scientist, but they're wrong. It's character.' How that quote haunts me at this moment, for two reasons. First, I have learned, since working in this lab, that Einstein's observation was exactly correct. And second, I have painfully discovered that my own character is lacking. I am now struggling with the question of whether one's character is set by nature, or can a weak character be made strong."

"I am here to apologize to you all. I know all of you, many of you well, and it is painful for me to stand here and tell you what I've done. Two years ago, I began having an affair with Sean Whitaker. Most of you know that he was the President of Sinai. I should have never let that happen, he is a married man, but it happened. Furthermore, both Sean and I, unbeknownst to each other, had sexual encounters with an underage boy named Steven who had been hired by the CEO of a biopharmaceutical company to seduce us. We both believed that he was nineteen, when in fact he was only seventeen. This CEO subsequently threatened Sean that he would have him arrested for having sex with an underage boy, which would destroy his marriage and career. The CEO told Sean that he would withdraw the threat only if Sean convinced me to give him extensive data from our research project. Sean asked me to steal the data, and I cooperated. It was not an easy decision. I knew it was unethical and illegal, but I nevertheless cooperated."

"There are many more sordid details that I could share, and there are, I am sure, more details to which I'm not privy. One detail you should know is that Steven was murdered, I am told, by an employee of this CEO. The fact that I was in some way associated with this boy's death will haunt me until I die. To go into more detail about this awful affair might leave an impression that I'm attempting to make excuses for my behavior. There are no excuses for my behavior, except that of a weak character." Tears began trickling down Craig's face.

"I have dishonored each and everyone of you by what I have done. I've compromised the integrity of this amazing research institution. I have instilled misgivings to the two individuals who have been so generous in their mentoring. Dr. Green and Dr. Blumenthal, I am so ashamed." Craig looked down and wiped his tears with his shirtsleeve.

"Dr. Green has inexplicably allowed me to continue my work here. I hang on to the possibility that character is not set by nature, but rather character can be hammered and forged into a higher order by hard work, being good, and rejecting unethical temptations. Henceforth, I will do my utmost in my personal and professional life to better my character, so that in the end I can become a scientist worthy of your trust."

Craig walked back to his position against the wall. There was utter silence. After a moment, Jason broke the silence. "Okay, we'll start our usual conference. The research assistants can get back to work now. Thank y'all for coming." For the next two hours, each postdoc fellow gave his or her usual update on the various projects, and there were the usual vigorous discussions after each presentation. Jason once again astounded all of the postdoc fellows and PhD students by the depth of his knowledge of each research project and by the fundamental questions that he asked, which usually resulted in a change in research direction or solution to a problem. Craig sat quietly through the two hours, although Jason detected a hint of a smile or a look of surprise each time Jason asked one of his questions. Jason knew, after that conference, that he had made the correct decision.

# CHAPTER 18

Friday evening, after the conference, Jason rushed home to Kevin, Julia, and Alejandra. The four left immediately to spend the weekend with the entire Olsen family as well as Jonathan and Sophia, who had driven to Wilton earlier in the afternoon. Jason noticed that the back of his Murano was packed with three large suitcases. Alejandra commented that she and Kevin had over-packed, an excuse that left Jason unsettled. But he quickly forgot as he listened to Alejandra and Julia conversing in Spanish, and Kevin and Julia conversing in Mandarin.

Jason smiled to himself as he took Kevin's hand, rubbing his palm with his thumb. Jason was astonished at Julia's command of the two languages, and equally amazed at her reading abilities, which were similar to his own at that age. Jason was equally stunned at the close relationship that Julia had with all four grandparents. He had never experienced that relationship. His father's parents had died when he was very young, and his mother was estranged from her parents and Jason had never met them. It was only when Jason had observed the bond that Julia had with Jonathan and Sophia, and with John and

Evelyn Olsen, that he understood what he had missed growing up.

But as stunning as the bond between Julia and her grandparents was to Jason, the bond between Jason and Julia was exponentially more intense. Jason had become obsessive about every aspect of Julia's existence, questioning Alejandra, Kevin, Jonathan, and Sophia about every detail of every outing, critiquing every element of every activity, and lecturing them when he thought some aspect of an excursion was suboptimal. His father laughed at him after an excursion to the art museum when Jason told him that it would be preferable to stick to the old masters and leave the impressionists and modernists until she was older. Jason said he was worried that some of the works of artists like Picasso would frighten her. As Jonathan was laughing, Jason displayed a rare fit of anger at his father, whom he adored, which made Jonathan laugh even more. "Jason!" Jonathan said, still laughing, "You need to relax. She loves the colors, and the weird works of Picasso make her laugh."

Jason knew that his attachment and worries about Julia were neurotic, but he was helpless. Kevin had even gently suggested that he see a counselor, which resulted in a rare argument and temper tantrum. The altercation ended when Kevin smiled, put his hand tenderly on Jason's face, and said, "I wish you could hear yourself."

As they drove up the long roadway to the Olsen mansion, Jason thought to himself how time did diminish his heartache. Tears had been usual as he drove up this roadway for the year after Philip's death. Philip's presence and absence were still profoundly extant, but time did diminish the tears. There were feelings of guilt for that absence of tears, for the deep love he had for Kevin, for Philip not being able to experience that inexplicable connection with Julia. How he missed Philip, how he still missed his mother. And yet, despite that ever-present void, Jason thought that he was still a happy person, so lucky to have Kevin, and Julia, and his father, and the Olsen family, and a fulfilling career.

As they pulled up to the front of the mansion, the door opened and Philip's younger sister, Anna, bounded out the front door, running to Jason as he got out of the car. Anna had matured into a physically stunning woman, much like her mother, as beautiful as her older brothers, Philip and Paul. She had become one of the most respected presidents of a large university medical center in the US and had developed the University of Pennsylvania medical facilities during her five-year tenure into an innovative and profitable medical system. After many failed relationships, it appeared that she had finally met her future husband to the great relief of Jason and the Olsen family. In truth, she had finally met her match, personally and professionally. David Kramer was an MD and PhD researcher at the University of Pennsylvania who had become famous in the scientific world for discovering the genetic defects in a host of rare genetic diseases, and, like Jason, was working on genetically based cures for those diseases. He was Jason's age, four years older than Anna, had been in one failed marriage, and according to Anna was very good looking with an engaging personality. Jason had never met him but had read and often cited his work in his own writings long before Anna had connected with him.

"God, Jason, I'm so happy to see you," Anna kissed and hugged Jason tightly. She grabbed Julia out of her car seat, held her up, and then kissed her. "My goodness, you are gorgeous."

"Hi, Aunt Anna," Julia smiled. Julia and Anna did FaceTime at least once weekly and would frequently talk for thirty minutes at a time, much to Jason's dismay. Jason was never one to spend time talking on a telephone. Anna kissed and hugged Kevin, whom she had grown to love, and hugged Alejandra as they all walked into the house. Paul, Amy, and their children came to the entryway to greet them. Jason walked into the living room, kissed John, Evelyn, his father, and Sophia.

"I'm so glad to finally meet you," Jason said as he walked to David Kramer and shook his hands. "Anna has talked so much about you that I feel like I know you already."

"And I can say the same about you. What a great pleasure to meet you." David smiled as Kevin walked in to greet everyone.

"David, this is my husband, Kevin, and here comes our little one, Julia." Julia ran in and jumped into Jason's arms. Jason took Julia around so that she could kiss everyone, and then she squirmed down and rejoined her cousins on the lower level.

Jason invited David to sit in a corner niche of the lavish but tastefully furnished and expansive living room. "I'm thrilled that you and Anna have found each other," Jason started the conversation.

"Not as thrilled as I." David laughed. "And even more so, because of her wonderful family, including you. I've read about you for years. I've read all of your research, which is amazing. Is it true you run fourteen separate laboratories?"

"That's true, but, in fact, they run themselves. The talent in each of those labs is incredible. I'm actually superfluous."

"You know, I'm not stupid enough to believe that for a second. I run a lab myself, so I'm not naïve regarding what it takes to run a lab, much less fourteen."

"Well, if you've read some of my papers, then you know that I cite much of your research in my discussion sections. You do amazing research, and what amazes me more is that the diseases you are studying are quite rare. I would imagine your funding is a struggle?" Jason said as if asking a question.

"You're right about that. We get some funding from the NIH, and some from private grants. But it's a constant battle. Even the funding committees at the NIH don't see the broader implications of my research. It's frustrating." David frowned as he affirmed Jason's speculation.

"Have they endowed your professorship?" Jason asked.

David laughed. "Are you kidding me? First of all, I'm not one of the chairman's pets." Jason knew that he was referring to the chairman of the department of medicine, who was an old timer heavily involved in the politics of medicine. "And secondly, endowed professorships only go to those whose funding is firm and long term."

Jason paused, staring at David, and then said, "I know that we just met, and I know what I'm going to ask is a bit forward, but what are the prospects for you and Anna?" Jason's face turned bright red.

David chuckled. "Anna said you flushed when you were embarrassed. Well, you're the first to know, but we will have an announcement at supper in a few minutes."

"Oh, fantastic. I'm so happy for you both." Tears welled in Jason's eyes, wiping them with his hands. "So what if I told you there is the possibility, even the probability, that you could have an endowed professorship, no, an endowed distinguished professorship, at Sinai. Would you be open to that?"

"That's certainly flattering and unexpected," David answered with a perplexed look. "But I wouldn't leave Anna, and she loves what she is doing."

Evelyn Olsen interrupted everyone's conversations. "Soups on everyone."

The thirteen sat at the elaborate dining room table, which could seat up to twenty people. As usual, Evelyn Olsen prepared the entire meal, which was elegantly served family style.

Evelyn smiled. "Jason, you're up."

"Julia, will you sing the prayers with me?" Jason lit the candles and, together, Jason, in a perfect tenor pitch, and Julia sang the Sabbath prayers, after which everyone clapped and began eating.

Shortly after the meal began, David clinked his wine glass and stood. "I'm so happy to be here with you all tonight, with the people who mean so much to Anna. About a month ago I drove up to Wilton in order to ask Mr. Olsen for permission to marry Anna. I think that he anticipated why I was coming here that day because he seemed to know a lot about me. I suspect Kevin had something to do with that." Everyone laughed, and Kevin blushed. "In any case, I apparently passed the test, because permission was granted. After that, all I had to do was convince Anna to marry me, and she has made me the happiest man on the planet by saying 'yes.'" Everyone clapped and stood, all hugging and kissing the two newly engaged couple.

After everyone was seated, Jason stood. "First of all, congratulations to you both. I cannot tell you how thrilled I am. David, I can only tell you that you are marrying a precious jewel. And Anna, I'm glad that you waited so long. Although I've just met David, I know of his work and reputation, and I know how picky you are, so I suspect yours will be the perfect marriage. I wish you both many years of good health and happiness together, and I'm hoping for a few more nephews and nieces." Everyone clapped and drank. "I'm not through. Nothing would make me happier, and I'm certain nothing would make our parents happier, than to see you two move up here where you belong. I know this is most unusual, but I have permission from the board of trustees of Sinai to offer Anna the Presidency of Sinai Medical Center. As you know, Anna, that position was recently vacated, and, when a committee was formed to search for a new president, I approached the committee. Because of your reputation and accomplishments, I was granted the privilege of offering you this position. And, David, I have just vacated the Harvey Glassman Distinguished Professorship and have occupied the Human Rights Distinguished Professorship, which has been vacant since Philip passed away. The Glassman Professorship is now open, and I have been given permission to offer you that professorship. I know that this may seem surreal to you both. It does to me. I never dreamed that my scheme would come to fruition. But, obviously, the powers that be saw the tremendous talent that you both possess. So I hope you give these offers consideration. I plan to pressure both of you, and I hope that the rest of the family pressures you to the point you'll have no choice but to move here. Thomas Jefferson said: 'The happiest moments of my life have been the few which I have passed at home in the bosom of my family.' So Anna, come home, and David, come to your new home." Anna and David looked at each other with stunned expressions, and wide-eyed smiles of hope were seen on the faces of John, Evelyn, and Paul Olsen.

The remainder of meal was filled with lively chatter, mostly about the children, with no further discussion of Jason's offers. Jason and Kevin pressed their legs against one another frequently during the meal, causing them to simultaneously smile or chuckle, something that Jason could see was obvious to everyone. Jason had confided to Kevin shortly after their marriage that Philip and he had a ritual of pressing their legs against each other, resulting in laughter that was inexplicable to others around them. Kevin had begun that same ritual shortly thereafter. At first, Jason was resistant, but Kevin, in a tender moment, explained to Jason that he was not trying to replace Philip, but in some way was trying to become Philip, in addition to being himself. Kevin explained that he knew how much Jason missed Philip, that he also deeply felt Jason's loss and pain, and that his resumption of that ritual was one way that he thought could ease that pain. And, in fact, it worked. That silly ritual brought back memories and happiness and intensified Jason's love for Kevin.

The following morning, Jason, Kevin, and Paul went on their usual seven-miles run. Despite Jason approaching forty years of age, Kevin and Paul struggled to keep up with him. Jason continued to be as obsessive about his running as he was obsessive about his daughter. At the end of the run, the three stood outside the mansion, catching their breath.

"Jason, I have to tell you something," Kevin said still breathing heavily. "You and I are going to St. Maarten tomorrow. I've made reservations for a week stay at La Samanna."

"What are you talking about?" Jason asked.

"You've not had a vacation in ten years. You and Philip didn't even go away after you were married. We've not been away together, alone, and you need a vacation. We're flying down in the corporate jet, and they will pick us up in a week." Jason stared at Kevin with a frown, not responding. "Jason, we need a vacation together. I've arranged everything. Eric knows, and he assures me everything will go smoothly in your lab. Julia and Alejandra will be staying here for the entire week. It's time Julia got to spend some time with John and Evelyn, and they're excited about it."

"It's out of the question," Jason responded with finality. "I'm not leaving Julia. I don't need a vacation. Every day with you, Julia, and the family is a vacation—"

Paul interrupted Jason. "You do need a vacation. You've been through a lot recently, you're uncharacteristically crabby, and Kevin is right, you two need time alone for a week. And it would do Julia good to be separated from you for a week."

"What are you talking about?" Jason said loudly. "Forget it. It's out of the question. I'm not leaving Julia." He abruptly turned around and began running, leaving Paul and Kevin speechless and shaking their heads.

Jason returned about forty minutes later after repeating the seven-miles run and went immediately up to his bedroom to shower, without acknowledging the rest of the family, all of whom were gathered in the living room.

As he was dressing, John knocked on the door, walked in, and sat on the bed as Jason dressed. "Son, I know you're upset about the prospect of leaving Julia for a week," he said quietly.

But Jason always listened to him. John was an imposing figure, one of the few people from whom Jason ever sought advice.

"Dad, I can't leave Julia. I just can't."

John paused, and then said, "The most important thing for Julia is for you to be happy, and even more important, that you and Kevin have the best possible marriage. You have been overtly stressed and for good reason. But that stress has worn on your happiness, and I suspect it has worn on your marriage, although I know that Kevin is incredibly accommodating. Nevertheless, you cannot ignore your marriage, because it's the most important part of Julia's upbringing. To see you two happy makes her happy, but to see you two stressed and not particularly happy? Do you think for a second that she doesn't notice that?"

"Did Kevin say we were having problems?" Jason asked, concerned.

"No, not at all, but it's obvious to everyone that you're stressed and that it has affected your relationship not only with Kevin but with all of us. You need to de-stress and relax for a week. You and Kevin need to catch up. You'll be doing everyone a favor."

"But I'm afraid Julia will think I'm not coming back."

"Julia will be fine with us. She'll be with us twenty-four seven, she loves playing with Ari and Zach, and she'll know you're coming back. You can FaceTime with her every day."

Jason stood up and began pacing back and forth. He realized that he depended more on Julia than probably Julia depended upon him, and he knew that he was completely neurotic about his attachment to her. Maybe what really worried him was that Julia would not miss him. He knew that he hadn't been as attentive to Kevin as he had been prior to the Thompson affair. Prior to that time, there had rarely been a day that they didn't have sex, but over the past few months, their sex life had deteriorated to once weekly, if that. Jason had been shunning Kevin's advances for the past month, although Kevin had seemed amazingly understanding. Jason saw John watching him as he paced back and forth.

"Let me talk with Julia." Jason left John sitting on the bed and quickly went two flights down to the lower level without saying hello to the rest of the family, all still congregated in the living room. Julia, Zach, and Ari were playing a math video game on the seventy-inch flat screen.

"Julia, come here a minute." Julia jumped up and went to the corner chair where Jason sat. Jason pulled her up on his lap and she hugged him. "What do you think about Kevin and me going away next week for a rest? We would come back here in one week and pick you up and drive back to our home. Do you know how much a week is?"

Julia laughed. "Of course I do, Daddy. A week is seven days. Papa told me that you were very tired and needed to rest. And Grandpa wants me to stay with him and Grandma for a week. They told me you would come back rested and happy."

"How do you feel about all this?" Jason asked, kissing her on the forehead.

"I want you to be happy, and I want Daddy Kevin to be happy too. Grandpa said you'll call me everyday."

"Of course, I will. But I don't want to leave if it will make you feel sad or worried," Jason said, almost wishing that she would tell him not to leave.

"I won't be sad or worried. I'll be happy because you'll be happy."

Jason hugged her and kissed her, suppressing tears and smiling at the same time. He suddenly understood that Julia was far more grounded than he.

Jason returned to the living room where everyone was gathered. He sat next to Kevin in the oversized leather chair, and everyone stared at him in silence. Jason's face turned red as he said, "Okay, St. Maarten, it is. I know I'm neurotic, and Kevin and I can use the time away." Everyone smiled, and Kevin took his hand. "I want to go visit Philip's grave," Jason said. "Does anyone want to come?"

Anna, David, Paul, and Kevin piled into Jason's Murano, and they drove the five miles to the cemetery where Philip and several generations of the Olsen family were buried. Jason held Kevin and Anna's hands as they approached the grave. The gravestone read: *Philip Green-Olsen, 1975-2015, Husband to Jason, Father to Julia.*

Jason had protested to John and Evelyn that other family members should be noted on the headstone, but they insisted that it was Jason and Julia that defined Philip. They stood silently for several minutes, tears trickling down Anna's cheeks, staring at the headstone. Jason had visited Philip's grave on every one of his frequent visits to Wilton, and as was his custom, he took a small stone from his pocket and placed it on the headstone, a Jewish tradition, signifying that the deceased had not been forgotten. The five stood silently for another few minutes and then rode back to the Olsen mansion in silence, Kevin holding Jason's hand the entire way.

The following morning, Jason and Kevin boarded the Olsen Law Firm's private jet, after saying goodbyes, and flew the four hours to St. Maarten. La Samanna was an exclusive beach hotel on the French side of the island with only about eighty rooms. The dining was open air and romantic, overlooking the beach. The French chef came to their table each night to ask them what dishes they would like him to prepare. Jason had never experienced more exquisite meals. The room was luxurious, and Kevin and Jason slept ten hours each night. They made love every day, and his intimacy with Kevin deepened further, something that Jason thought impossible. Jason talked to Julia daily, relieved that she was happy and content. By the end of the week, Jason understood that everything John Olsen had expressed was true. On the plane ride home, Jason thanked Kevin for the week, they kissed passionately, and Jason pleasured Kevin just prior to the start of their descent into the Danbury Municipal Airport.

# CHAPTER 19

Jason had contracted with Corigian Pharmaceuticals to produce the Blumenthal protein to FDA standards. Corigian was one of the largest and most respected pharmaceutical houses in the world, with headquarters in Princeton, New Jersey. Jason had met with the president and CEO of that company and had worked out an arrangement that Sinai Medical Center would receive twenty percent of the gross sales of the drug, should clinical trials be successful and the drug be put into production. In return, Corigian would produce the drug for the clinical trials, pay the cost of performing the clinical trials, and, assuming successful clinical trials, produce and market the drug worldwide.

In addition, Corigian agreed that Jason, who was designated as principal investigator, would have to agree and sign off on virtually every aspect of the clinical trials and subsequent production and marketing of the drug. Producing the drug for clinical trials and paying for those studies would cost Corigian millions of dollars, but after looking at the animal data and because of Jason's reputation, Corigian readily agreed to the proposal. The research committee at Sinai and their lawyers agreed to the contract, and the new President of Sinai Medical Center, Anna Olsen Kramer, signed her name to that agreement with Jason looking over her shoulder.

Peto Research was the company that Jason had chosen to design and help perform the clinical trials. Peto had the best clinical research designers in the world and had excellent relationships with both Corigian and the FDA. It was agreed that the phase one study would be performed at Sinai, which had a large oncology unit and hundreds of patients with pancreas cancer. A phase one study would be performed on patients who had terminal pancreas cancer that was either not amenable to or had failed other chemotherapies. This study was designed to test which doses were safe, the adverse effects of the drug, how long the drug remained detectable in the blood, and how the drug was eliminated from the body.

Jason believed that this protein had such a high affinity for the peptide on the surface of the pancreas cancer cell that it would quickly disappear from the blood stream and bind to any cancer cell that it came in contact with. Jason and the Peto scientists had decided to administer the protein in a saline solution over an hour and measure blood and urine levels for six hours after administration. Eric Adelman and Jason had also devised a complex computer program, which would determine the optimal dosage based upon a rough estimate of the tumor burden in an individual patient. In other words, based upon MRI scans, the radiologists could give a rough estimate of how many grams of tumor were in an individual's body, and based upon that rough estimate, the computer program could give a rough estimate of how many milligrams of the protein would be required to bind to all of the pancreas cancer receptors. Jason decided to start at ten percent of the calculated dosage, and test between three and five patients, depending upon the response. The dosage would then be increased in ten percent increments until the optimal dosage was reached, or until adverse effects prevented any further increase in dosage. This study design was unusually sophisticated and based upon a unique computer program for which there was no precedent. All of the involved scientists were very excited.

Corigian had established the FDA approved facility to produce the drug, and by January of 2019, the phase one trial began. Jason had personally interviewed the first three patients, all of whom had terminal pancreas cancer and were eager to participate in the study. The first man was a fifty-four-year-old New York Supreme Court Justice who had just resigned his position because of his pancreas cancer. Traditional chemotherapy had failed to halt the progression of his cancer, and he and his family had accepted his oncologist's prognosis of only a few months. The second patient was a forty-six-year-old woman with an adoring husband and three teenage sons. Her pancreas cancer was widespread when discovered, and she refused any traditional chemotherapy because she had seen her sister suffer tremendously through chemotherapy for breast cancer. The third patient was the wife of a genetics professor at Columbia University. She had her pancreas removed a year earlier followed by chemotherapy, and for eight months she showed no evidence of any persistent cancer. However, a scan four months ago showed tumors throughout her liver and lungs, and chemotherapy caused an almost fatal adverse reaction, resulting in refusal of any further chemotherapy. Jason spent considerable time with each patient and their families, explaining the new drug, the results of the animal studies, and the purpose of this study.

The three patients were admitted to the oncology service on Tuesday, January second. The unit was staffed with specialty nurses, an oncology professor, two oncology fellows, a medical resident, and a medical intern. The entire unit had heard about this revolutionary new therapy that Jason Green had developed and were eagerly anticipating the arrival of the three patients. While the three patients were being admitted to the unit, dressed in hospital garb, intravenous lines started, cardiac monitors attached, automatic blood pressure and temperature monitors applied, and papers signed, Jason gave a thirty minute lecture to the group of doctors and nurses about the development of the Blumenthal protein, the results of animal studies, and the dosing rationale for the phase one study.

Dr. Susan Knopf was the oncology professor who was in charge of the oncology unit, her own research and clinical expertise being breast cancer. She had been collaborating with one of Jason's labs regarding a similar protein found on the cell surface of breast cancer cells in animals and humans, and was extremely excited about this phase one study. "Jason, what will the plan be with these three patients should there be no adverse reactions? Will they be able to receive increased doses, or are they only to have one dose and then that's it?"

"That's a good question," Jason replied with a smile. "Ordinarily, as you know, study subjects are allowed only one dosage. But because of the nature of this protein, the fact that it has a specific target molecule, we've gotten permission from the FDA and the clinical research committee to offer the same subjects increasing doses. We are however obligated to take at least three new subjects with each increased dose. So we're not going to abandon these three subjects after one dose like it happens in most phase one studies."

One of the oncology fellows raised his hand, and Jason nodded to him. "Where did you find this computer program? I've never read about such a thing."

Jason smiled again. "You haven't read about it because this is the only program of its kind. I have a computer genius in my lab, Eric Adelman, who wrote this program."

Dr. Knopf started laughing and looked at the fellow. "Don't be fooled. You are looking at the genius behind the program."

Jason's face turned red. "Okay, let's go see what happens." He took three bags of intravenous fluid containing the new drug out of his cooler. Each one had doses specifically calculated for each patient based upon the estimated amount of tumor each had. Jason personally went to each patient, attached the bag to the intravenous line that had already been inserted into the vein, and started the drip so that it would be completed in sixty minutes. He held each patient's hand after starting the drip, smiled at them, thanked them for participating in the study, and assured each one that all of the doctors and nurses, as well as himself, would be around all day to observe them and react to any problems that could arise.

The nurses collected urine and blood samples hourly after the infusions were completed. At two hours following completion of the infusion, all three patients developed a fever and chills and felt generally poor. Jason ordered blood work on each patient, which indicated elevated potassium, uric acid, and phosphorus levels. The doctors congregated around Jason as they read the blood results on the computer screen. One of the fellows asked, "What do you think is going on?"

Jason smiled. "This is called tumor lysis syndrome. Tumor cells are being rapidly destroyed because the drug is allowing a vigorous immune response to the tumor. This is a very good indication that the drug is working. But this syndrome can be fatal. So we need to give the patients allopurinol, in order to prevent uric acid formation, kayexelate to prevent elevated potassium levels, and lots of intravenous fluids to prevent kidney damage. So get to it right now." The doctors quickly disappeared to follow Jason's directions. Jason went to each patient, reassured them that their reaction was a good sign, and that they would be receiving some additional medications to prevent complications. He held each patient's hands as he spoke with them and then went to the families who were waiting in a lounge area to explain what was occurring.

The fever and chills continued throughout the day and into the night. Jason would not leave the unit and went to each patient frequently through the night to reassure them that all was going well. By morning, the fever and chills had resolved, and the patients were feeling much better. All of the chemistry abnormalities had been corrected.

Jason insisted that each patient remain in the unit until at least late afternoon, and Dr. Knopf agreed that if blood chemistries remained normal by late afternoon that the patients could be released.

The following week Jason received results of the blood and urine tests, which showed no detectable levels of the new drug in the blood or urine during the six hours after completion of the infusion. This suggested that the drug was quickly binding to the pancreas cancer cells. Two weeks later the three subjects received MRI scans and PET scans to determine if there had been any decrease in the tumor burden since the infusion. The results were astounding. The judge and the housewife had no evidence of any tumor on both the MRI and PET scans, and the professor's wife had reduced her tumor burden by at least eighty percent. The patients and the families were ecstatic, as were the scientists at Corigian and Peto.

The protocol was altered by pretreating each patient

with allopurinol, in order to prevent elevation of uric acid, administering medication in order to prevent elevation of potassium, and infusing relatively large amounts of fluids during the treatment to prevent kidney damage from destruction of tumor cells. Over the next ten weeks, sixty-three infusions were administered in increasing doses on thirty-four individuals, with the maximum dose being sixty percent of the optimal dose as determined by the computer program. It was decided by Jason and the scientists at Corigian and Peto to stop at sixty percent because all of the patients, even the first-time patients, had complete destruction of the tumor at fifty-percent as determined by MRI and PET scan testing. It was decided that each future patient would receive one infusion after initial MRI and PET scans at a thirty percent dosage, and that if there were residual tumor present at three weeks after the first dosage, another infusion at a fifty percent dosage would be administered. There were no serious complications during any of the infusions, although all patients had severe fever and chills and felt awful for twenty-four hours after the drug infusion. It seemed that the greater the tumor burden, the more intense the reaction, but, in all cases the reaction resolved within twenty-four hours after each infusion.

The results of these studies were stunning. It appeared, at least on the surface, that a cure for pancreas cancer had been discovered. Time would tell whether recurrences would occur in these patients, and if recurrences should occur, whether there would be similar responses to the new drug. The animals that had been treated with the drug had remained cancer free for over two years, so at a minimum this drug offered for the first time hope of long-term survival. Jason and Eric quickly wrote a paper for publication in the *New England Journal of*

*Medicine*, and after reviewing the paper, the editors agreed to expedite publication of the news.

Without exception, phase two and phase three studies were required before a drug would be approved for market, since these two phases were designed to study the safety and efficacy of new drugs. However, it was clear from Jason's phase one study that the drug was both safe and highly effective. Because of Jason's reputation and the stunning results from the phase one study, which Jason presented to an emergency committee assembled at the FDA, distribution of the drug to the seventy-six cancer treatment centers designated by the National Cancer Institute using the protocol developed by Jason and the Peto scientists was approved. Reports of responses for every patient was required to be submitted to the FDA and to Jason, and Jason was to be available for consultation should any untoward event occur. Peto and Jason were to compile statistics from the next five hundred patients and present the results to the FDA as expeditiously as possible. If Jason's results were confirmed, Corigian would be allowed to market the new drug.

In late March 2019, oncologists from the seventy-six cancer treatment centers assembled in the Philip Olsen auditorium on the first floor of the Olsen Research Building at Sinai Medical Center at eight a.m. All of these clinicians knew of Jason Green, but literally none had ever met him. Jason mingled easily among the clinicians, introducing himself and complimenting each on their work, all of which he had read and retained in his memory. After thirty minutes of introductions, Jason asked that everyone be seated. Over the next forty-five minutes, Jason reviewed their basic research, the discovery of the peptide on the pancreas cancer cell surface, the role of this peptide in inactivating killer T-lymphocytes, the creation of the Blumenthal protein which inactivated the cancer peptide, the animal studies which demonstrated the pancreas cancer cure, and the human data from the phase one study. The presentation was presented so dynamically and in such clear fashion that, except for Jason's voice, there was not another sound in the auditorium—no coughs, no sneezes, no crackling of papers—only Jason's voice.

After Jason completed his presentation, there was stunned silence until Dr. Stanley Morganthaler, one of the most prominent cancer specialists and researchers in the world from MD Anderson stood and said, "Dr. Green, thank you for arranging this meeting and presenting your remarkable research to us. Your results are astounding, and I think that I speak for everyone here that we are all excited to participate in this next phase."

"Thank you for that, Dr. Morganthaler, and I thank y'all once again for coming here today. My primary interest is getting this drug to the hundreds of thousands of people around the world suffering from this terrible disease, and, with your help, I think that can be done expeditiously. The protocol for using this drug is simple, and I have folders for each of you that spell everything out. In addition, you'll find three compact discs in your folders, which contain the computer program for calculating the dose of the drug. This program can be used for research and clinical purposes in calculating dosages of drugs based upon tumor burden rather than conventional methods based upon height and weight, and we're happy to provide you with this valuable tool. My colleague, Dr. Adelman—would you stand up, Eric?—is the genius behind this program and will consult with your computer people if they run into problems. I would be happy to answer any questions."

Over the next two hours, Jason answered scores of questions. The meeting finally ended at noon, and Jason hosted a lunch in the faculty club for about twenty of the researchers who either had late flights out of New York or who were staying overnight. Jason mingled easily among them, declining multiple invitations for dinner. Dr. Morganthaler sat next to Jason during lunch and at one point said, "So Dr. Green."

"Please call me Jason."

"Jason, rumor has it that you never come to our meetings because you refuse to leave your daughter."

Jason laughed. "I'm reminded of the Mark Twain quote: 'the rumors of my death have been greatly exaggerated.' But, in fact, although I'm surprised that I'm the subject of any talk, that particular rumor is true. I'm admittedly very neurotic about my daughter. I've recently become a bit more laid back in that regard, thanks to my husband, so perhaps I'll start coming to some of the meetings."

"Good." Dr. Morganthaler smiled. "Your absence at these meetings is a crime. You can see I'm good at Jewish guilt. Your postdocs are wonderful presenters, but it's not the same. And you should call me Stan, even though I'm old enough to be your father."

❧❧❧

Over the next twelve weeks, over eight hundred patients with terminal pancreas cancer were treated with the Blumenthal protein. Seventy percent of the patients had complete remission at thirty percent of the calculated optimal dosage, and virtually all patients had complete remission at the fifty percent increment. Every patient had complete disappearance of their tumors based on MRI and PET scanning. There had been only one serious complication. That one patient had a cardiac arrest because of an elevated potassium level that was not adequately treated, but, fortunately, the patient was revived and survived unscathed.

By the first of August, Jason had compiled all of the data, had written a follow-up article for the *New England Journal of Medicine*, listing all seventy-six researchers as coauthors, and presented the data to the FDA. Immediate approval was given for Corigian to produce and mass market the new drug.

Jason signed a release to allow Corigian to begin mass production of the drug, but he refused to sign a release for marketing until he met with the relevant individuals at Corigian to determine their marketing strategy and their cost structure. On the first Monday in September, Jason drove to Princeton, New Jersey, to meet with the corporate individuals responsible for marketing. To his surprise, the CEO met him in the waiting lounge and brought him to the conference room where five marketing executives were waiting.

After cordial introductions, the CEO said, "Dr. Green, we want to answer all your concerns about the marketing of this remarkable drug. Perhaps it would be best if you enumerated those concerns."

Jason smiled. "First of all, it has been a great pleasure working with Corigian. Your company has been extraordinary in expediting the release of this drug. I have a few major concerns. First, in order for proper dosing, tumor mass has to be estimated, which requires an MRI and PET scan. Most radiology groups do not have the expertise to measure tumor mass, particularly in smaller communities and rural areas. How do you plan on solving this issue?"

"We have anticipated that concern," the head of the marketing group stated. "We have contracted with six radiology groups, including yours at Sinai, all of whom have great expertise at estimating tumor mass based on three dimensional MRI scans and PET scans. When an oncologist wishes to use the drug, they will be required to contact Corigian to request the proper dosing based on tumor mass using your computer program. If they don't have access to a radiology group, they will overnight the MRI and PET scan discs to one of the six radiology groups who will estimate tumor mass, we will plug the results into your computer program, and then overnight the drug to the oncologist. So there would be a forty-eight hour delay in administering the drug in those instances."

Jason nodded. "How will you know whether the oncologist is being truthful regarding tumor mass?"

"We will require that a report from the radiologist be emailed or faxed to us, and based upon that, we'll determine the dosage to send to the oncologist. We will require an official report. Word of mouth will not suffice."

"Good," Jason answered. "I'm not concerned about marketing. The drug will market itself, and I believe little marketing will be required other than to educate the oncologists on how to obtain the drug and the protocol for administering the drug. Am I correct on that point?"

"That is correct," the market finance officer answered. "Our costs for marketing will be relatively minimal compared to almost every other drug that we bring to market."

"Good," Jason nodded. "My only other concern is your cost structure. I believe we have agreed, and the FDA has consented, that each patient will receive two infusions one month apart and that the infusions will be at fifty percent of the optimal calculated dose. What is your plan for cost?"

The CEO leaned forward. "We have already been in contact with the major insurance companies, Medicare, and various Medicaid plans. We believe that a cost of twenty-five thousand dollars per infusion is a reasonable charge. The insurance companies have balked at that cost, but we have shown them that the cost of caring for the average individual with pancreas cancer between the time of diagnosis and death is between three and four hundred thousand dollars. This cost will result in a huge savings for the insurance industry."

"What about the uninsured or those individuals that have huge deductibles?" Jason asked.

"There are ways those individuals can get the necessary monies. There are various charitable organizations, friends, private savings, and assets. We are still in a free market system, after all," the CEO responded, smiling.

"Let me ask you something," Jason continued with a grimace. "How much have you spent thus far developing this drug? I mean, all costs: The new facility, employees, everything. We have given you the method of producing the drug, so that shouldn't enter into the cost. Just the cost thus far."

"We have spent about thirty-five million dollars thus far," the CEO said, the smile having disappeared.

"So in this country alone, there are fifty thousand new cases of pancreas cancer every year. Let's leave out the other hundred thousand plus cases that occur yearly outside the US. So, in this country alone, you are talking about fifty thousand cases times fifty thousand dollars per case. That is two point five billion dollars a year in annual sales, at a cost of let's say, and I am being very generous here I believe, two hundred and fifty million including marketing and production. Now I know twenty percent or about five hundred million will be going to Sinai, leaving you about two billion in gross proceeds in the US with a cost basis of about two hundred and fifty million. I'm not very good at math, so let me know if I'm way off base." There was complete silence in the room. "Please gentlemen, let me know if I'm way off regarding your costs."

"Dr. Green, you're correct regarding the costs. In all honesty, our costs will be substantially less than your generous estimate of two hundred and fifty million," the head of marketing quietly said, eliciting a frown from the CEO.

"Thank you for that, sir. Then don't you think that a two billion dollar yearly return on a cost basis of two hundred and fifty million is a bit obscene? I don't know of a business that has that sort of margin." Jason could see that the CEO was very uncomfortable.

"Dr. Green, as the CEO of this company, I have investors that I have to satisfy."

"I am sympathetic to that concern, sir. I do my own investing, and I expect a decent return on my money. But a return of ten times the cost of a product is not ethical in my opinion. I cannot agree to that kind of cost structure in this country unless you agree that all uninsured patients will not be charged for the drug and those individuals with high copays will be relieved of their copay obligation. I'll go along with whatever you end up negotiating with Medicare, the Medicaid plans, and the various insurance companies, but the drug should not be withheld from anyone for financial reasons. I would estimate that agreeing to this might decrease your proceeds by four hundred million dollars annually, based on my research into the economics of this problem. That still gives you a very high return based on your cost. Your investors should be very pleased."

"You realize that if we agree to this, Sinai will receive a hundred million dollars less yearly," the CEO said with obvious resignation.

"I'm certain that Sinai will be very pleased with whatever revenues result from your sales. Sir, you have been handed a revolutionary drug for which you have had minimal costs to develop. The amount of good will that your company will receive for agreeing to my proposal will far exceed any lost revenue. Surely you see that."

"Dr. Green, quite honestly, I had not thought of the good will aspect, and I'm embarrassed to admit that. But you are correct, and we'll draw up the agreement. What about marketing outside the US?"

"Oh, I'll leave that up to you. I suspect that other countries will drive a much harder bargain. I hope that you would be generous to individuals, wherever they may be, who need the drug and have no means to pay for it. I'll leave that to your own good will."

# CHAPTER 20

The day following publication of the *New England Journal of Medicine* article, the headline in virtually every newspaper in the United States and around the world was *Cure for Pancreatic Cancer* or something to that effect. The *New England Journal* article was the lead story on every major network and cable news program.

All seventy-six coauthors of the *New England Journal* article were interviewed by their local as well as national news organizations, and each researcher referred the interviewer to Jason Green, whom they all acknowledged was the individual responsible for the discovery.

Jason sat on his couch at home with Kevin and Julia watching an extensive report by Dr. Gupta of CNN at six p.m.

Dr. Gupta ended his report by saying, "We have tried contacting Dr. Jason Green at Sinai Medical Center in New York City, the scientist who discovered this drug, but, as of now, he has been unavailable for an interview. We understand he does not like publicity and is a very private person."

Julia yelled out, "Daddy, is he talking about you?"

Jason laughed. "Yes, sweetheart."

Kevin said, "Why don't you give an interview? You're famous, people want to hear about your discovery from you, and they want to know about you. It's really not right."

Jason frowned at Kevin. "You know how I hate interviews and publicity. I couldn't care less about it." At that moment there was a knock on the door, and in walked Anna. Jason jumped up. "Anna, what a surprise." Julia jumped up and ran to her, hugging and kissing her.

"Just on my way home, and thought I would stop by and coerce you a bit," Anna smiled.

"Anna, I don't want to give interviews. Everything is in the article, and the coauthors of that article have done a good job explaining the results."

"Jason, my phone has not stopped ringing. I'm not kidding you when I tell you I've spoken to the presidents of every major news organization in this country and many others. You should give interviews, if for no one else, for the medical center. It's great publicity for us, and we're not shy about wanting good publicity."

"Anna, Sinai is going to get about four hundred million dollars yearly for this drug. Sinai doesn't need publicity."

"You know that's not true. I've taken the liberty of arranging a news conference tomorrow at the medical center—"

Jason interrupted. "Anna, I don't want to do that—"

"Just do it. You're being selfish. Everyone wants to hear about this from the one who discovered it. Just do it." Jason began pacing back and forth. Anna went to Kevin and kissed him, and they watched Jason as he paced back and forth for several minutes.

"Where? What time?" Jason asked, obviously annoyed.

Anna chuckled. "In the Philip Olsen auditorium, at ten a.m."

"Who'll be there?"

"It will be packed. Over five hundred reporters have made reservations. We printed tickets that have to be presented before they're allowed entrance. Cameras from every major network will be there."

Jason began pacing again. Anna and Kevin looked at each other, both shaking their heads. Jason went into the kitchen and drank some water. When he returned, he continued pacing, and Julia ran to him. "Is everything okay, Daddy?" she asked. Jason picked her up and began pacing again, holding Julia tightly.

Jason stopped and asked Anna, "What is expected of me?"

"Just give a ten minute summary of your findings, and then take questions. Be generous in allowing them to ask questions. They are all very curious about you."

"Anna, I'm doing this just for you. Repay for you and David moving here. Don't ask me again." Jason sounded serious.

"Sweetie, thanks. But I can tell you CNN, ABC, Vanity Fair, Time, and the New York Times have all asked for exclusive interviews. You should consider it."

"Goodnight, Anna. I love you." Jason took her arm and led her to the door. Anna kissed him and left.

"That wasn't very nice." Kevin chuckled. "Why don't you want to do these interviews? Most ambitious people would love the publicity."

Jason shook his head. "You know how I hate this. It's not important to me. What's important to me is right here in this room."

The following morning, Jason got up at his usual five a.m., ran his usual six miles, was in his office by seven a.m., and made his usual rounds of the fourteen labs. He spent an inordinate amount of time with Ellen Mirowitz, a postdoc fellow from Israel, and her PhD student who were working on a breast cancer surface protein that seemed to have similar activity as the Blumenthal protein. By the time he had finished his rounds, it was already ten o'clock. Jason grabbed his jacket and rode the elevator down to the second floor entrance to the Philip Olsen auditorium. The lobby was filled with mostly angry people who were complaining that they were not allowed to enter the auditorium. Jason worked his way through the crowd and was stopped at the entrance by a security guard who asked for his reservation ticket. Jason explained that he was the speaker, which made the security guard laugh. Jason frowned and said, "Sir, do you know what this whole affair is about?"

"Yeah, some dude found a cure for cancer," the security guard replied.

"Well, sir, I'm that dude. Now please let me pass by," Jason said with a smile. Another security guard whom Jason recognized approached and motioned for the guard to let Jason pass through.

Jason entered the five hundred-seat auditorium packed with reporters, men and women with cameras and video equipment, people lined against the walls, reporters talking into microphones. Jason walked quickly down to the podium, and, suddenly, there was complete silence, except for the rapid clicking of cameras. Jason attached the small microphone to his shirt and looked out at the audience. He was immediately stunned. In the first row sat Anna and David, John and Evelyn Olson, his father and Sophia, his sister Susie, Paul and Amy Olsen, and Kevin with Julia. In addition, Seth Goldberg, Eric Adelman, and many other professors at Sinai occupied the remainder of the first and second rows.

Jason's eyes suddenly moistened and a few tears began to trickle down his cheeks. Julia jumped out of her seat and ran to Jason, handing him a handkerchief. Jason kissed her, she ran back to her seat, and Jason took a deep breath. "Welcome, ladies and gentlemen. My name is Jason Olsen O'Malley Green. Most people know me as Jason Green. I had no idea that this event was so important that my family would be here today. So the first thing I'm going to do is to introduce to you what is most important to me in this world: My family. That little girl who just gave me the handkerchief is my daughter Julia, and sitting next to her is my husband Kevin O'Malley. There sits my father and mother, Jonathan and Sophia Green, my sister Susie, my other father and mother, John and Evelyn Olsen, and then my other sisters and brothers, Anna and David Kramer and Paul and Amy Olsen. And I am honored that several of my close friends and esteemed colleagues who make Sinai Medical Center the great institution that it is are also here." Jason paused as cameras clicked and wiped away residual tears.

"Albert Einstein said: 'We owe a lot to the Indians. They taught us how to count, without which no worthwhile scientific discovery could have been made.' The point is, what we discovered in our lab was made possible only because of the hard work and imagination of literally thousands of scientists over many decades who have given us the tools to make our work even possible."

Jason spoke slowly in his deep southern accent. "Let me tell you concisely what we have found, and then I'll take questions. For the past several decades, the Harvey Glassman labs have been working on the nature of cancer cell surface proteins. These are proteins that are on the surface of all cells, normal cells as well as cancer cells. All of these proteins serve a purpose. Some allow nutrients to pass in and out of the cell, others allow waste products of the cell to exit the cell, others are signal proteins that result in chemical reactions inside the cell. For example, certain proteins on the surface of cells that produce insulin result in production and release of insulin when food is ingested. Are y'all following me?" There were nods from most of the audience.

"Good. It was discovered years ago that cancer cells have proteins on their cell surface that are not found on the surface of normal cells. Several years ago, we stumbled upon one of these proteins that occurs on the surface of pancreas cancer cells. We found that this protein attaches to certain types of T-lymphocytes called killer T-lymphocytes. We all have these killer T-lymphocytes. They are an important part of our immune system because they destroy cells that shouldn't be occurring naturally in our body. In other words, these killer T-lymphocytes will destroy cancer cells. It turns out that this little pancreas cancer protein that we stumbled upon attaches to a particular surface protein on the killer T-lymphocyte that sets off a chain of chemical reactions in the lymphocyte, resulting in self-destruction of the lymphocyte. Hence, this pancreas cancer cell protein results in destruction of the killer T-lymphocyte before the killer T-lymphocyte is able to destroy the cancer cell. Pretty clever on the part of those cancer cells, I would say. Are y'all still with me?"

Again nods from most in the audience.

"What we were able to do was to make a new protein that neutralized that nasty protein on the surface of the pancreas cancer cell. By neutralizing that protein, the killer T-lymphocytes are able to destroy the pancreas cancer cells. I will not go into all of the years of hard work that allowed us to be able to make this neutralizing protein. In large part, it was because of the hard work of that man sitting there, Dr. Eric Adelman, who invented a unique computer program that allowed us to literally design this neutralizing protein. Because of that computer program, and the hard work of Dr. Blumenthal, Mr. Henderson and others in our lab, over several years we have been able to design and make this neutralizing protein. And I know everyone here has read the remarkable results we have had in treating patients with terminal pancreas cancer. In literally one hundred percent of the patients treated thus far, treatment with this protein has resulted in complete disappearance of the cancer. Questions?"

At least a hundred people started shouting questions.

Jason raised his hand and yelled, "Please everyone, quiet." Silence was slowly restored, and Jason said, "I've never had a press conference before, so I'm not good at this. Let's do this like it's a classroom. I'm going to ask y'all to raise your hands, and I will point to the person who's to ask the question."

"How confident are you that these patients have been cured?"

"I'm hopeful, not confident. Time will tell."

"When will the drug be available for general use?"

"The drug is currently in production and has been approved for release by the FDA. It will be distributed by Corigian Pharmaceutical, and I suspect it will be available within the next month or two."

"How much will it cost?"

"It will be expensive. I'm not certain of the exact pricing, but every person receiving the drug will require two infusions. I can tell you that the drug will be made available to everyone with pancreas cancer, whether or not they are insured, and if there is a high deductible, that deductible will be forgiven."

"Has Corigian agreed to what you have just stated?"

"Yes, it was at Corigian's insistence."

"Where will the money come from to pay for uninsured patients?"

"Corigian will foot the bill."

"I understand that the CEO of another pharmaceutical company tried to bribe you into giving him rights to your discovery, and that he is now in jail."

"Is there a question?"

"Could you comment?"

"That is all a matter of public record. You can get all of the gory details without my help."

"Could you let Dr. Adelman speak as to how he came up with this computer program?"

Jason hesitated, but Eric quickly stood, walked to Jason, and took the microphone. Jason looked to the side and saw Dr. Blumenthal and Mr. Henderson standing toward the front of the auditorium against the wall. It was obvious that Henderson had been tearful.

Eric spoke authoritatively. "This computer program is literally revolutionary. There is nothing like it anywhere. And this drug could have never been constructed without such a program. Furthermore, to develop this program requires an extraordinary knowledge of molecular structure and computer programing, in addition to an imagination that I have difficulty fathoming. I daresay there are not a handful of people on this planet who have that ability, and perhaps there is only one. I did not invent this program.

"Dr. Green developed this program in 2005 when he first came to Sinai as an intern, working in Dr. Harvey Glassman's lab. When I arrived in 2006, the program was already written. With Dr. Green's help, I have been able to refine the program over the years."

Eric handed the microphone back to Jason, who was red-faced.

"Dr. Green, how were you able to write this program as a young intern, and why haven't you made it available to other laboratories?"

"This drug is the first designer molecule that we have synthesized and have had success regarding a clinical outcome. We didn't want to distribute a program that didn't show promise."

The same man persisted, "You didn't answer the first part of the question. How were you able to write this program as a young intern?"

"I didn't answer it because I don't know the answer." Jason pointed to the next questioner.

"Are you going to make your computer program available to other labs?" the man asked.

"Yes, Dr. Adelman is in the process of writing a comprehensive article on this program which will hopefully be published in the next six to twelve months. We will make the program available to any research lab that can use it."

"How much will you charge for that program?" the same woman asked.

"There will be no charge."

"How much money are you personally making for discovering this drug?"

"I have no personal monetary gain. Sinai Medical Center will be getting twenty percent of the gross sales of the drug. That money will be used for research grants, scholarships, and other needs of Sinai Medical Center and The Olsen Research Center. I suspect that Anna Kramer, the President and CEO of Sinai Medical Center, and the board of trustees will determine how those monies are used."

"Why are you not receiving compensation for developing this drug?" the same man asked.

"I am being compensated. I get my salary from Sinai

Medical Center, and my salary is paid to me for the research that I do."

The man shook his head. "It seems to me that you should get some extra compensation for your discovery."

"Sir, I do appreciate your concern for my financial wellbeing. But don't worry yourself. I'm doing just fine. Next question."

Everyone laughed.

"Do you have any more promising discoveries?"

"We are working on a number of different types of cancers. We are particularly interested in breast cancer and melanoma, and we are making some progress in those areas."

There was another fifteen minutes of questions regarding the new drug, the research that went into designing the drug, and the prospects for new drugs. Then a young lady whom Jason recognized from one of the television stations asked, "Can you tell us something about your personal life, Dr. Green. Everyone is very curious about you."

"This is not about me. I promise you that it is only because of my brilliant colleagues in the Glassman lab that we have accomplished this."

"Just a little about you, Dr. Green," the same reporter persisted.

"I'm happily married to Kevin O'Malley. We have a beautiful daughter, Julia, and a wonderful and loving family. What more is there?"

"Dr. Green, in 2006 you were shot in the chest and almost died. There are many rumors that it was an assassination attempt revolving around research that you were doing in Dr. Glassman's lab, that one or more Chinese nationals were involved, and that the President of the United States met with you and even presented a medal to you. Do you care to comment?"

"I love rumors. I learn so much about myself that I didn't know." Laughter erupted in the audience. "Ladies and gentleman, thank you so much for being interested in our research at Sinai Medical Center and The Olsen Research Center. I hope that everyone prays, in their own way, that these men and women with pancreas cancer who are being treated with this new therapy live long and happy lives. Thank y'all for coming and have a nice day." Everyone clapped and then the talk among the five hundred reporters became almost unbearably loud. Jason went to Kevin and kissed him, picked Julia up, and then went to each of his family and kissed them.

Anna put her hand on Jason's face. "Sweetie, you were superb, and thank you. I know you hated doing that."

"Like I told you, I owed you. But no more," Jason said with impish seriousness.

"Only a New York Times interview, and here comes Dr. Gupta. Be nice."

Dr. Gupta shook hands. "Dr.Green, it's an honor to meet you."

"And likewise. I'm a big fan."

"I would be grateful if I could do a story on you and your research. I know you dislike publicity, but your story and research are compelling, and it would be a mitzvah for you to do it." Dr. Gupta smiled, not letting Jason's hand go.

Jason chuckled. "You do your homework, Dr. Gupta, and where did you learn about Jewish guilt?"

"Well some of my best friends are Jews, Dr. Green." Dr. Gupta laughed out loud. "I'm serious, this is an important story."

"Well, email me, and we can set something up. I won't travel though. You should know that upfront."

Dr. Gupta nodded. "I know, I know. I heard it would take an act of congress to get you to leave Julia. We can do the interview here or at your home, your choice. I'll email you. I'm really looking forward to getting to know you." Dr. Gupta introduced himself to the other family members, talked with Julia and Kevin for a few minutes, and then left the auditorium, which was still filled with reporters taking pictures and looking at the family members. All of the professors came and shook Jason's hand. Seth Goldberg hugged Jason and patted him on the cheek.

John suggested that everyone go for lunch. "Dad, I'm really sorry. I would love to, but I have some pressing work that I have to do this afternoon. We'll be coming to Wilton on Friday, though."

"Jason, I didn't invite you. I was talking to everyone else. Get to work." John laughed with everyone. Jason talked with his sister, Susie; said goodbyes; kissed Julia and Kevin; and walked through the remaining two hundred reporters in an attempt to get to the bank of elevators. He was stopped by numerous people who asked for interviews, and Jason responded each time with a smile that he or she should email him through the Sinai Medical Center website. He rode the elevator, thankfully by himself, up to his office on the seventeenth floor, exhausted and grateful to be back in a familiar setting.

# CHAPTER 21

The following day, virtually every major newspaper in the US printed a story about the press conference with pictures of Jason, Kevin, and Julia. The most prominent New York City tabloid had a large picture of Jason holding Julia and kissing Kevin with the headline: *New Power Couple*. The article was a detailed biography of Jason from his youth up to the present, his success as a clinician including details on how he twice saved Judge Lackland's life as an intern at Sinai, and all of his successes as a researcher.

The article recounted his first marriage to Philip, their adoption of Julia, Jason's devotion to his daughter, Philip's tragic death, and the introduction of Kevin to Jason by Philip's own parents. The article then described Kevin's upbringing, his estrangement from his parents, his military service as the president's aide, and Kevin's tremendous success starting and operating his own security firm. The author estimated Kevin and Jason's combined wealth at around fifty million dollars. The article ended by stating that not only were Jason and Kevin the newest and most influential power couple in New York

City but they were also by far the most attractive couple in New York City.

Someone from his lab had laid the tabloid on Jason's desk before he arrived, and, after reading the article, Jason had a panic attack. He closed his office door and paced back and forth.

The last thing that he wanted was publicity, and especially this sort of publicity. How could this reporter possibly get all of those details, particularly regarding Judge Lackland, and how could he possibly know their assets? Jason did his own investing and had been extraordinarily successful, but his assets were not public knowledge. At least the article didn't report his first meeting with Kevin at Camp David. Jason's panic turned to fury. He was determined to give no further interviews. He would not expose Julia, Kevin, or himself to the public in this way. He had never read a tabloid newspaper in his life, and now he was on the cover of one.

There was a soft knock at the door. Jason continued pacing, and the knock became louder. Jason opened the door. "Jason, I'm so sorry," Anna said, walking in and closing the door. "I see you have that article. I knew you'd be upset. It will all blow over." Anna tried to kiss Jason, but he kept pacing back and forth. "Jason, stop, sit down!"

Jason walked back to his chair. "Anna, I hate this. I just want to work and enjoy my family in peace. And to be on the front page of a tabloid newspaper like some publicity-seeking socialite. Kevin is going to be furious. And where did this guy get all of his information?"

"Sweetie, I don't know. They have their ways. They're good at what they do."

Jason stood up and began pacing again. "Well, you know what Socrates said."

"Another lesson from Jason. You used to annoy Phil by giving him all these Socrates and Mark Twain quotes."

Jason continued unchecked. "Great minds discuss ideas. Small minds discuss people." Jason stopped pacing and looked at Anna. "Philip told you I annoyed him with those quotes? I never knew that. He would always just smile and go on his way."

"Jason, this will all settle down. Like it or not, you are famous. You've discovered a cure for a common and deadly cancer, and you have to answer for that. You agreed to an interview with Dr. Gupta, and I am asking you to do an interview for the New York Times. That's all I'm going to ask. And you can just talk ideas with them. If they start asking you about your personal life, or about people as Socrates says, then just simply decline."

Another knock on the door interrupted their conversation. Anna opened the door, and Kevin walked in. Jason went to him and hugged him. "I'm so sorry this happened," Jason said, looking at Kevin to see if he was angry. "Are you upset or angry?"

Kevin smiled. "I'm not angry. I just came to make certain you didn't jump out of one of these windows. It's a long ways down. I knew how upset you'd be."

"Upset is not the word. I'm humiliated. And I've put you and Julia in a terrible position. I don't know how they got all of this information."

"Nothing is private anymore. I can also tell you that a Freedom of Information Act request was made regarding the 2006 espionage business, and that entire story is going to come out. So just be prepared."

"How do you know that?" Jason asked with a puzzled look.

Kevin laughed. "I'm in the business of getting information. I have friends in Washington. And by the way,

I hope that you don't think that I'm weak minded, as Socrates says, because of the business I'm in."

"Don't be ridiculous," Jason sat down, calming somewhat. The three sat in silence for several minutes. "Are you coming to Wilton this evening?" Jason asked Anna.

Anna chuckled. "Of course, if you promise to improve your mood."

"Your parents are not going to be happy about this." Jason's mood turned broodingly.

"I've talked to Dad already. He thought it was funny. Okay, I'm leaving. Cheer up. See you this evening. Love you both." Anna got up and left. Kevin stood and shut the door. He went to Jason, sat on his lap, and began kissing Jason passionately, deeply. Jason responded, becoming quickly aroused.

"Kevin, I can't here. I have to be careful. There are too many people in and out of here." Kevin persisted, but Jason finally pushed him away. "I'm going to orgasm if you continue this." Kevin laughed and stood up, both smiling at each other's bulging pants.

Jason loved, even craved, having sex with Kevin. They had sex almost daily now, and it seemed that both could not get enough of one another. Jason would sometimes have vivid memories of having sex with Philip when with Kevin, and when that happened he would shake with a startle. He suspected that Kevin knew what this reaction was, although they never discussed it. Jason also continued to have vivid nightmares, which would result in his awakening in a sweat and shaking. Jason had warned Kevin when they first went out that he had suffered vivid nightmares since childhood and that he was embarrassed about it. But just like with Philip, every time it occurred, Kevin would hold him tightly until he fell back to sleep. And just as with Philip, and what pleased

Jason most, was that they slept each night entwined with one another. The great comfort that Jason felt sleeping with Kevin was, as it had been with Philip, surprising and inexplicable.

Jason started his laboratory rounds thirty minutes later than usual because of the unexpected article. When he arrived at the Blumenthal lab, Marcus Blumenthal got up from his desk with a smile.

"Dr. Green, that was an impressive news conference you gave yesterday. And you were generous in mentioning our names."

"There was nothing generous about it. You and Craig should get your due credit for this research. Where is Craig?" Jason asked.

"He's over at the Mirowitz lab, helping them with a problem. I'm sure you know that he has been working day and night since all the trouble. He is literally here until ten or eleven every night, he arrives here at five every morning, and he is here most of every weekend. He has no life outside this lab. Yesterday when you mentioned his name, he started crying."

"I know. I saw that. Does he seem depressed?" Jason asked

"He seems fine. He laughs when someone tells a joke, he's animated and incredibly engaged in the research, and he's always helping the other PhDs with problems or writing. I've invited him over for dinner several times, but he always declines, saying that he has too much work to do. And sure enough, the volume of work he's doing here is pretty staggering."

"Well, first of all, I think it's time you start applying for a professorship to get your own lab. You'll be able to go wherever you like, and you deserve it. I'll look forward to collaborating with you."

"It would be an honor. My wife, Jeanne, is from Ann Arbor and she really wants to go back there to be near her family, although I hate the winters there."

"Dr. Dodsen, the new Department of Medicine Chairman, has called me several times already, asking me to push you back to Ann Arbor. I'm certain there's a position awaiting you there. And you tell him that you will accept only if you are tenured on day one. I know that is unusual and rare, but I've made it clear to him that you are not a risk and that if you are not hired with tenure, then I would see to it that you would be hired here with tenure. You should get in touch with him soon."

Dr. Blumenthal turned pale with a look of shock on his face, which made Jason smile. "Don't you sell yourself short. You do what I'm telling you. Secondly, I know you're working hard on these melanoma surface proteins, but I want you to collaborate with Mirowitz on the breast cancer proteins as well. You can hire a couple more research assistants if you need to. Craig won't get his PhD for another year after you leave. Do you think he can head your lab?"

"I'm certain he can. But that may cause some rancor among the other PhD candidates."

Jason paused. "Hmm, I'll have to give that some thought. Have you reviewed all of the technical papers he's written over the past four months?" Blumenthal nodded. "They're all suitable for publication, they're all perfectly written, and they all have you as first author and me as last author. I've never seen anything like this come from a PhD student."

"Oh, I have," Blumenthal replied, laughing. "Have you reviewed your own bibliography from 2005 to 2008?"

Since the Thompson affair, Craig had never initiated a conversation with Jason, even during his daily rounds.

When Jason asked him a question regarding his research or when critiquing one of the technical papers he had written, Craig would answer thoroughly, but Jason sensed something was not right. Perhaps he was depressed, or maybe he was just embarrassed by his behavior. In any case, Jason was bothered by his complete immersion in his work, shunning any outside activity. Jason finished his rounds, met with Eric Adelman regarding the direction of the fourteen labs, took a call from Dr. Sanjay Gupta who arranged for an interview at his lab the following Wednesday, and agreed to be interviewed by the main editor of the New York Times on Thursday after a pleading call from Anna. Anna had also informed him that she had over four hundred calls and emails requesting interviews but assured him that the New York Times interview was the only one that she would ask of him.

At two-thirty p.m. Jason walked into the conference room where the postdoc fellows and PhD students had already gathered. As he walked in everyone stood and began clapping. "So what's this all about?" Jason asked, waving the men and women to sit down.

Sally Mosley, an effervescent PhD student who was never afraid to speak her mind yelled out, "We are all just so excited to be working for the new power couple, and we thought that deserved a standing ovation." Everyone looked at her, and then at Jason, not knowing what response to expect. "And also, there are about thirty of us here. If you could give up just thirty of those fifty million dollars, we could all go home and forget all of this drudgery."

There were several murmurs after she made that statement.

"Sit down, everyone," Jason said with seriousness, and then there was complete silence as everyone sat, waiting for Jason's response. "Ms. Mosley, knowing the little I do know about you, that one million dollars would not last very long, and then what? I would suggest that you stick to your day job." Laughter erupted. "And let me show you the power of this power couple thing. Ms. Mosley, you can now add an extra year of drudgery to your PhD program for those ill-advised comments."

Laughter once again erupted.

"Well," Ms. Mosley boldly persisted, "that extra year won't be so bad. The one statement in the article I know to be true is that you are the best-looking power couple around, so looking at you and occasionally Mr. O'Malley will ease the pain."

More laughter.

"Okay, you get the last word in this two-way conversation, Ms. Mosley, but I'm keeping my eye on you." Again laughter erupted. "So, apparently, Dr. Blumenthal's and Mr. Henderson's research has put me in an unwelcome limelight, and I suspect that there will be more tabloid articles with all sorts of rumors. As I said yesterday, for those of you who were not at that ridiculous news conference, which was by the way forced upon me, I love rumors. I learn so much about myself that I never knew." All laughed again. "So this is the last I want to hear about any tabloid articles. I don't want anyone putting another tabloid article on my desk. Occasionally, ignorance is bliss, or at the least ignorance prevents panic, to which I am prone. Some of you may have seen the door to my office uncharacteristically closed this morning. That was so I could have my panic attack in private after having read that article.

"On a more serious note, we're all on to something in these fourteen labs, and each of you has a great opportunity to greatly further your career. In the future, there will be more overlap, collaboration, and cooperation among the fourteen labs, and I suspect that our future publications will have most everybody in this room listed as a coauthor. Dr. Adelman will be working with each lab to revise projects in order to make collaboration more efficient and increase productivity. Having said that, I want everyone to go to your lab right now, shut everything down, and take the weekend off. I don't want any of you here unless timing requires you to be here, in which case I prefer your research assistants complete the task. I mean it. No one here this weekend. Take the weekend off, do something fun. Ms. Mosley, go spend some money." Everyone laughed but appeared stunned at the weekend respite. As everyone left the conference room, walking by Jason and smiling or wishing him a good weekend, Craig Henderson passed Jason, with his head down, eyes pinned to the floor.

"Mr. Henderson, could you come to my office?" Jason directed Craig to follow him. "Shut the door please, and sit."

Jason sat at his desk, taking a few memos from his desk and putting them into his briefcase, the same Tumi briefcase that Philip had given him many years ago. "Mr. Henderson, you've been working very hard. I'd like you to spend the weekend with my family and me in Wilton. It's very relaxing, and it would be good for you."

"Sir, I have a lot of work to do, I really can't, but thank you so much for the invitation."

"I won't take no for an answer. That work can wait," Jason persisted.

"Sir, I couldn't impose. Really I can't."

Jason wrote his address on a memo sheet. "Here's my address. The concierge will let you up to my home. Be there at five. Just bring casual clothing." Jason stood and went around his desk. He put his hand on the young man's shoulder. "Craig, don't disappoint me. Be there at five." Craig slowly got up and without saying anything left Jason's office.

Jason finished reviewing a rough draft of Eric Adelman's computer program article and walked down to Eric's lab. Eric was in the process of shutting his computers down to a sleep mode. "Great paper, Eric. By the way, I took the liberty of renegotiating your salary up another hundred thousand dollars."

Eric laughed. "How in God's name did you do that."

"I didn't do it in God's name. I made a compelling case that you were worth twice that, I reminded them of all the money they are getting because of the drug that you, in large part, developed, and that was it."

"Well, I'm grateful. I get paid far more than any other PhD around here. I'm afraid there will be a lot of resentment among the other faculty."

"Well, we fixed that. Your reported salary will remain the same. The extra will be paid in bonuses at the end of the year. So your official salary as far as the medical center printed information is concerned will remain the same."

Jason rushed home and arrived just as Alejandra and Julia were walking into the building. Jason scooped Julia up and began ticking her neck with his lips and nose. She started squealing as usual and then said, "Daddy, I'm getting too old for that. Don't do that anymore."

"My goodness, seven years is too old for tickling?" Jason asked, amused.

"Yes, it is. Are we going to grandma and grandpa's?" Julia asked.

"Yes, we are. We're staying the entire weekend. Thanks, Alejandra, I'll take her from here. Have a great weekend." They walked into their home and Kevin was on the telephone, explaining to John Olsen that they were bringing Craig Henderson with them for the weekend because of the concerns that Jason had about his mental health. Julia ran to him, and Kevin picked her up, giving her a kiss.

At five p.m. the doorbell rang, and Julia ran to open it. "You must be Mr. Henderson," she said loudly.

"Yes, I am. And you must be Julia," Craig answered.

Julia laughed. "You're right."

Jason came from his bedroom where he was packing a few things. "I'm thrilled that you came, Craig. You remember Kevin?"

"Of course. Hello, Mr. O'Malley." Craig held his hand out to shake Kevin's hand, but Kevin hugged him instead, resulting in an obvious look of surprise from Craig.

The four got into Jason's Murano and drove the ninety minutes to Wilton. Craig spoke Spanish fluently, and he and Julia conversed in Spanish most of the way to Wilton. John Olsen emerged from the mansion as they drove up the long driveway, waving them up to the front entrance. John took Julia out of her seat and kissed her, and then Julia ran into the house. After hugging Kevin and Jason, John laughed, "Ah, the new power couple, and, Jason, this must be the young man who's after your job." John walked to Craig. "I understand that you just might be the next Jason Green, young man." John put his arm around Craig's shoulder, and they all walked into the mansion, where Paul and his family, and Anna and David were all waiting in the living room. The dinner began after Julia sang the Sabbath prayers, and the talk was lively, mostly revolving around politics. Craig was quiet most of the dinner. At one point, John said, "So Craig, I'm surrounded by liberals here. Are you going to help me out?"

Craig turned red in the face., "Mr. Olsen, I don't want to wear out your warm welcome so soon, so I'm afraid I'll have to refuse to answer that question." Every-one laughed, and the chatter resumed.

The next morning, Jason knocked on Craig's door at eight a.m. and walked in, finding Craig still lying in bed. "Hey, sleepyhead, are you awake?"

"Sorry Dr. Green, I just woke up. I haven't slept this late in a long time."

"First of all, this weekend you call me Jason. Back at the lab, Dr. Green is fine. Are you up for a run?"

"I haven't run in months. I'm really out of shape, and from what I hear, there is no way I could keep up with you."

"Here, these are some running shorts and a tee shirt, and these shoes should fit you. I'll be waiting down-stairs."

Ten minutes later, Craig came downstairs in his run-ning shorts and tennis shoes, and Jason announced to the rest of the family that they would return in about forty-five minutes. They started the seven-miles run, and two miles into the run Craig had to stop. "I'm sorry Dr. Green. I'm holding you back. You go on."

"Craig, this weekend I'm Jason. Let's walk." They continued at a slow pace while Craig caught his breath. Jason said, "You know, Craig, I've been very worried about you. I'm not only interested in my students' aca-demic achievements. I'm also interested in their personal lives and particularly their mental and physical health. And you've seemed depressed to me lately."

"After what I did, anyone with a conscience would be depressed. And I don't understand why you've been so good to me. What I did was criminal."

"Are you suicidal? Be honest with me."

"I've thought about it. But I wouldn't act on those thoughts."

"Would you agree to see a psychologist?" Jason asked.

"I don't want to spend the money. Besides, I know what I did, and I understand how I've responded. I don't need any help figuring that out."

"That's not the point. I tell you what, I know a great counselor. I want you go see him. The lab has extra money for exactly this purpose. There's no cost to you." Craig did not respond, continuing to walk with his eyes to the ground. "You know, Craig, I'm a big believer in second chances. There is a lot of history behind that belief. I guarantee you, had it not been for second chances, I would probably be packing groceries or maybe dead. I can also tell you that you have more potential than any PhD student I've ever mentored. The bad news is that if you don't get your personal life straightened out, make peace with your past actions, and find a soul mate, you'll not be very successful or happy in your personal or professional life. So promise me that you will go see the counselor."

Craig began to sob. Jason held him until the crying diminished, and then he held Craig's shoulders, looking at him in the eye. "Look at me, Craig, will you see the counselor?" Craig nodded, and Jason smiled. "C'mon, let's run." Both men ran the entire four miles remaining without having to stop.

The remainder of the weekend was jovial. Anna announced that she was sixteen weeks pregnant and was expecting a boy whom they planned to name Philip, resulting in tears from Jason and Kevin. Craig spent a lot of time playing with the children. Kevin and Jason spent a lot of time together in that oversized leather chair talking with John, Evelyn, Anna, and David. At the end of the weekend, Jason was greatly relieved regarding Craig's demeanor, and on the car trip back to the city Jason saw in the rearview mirror Craig's smile when Kevin took Jason's hand, which he held for the entire ride home.

# CHAPTER 22

Over the weekend, stories were printed in newspapers all over the US, in Europe, and in Asia about Jason's discovery and about his personal life. Much of what was printed was based on rumors and half-truths. Many stories in the tabloid press concentrated on Jason's homosexuality, some articles alleging that he had been promiscuous as a young man. Jason refused to read any of the articles, although he was aware that he had become the focus of much attention.

He was refining an article written by Dr. Mirowitz when there was a knock at his door. Anna walked in and sat down. "So, when you walk all the way over to my office on a Monday morning, it can't be good news." Jason got up and went around his desk to kiss Anna.

"It's not bad news," Anna replied. "But as you probably know, there've been hundreds of articles written about you the past several days. I mean all over the world. And a lot of ridiculous things have been written about you."

"I know I'm apparently the topic of conversation. It's laughable. I understand the interest in the new drug. But there are so many other important and awful things going on in this world to talk about. Why anyone would have any interest in my personal life...well, it says something about the human condition."

"Look, Dr. Gupta is interviewing you on Wednesday. The New York Times editor is going to be present at the interview, and may have some questions for her article after Gupta is finished. I told Dr. Gupta that you were interested only in discussing the science and would not discuss your personal life. Dr. Gupta made a strong case that you should open up about your personal life, and I agree with him. There are so many ridiculous rumors out there about you now, and your personal life is becoming more important than your discoveries. I know this is not what you wanted or expected, but just answer his questions. When people find out how boring you really are, then the science will come to the forefront."

Jason chuckled. "Well, thanks for that." He paused and then said, "I give up. I'll do my best."

"So, they're making a big deal of this. It's going to be a two-hour special in prime time. Gupta's team would like to come here tomorrow and do a video of your labs. He won't interview you then. They may talk to some of your people as they are recording. Your people can continue doing their usual activities, and they promise to be as discreet as possible. And then what Gupta would really like to do is to interview you at your home in a more relaxed setting Wednesday evening. They will set everything up Wednesday afternoon, and then when you get home, you can get a bite to eat and then do the interview. Are you okay with that?"

"It seems everything has been planned for me. Why not just interview me here?"

"He wants you to be relaxed, and he wants Kevin and Julia to be there."

Tuesday morning, Jason arrived at the Olsen Research Center as usual at seven a.m. after his six-mile run, shower, and breakfast. At the entrance was a large CNN van with men removing cameras and lighting equipment. Jason quickly walked to his office, put down his briefcase, and began pacing, wondering why he had agreed to this. All he wanted to do was work and go home to his family. He left his office and went to each of the fourteen labs, explaining to everyone that CNN was doing a show on the Glassman labs and that they should continue their work as if the camera crew were not there. He went back to his office and began completing his review of Eric Adelman's computer program article. An hour later, there was a knock on his door, and Sanjay Gupta walked in.

"Dr. Green, good morning. I'm really grateful you are letting us do this. I promise that you'll like the end product."

"Well, Dr. Gupta, I don't think I had a choice. The power players around here insisted that I do it, and although I'm not thrilled about all this publicity, I'm glad you are the one handling this. By the way, why aren't you in an operating room somewhere cutting on someone's skull?"

"This is much more important. I'm not going to bother you anymore today. I just wanted to say hello. We'll be waiting for you at your home tomorrow evening when you arrive. The interview shouldn't last more than one or two hours, just depends on how difficult it is to drag information out of you."

"I'm not that interesting, Dr. Gupta. I suspect it will be a short interview."

Jason went to each of the fourteen labs over the next three hours, trying to avoid the CNN crew and Dr. Gupta who were making videos of the various labs. While he was in the Blumenthal lab talking with Marcus and Craig, the CNN crew came to the door. "Dr. Green, is this the lab where the research for this new drug was performed?" Dr. Gupta asked.

"It is." Jason stood up to leave. "This is Dr. Marcus Blumenthal, the postdoctoral fellow in charge of this lab, and this is Craig Henderson, the PhD student who has been working in this lab with Dr. Blumenthal for the past two and a half years. These two men have had primary responsibility for the research in this lab. And those men and women over there are the research assistants who have contributed tremendously to the work in this lab. Excuse me, Dr. Gupta, I'll leave you to your work. I'm going to continue my rounds." Jason quickly walked out and finished his rounds. He called his friend, Seth Goldberg, and asked if he could meet him in the faculty club for lunch.

Jason walked into the faculty club and went to the table where Seth was sitting. "There must be something terribly wrong, Jason. You haven't called me to have lunch in over a year."

"No, I just had to get away from my office, and I didn't want to have lunch by myself. And besides, Kevin and I have not seen enough of you and Sherri lately. Can you have dinner with us this Saturday."

"Of course. What's going on in your office?" Seth asked.

"CNN is doing a story on this research, and they are up in the lab filming and interviewing the postdocs. I'm being interviewed tomorrow evening. Apparently, I'm on the front page of most of the tabloid newspapers these days."

Seth laughed. "You are. And I'm learning a lot of things about you that I never knew. Like I didn't know you were so promiscuous in your younger days. I thought you were just a shy little boy from Mississippi."

"Very funny." Jason settled down as he always did when he was with Seth, who had been his closest friend and confidant since his internship. Jason rarely lunched in the faculty club, and he noticed that he received stares from many of the other professors. Jason nodded and smiled to most as eyes met, but he knew that the stares were because of his newfound fame, or rather, notoriety. After ninety minutes of catching up, Jason hugged Seth and returned to his lab.

To his great relief, the CNN crew had left, and Jason finished the rest of the day in his office, concentrating on his work.

Wednesday evening, Jason walked the two miles home, unhappy about the interview that was about to occur. The CNN van was parked outside his building, and his heart began pounding. Maybe he would just not show up. Why was he so nervous about a silly interview?

He walked into his home and was almost blinded by the lighting. Julia jumped up from the couch, where she was sitting with Kevin and Dr. Gupta, yelling, "Daddy." Jason scooped her up and kissed her, unaware that the greeting was being filmed. Kevin and Dr. Gupta got up to greet Jason, Kevin with a tender kiss. There were several lighting umbrellas that were strategically placed. Two leather chairs had been moved to face each other for the interview.

Dr. Gupta laughed. "I was a little worried you would be a no show."

"The thought crossed my mind." Jason smiled, putting Julia back down. Alejandra had dressed her in a beautiful lace dress.

"Do you want to get a bite to eat before we begin?" Dr. Gupta asked. "We have been eating this wonderful food Alejandra provided. Thank you for doing that."

"I think I'll wait till the interview is over. I would

like some water with me. You'll have to tell me what to do. I've never been interviewed by a news organization."

"Just relax, we're just going to have a conversation. There'll be a lot of editing, so if I say something stupid, or in the unlikely event you do, it will be edited out. So just pretend it's a normal conversation. I'm going to ask you later some very personal things that you may not want to discuss in front of Julia. I can let you know, and perhaps Kevin could take Julia to another room."

"Julia can hear anything I have to say," Jason quickly answered.

"She's pretty amazing. I've been listening to Julia and Kevin talking in Mandarin, and then she speaks to Alejandra in Spanish. Do you speak Mandarin and Spanish?"

"I'm conversant in Mandarin but not Spanish. Whenever Julia doesn't want me to know something, she speaks to Alejandra or Kevin in Spanish."

"Let's talk about your science first. You head fourteen separate research labs that occupy the sixteenth and seventeenth floors of the Olsen Research Center at Sinai Medical Center in New York City. I have asked scientists around the country about this. They all say that most successful scientists run one lab, rarely two or three. No one comes close to fourteen labs. How is that possible?"

"First of all, when I first came to Sinai in 2005, I had the good fortune to start working in Harvey Glassman's lab. At that time, he headed seven separate labs. So there is one scientist who headed more than three labs. And by the way, these fourteen labs are still known as the Glassman labs."

"What you say is true," Dr. Gupta nodded. "Harvey Glassman was a Nobel Prize winner and was by all accounts a driven taskmaster. At that time, he headed more labs than anyone in the country, more than twice as many as any other researcher. That doesn't explain how you are able to head fourteen labs."

"It's only because I have somehow been able to attract brilliant postdoctoral fellows and PhD students. They are the ones who really head each of these labs. Without those individuals, it would not be possible. I really just coordinate the research activities and am more of a cheerleader for these young scientists."

Dr. Gupta smiled. "You know, I spoke with every postdoctoral fellow in these fourteen labs, and, without exception, they all say the same thing. That Jason Green has a computer mind, knows every detail of every experiment in each of the fourteen labs, is intimately involved in every project, and has an uncanny ability to direct each of the projects in the proper direction. One of the postdoc fellows told us that every Friday you have a two-hour meeting with all fourteen labs to review the week's progress. She described your performance at these conferences like that of a great symphonic conductor, and then she corrected herself and said you were more like a great composer, both composing and conducting a great symphony at the same time. She said there has been never a meeting at which everyone didn't walk away awestruck by your intellectual abilities."

"I must be paying her too much. Look, I've been blessed with an ability to retain a lot of facts. What I learned from my mentors, Harvey Glassman, Franklin Skor, Edward Berk, and others, is that fact retention is not so important. What is most important in any research endeavor is to ask the right questions. It's the most important lesson that I can teach my students. It seems like such an easy lesson, and yet it is so difficult to do. Once you learn to ask the right questions, the answers can usually be discovered, sometimes easily, most times with hard work. So what I do during my interactions with these young researchers is to try and teach them to ask the right questions. The greatest joy I have in my job is watching these researchers learn that lesson."

Dr. Gupta chuckled. "Well, Dr. Green, I can see I'm not going to get a straight answer out of you."

"I thought I answered the question."

"No," Dr. Gupta said, "I wanted you to tell me how you are able to effectively run fourteen different laboratories."

"You've heard John Donne's poem many times. *No man is an island, Entire of itself, Every man is a piece of the continent, A part of the main.* Well, I'm simply part of the main. Our success is a result of the work of scientists long dead, the hard work of many living scientists from around the world, and the hard work of the young scientists in the Glassman lab. I'm so grateful to be a part of this success."

"Okay, I give up," Dr. Gupta said. "So can you tell me in simple terms how you discovered this new drug that is an apparent cure for pancreatic cancer? Remember, I am a dumb neurosurgeon, so speak plainly."

"My mentor, Harvey Glassman, who headed this lab before he died of pancreas cancer seven or so years ago, along with other researchers elsewhere, discovered that cancer cells have certain proteins on their cell surface that are not found on non- cancerous cells. We know that the proteins on the cell surface of normal cells, whether pancreas or other organs, perform certain functions, such as moving nutrients in and out of the cell, as well as many other functions. Presumably, all of the proteins on the surface of a cell have some purpose. Scientists have been trying to discover what the functions or purpose are of these new surface proteins found on the surface of various cancer cells. Do these proteins somehow allow cancer cells to grow without restraint?"

"Cytotoxic T-lymphocytes are an important part of our immune system. These cells recognize infectious agents such as viruses and bacteria, and they also recognize abnormal cancer cells. When these T-lymphocytes recognize the presence of cancer cells, they would normally destroy the cancer cell. We also know that there is a specific protein...let's call it protein A...on the surface of these lymphocytes that, when stimulated, results in the self-destruction of the lymphocyte. Am I making sense to you?"

Dr. Gupta nodded. "Yes, please go ahead."

Jason looked over at the couch where Kevin and Julia were quietly watching intently. "Well, lo and behold, Dr. Blumenthal's lab stumbled upon a protein on the surface of mice pancreas cancer cells that attaches to this protein A on the surface of the cytotoxic T-lymphocytes, resulting in self-destruction of the lymphocyte. That was our first exciting discovery over two years ago. We tried to isolate this protein on the pancreas cancer cell, because if we were able to do that, we could easily create antibodies to this surface protein. But it was impossible to do. It was simply too small.

"But we were able to isolate the protein A on the cell surface of the T-lymphocyte, which was much larger, and we were able to characterize the structure of that protein. Knowing that structure allowed our computer program to design a synthetic protein that would bind to the pancreas cancer cell protein with a much greater affinity than the T-lymphocyte surface protein A. In other words, we wanted to design a protein that sticks to the pancreas cancer cell protein to a much greater extent, hundreds of times greater, than the lymphocyte protein A. Our computer program allowed us to do that. Are you still with me?"

Dr. Gupta waved. "Go ahead."

"We quickly made that protein and tested it in mice with pancreas cancer. They were all cured. This protein prevented the pancreas cell protein from binding to the T-lymphocyte, preventing self-destruction of the T-lymphocyte, thus allowing the T-lymphocyte to do its thing—destroy the tumor cells. We then started our human studies, and we found the same. So far, virtually all of nearly one thousand individuals with advanced pancreas cancer have had complete disappearance of their tumors."

"So basically, the drug you have invented prevents the pancreas cancer cells from destroying the T-lymphocytes, and therefore the T-lymphocytes are able to destroy the cancer cells."

Jason smiled. "You said it much better than I."

"It sounds so easy to do. Why hasn't this been discovered sooner?"

"It took literally thousands, probably tens of thousands of hours of work. Marcus Blumenthal and Craig Henderson worked day and night, usually seven days a week, with their research assistants, for almost three years to accomplish this. And what allowed us to finally create the drug was our computer program. So I don't want to minimize the difficulty of this. It wouldn't be fair to the thousands of researchers over the world who struggle with these problems every day."

"So it sounds to me like it was really your computer program that allowed the breakthrough. Am I correct?"

Jason was hoping to avoid the subject of the computer program because Eric Adelman had already made it clear at the news conference that Jason had developed the program on his own. "It was very helpful," Jason said and drank some water.

"I understand you wrote that program in 2005 when you were an internal medicine intern. And I also understand that the program is revolutionary, that no one has been able to develop anything like it."

"As far as I know, this computer program is unique. As I said in the news conference last week, we're going to make the program available to anyone who wants it. It was obviously very helpful in developing this drug, and I think it will be very useful to many labs working with protein structures. It will have wide applications."

"Where did you learn computer programming? How in the world could you develop a revolutionary program like this while an intern? It seems impossible to me."

"I taught myself computer programming in college, and I just don't have a good answer regarding how I was able to come up with that program. I just have been blessed with an ability to visualize protein structures. I don't know, it's not worth talking anymore about it. Let's change the subject."

"So do you think that these individuals who have been treated with your new drug have been cured?"

"Well, as I said in the news conference, time will tell. I believe they have been. It's certainly possible that these cancer cells will develop new ways of destroying the T-lymphocytes, and perhaps we'll have to come up with new strategies. I wouldn't be at all surprised. But, hopefully, this is the start of a new era of treatment for various cancers. I believe treatments for cancer are going to become much more effective."

"I understand you are working on other cancers in a similar manner?" Dr. Gupta asked.

"Yes, we're very excited. We have found similar proteins on the surface of certain breast cancer cells and melanoma cells. Hopefully, we'll have some good news in the next few years."

"Your mentor, Harvey Glassman, with whom you were very close, won a Nobel Prize. Would you like to follow in his footsteps with your own Nobel Prize?"

"I've never given that any thought. Far more satisfying than any prize is knowing that many people with pancreas cancer will, at the least, have much longer lives, and, hopefully, be cured, as a result of this research. Having said that, I should say that Harvey Glassman was an amazing mentor. He took a chance on me by letting me work for him while I was an intern and resident. He had an amazing influence on me, and most of all, he taught me to ask the right questions."

Dr. Gupta put down his notepad. "Let's take a short break here, and then I would like to ask you some personal questions." The cameramen turned off their videos and headed towards the kitchen.

"That's fine," Jason stood. "But tell me, why talk about my personal life. I know I agreed to do that. But it has no relevance to all of this."

"It does have relevance. Like it or not, you are a rock star. Everyone is very intrigued by you. You are obviously brilliant, you have model looks, you are married to an equally handsome man, you have a beautiful daughter, you are, by all accounts, very wealthy, and you have started a revolution in cancer treatment at forty years of age. I suspect you could be elected president."

Jason laughed. "Oh, sure, Americans are going to elect a gay New York atheist Jew with a southern accent."

"People like you are rare, and precious. If you don't set the record straight about your personal life, the tabloids are going to have a field day with you, and the lies and rumors will exponentially increase. People want to know about you."

Jason grimaced, walked over to Kevin and kissed him. He picked up Julia and kissed her. "Are you hungry sweetheart?"

"I'm going to wait for you, Daddy."

"We're almost finished. Dr. Gupta, how about Kevin and Julia sitting with me for the rest of the interview?"

Dr. Gupta hesitated. "I'm not certain you would want Julia to hear some of my questions and your answers."

"I don't think there'll be a problem if we're tactful. And Julia and I have already discussed some of the stories that have appeared in the press about me. Some of the kids at her school have already informed her."

The CNN crew rearranged the couch and lighting, Kevin sat on the couch next to Jason, and Julia jumped onto Jason's lap.

"Okay," Dr. Gupta said. "Are you all comfortable? How about you Julia, are you comfortable?"

"Yes, I am, Dr. Gupta," Julia said. "Are you, Daddy?" Julia looked around at Jason.

Jason laughed and kissed Julia's cheek. "Yes, I am, sweetheart."

"So, Dr. Green. I have talked to many people who know you professionally. Without exception, they all say that you are a genius, the most brilliant individual they have ever been associated with. Are you a genius?"

"Well, Dr. Gupta, I don't even know what that word really means. Are you talking about IQ, because I know people of average IQ who are innovative and have had extraordinary success as a result of common sense and hard work? On the other hand, I know people who have extremely high IQs who are unable to see the forest because of the trees. They have no common sense and are not successful in their personal or professional lives."

"Can you name some people you think are geniuses?" Dr. Gupta persisted.

"I can name hundreds, perhaps thousands of people who have created something that I consider a work of genius: For example, Beethoven, Einstein, Michael Jackson,

Somerset Maugham. I doubt that most young people to-day consider Beethoven a genius, and I doubt that my father considers Michael Jackson a genius."

"So a genius is someone who creates something unique or new?" Dr. Gupta asked.

"That might be one definition, although if that is the complete definition, I guess one would have to classify Hitler as a genius. That's not a very satisfying thought."

"Kevin, is Jason Green a genius?"

"You have no idea. One has to be with Jason for only a few minutes to realize that he has an extraordinary mind. I can't speak to the science part. I'm not a scientist. But all of his colleagues tell me that he is a scientific genius. What I can testify to personally is that he is a genius at being a husband and a father, and a genius at how he conducts his life."

"Julia, is your daddy a genius?" Dr. Gupta asked softly.

"No, he's my daddy," Julia answered with a frown. Everyone laughed out loud, including the crew.

"So, Kevin, is Jason perfect? I've yet to meet that person," Dr. Gupta asked inquisitively.

"Well, I'm not sure what you mean by perfect. He's perfect in my eyes. Like most geniuses about whom I've read, Jason can be emotionally fragile. Sometimes he lacks self-confidence. Hopefully, I'm good for him in that way. I'm not a genius, but I'm emotionally strong and confident." Tears welled in Jason's eyes, but he quickly controlled himself and took Kevin's hand.

"So, Dr. Green, when did you realize that you were gay?"

"I knew that I was different, gay, very early on. Certainly, by the time I was nine or ten years of age, I realized I was much more interested in the athletes than in the cheerleaders."

"You were an athlete, were you not?"

"Yes, I ran track in high school and college."

"What do you say to those people who believe that being gay is a choice?"

"I don't say anything to them. I subscribe to the Mark Twain philosophy: Never argue with stupid people. They will drag you down to their level and then beat you with experience."

"You grew up in a small town in Mississippi, Jewish and gay. How did you cope with that?"

"For some reason, I always felt good about being different, whether it was being Jewish or being gay. It never bothered me, even when I was taunted by my classmates. I guess I'm lucky in that way."

"When did you tell your parents that you were gay?"

"I was thirteen. I told my mother at breakfast one morning when my da—when my father was out of town on a business trip. She held me tight, told me I was an amazing human being, that she just wanted me to be happy, and that she wanted me to get married one day and bring her a grandchild. My mother died when I was in medical school. I wish she were here to enjoy Julia."

"How did your father handle it?"

"He told me about all of the famous gay people: Socrates, Aristotle, Michelangelo, Leonardo Da Vinci, Alexander the Great, T.E. Lawrence, Walt Whitman, Oscar Wilde, Emerson, Tennessee Williams, Cole Porter, Tchaikovsky, Elton John, Nuryev, Alan Turing, Sally Ride, James Dean, and hundreds of others. He told me that I would be on that list one day. He was wonderful."

"Your father told me that he and your mother knew you were a genius by the time you were five years of age."

"He never told me that. Let's change subjects."

"Okay, who has been the greatest influence in your life?"

"That's easy. My father. I am who I am because of him. We were the closest of friends from my earliest memories. We read books together from the time I was very young. He taught me tolerance and discipline, he made me think critically, he taught me to ask questions. I was very lucky to have him as a father."

"There are articles in the tabloids that you have been promiscuous since your college days. Do you care to respond to those articles?"

"Not really, but I will, only because some young people might watch this interview, assume that those tabloid articles are true, and as a result use my alleged behavior as justification for their own promiscuity. When I arrived in New York City in 2005 as an intern, I was sexually inexperienced. The first person with whom I was ever sexually intimate was my first husband, Philip Olsen, who was killed in a tragic car accident almost four years ago. The only other person with whom I've been sexually intimate is my husband, Kevin. I'm sorry to disappoint the tabloid press. I'm not judging people who are sexually active with multiple partners, or even promiscuous. I would only want them to know that serious diseases can be sexually transmitted, and that sexually transmitted diseases are epidemic. I would also tell them that having sex with someone with whom you are deeply in love is like magic, so to the extent that promiscuity diminishes that experience is a tragedy for those individuals."

"When did you meet Philip Olsen, and how did that relationship develop?"

"I met Philip early in my internship year at Sinai. One of my patients, Ellie Shapiro, fell and broke her hip. Philip Olsen, who was chief resident in orthopedics, consulted and operated on her hip. We began dating and it was really almost love at first site. We fell deeply in love with each other, I became very close with his family, and Philip and my father became very close. We married in 2011 when same-sex marriage was legalized in New York, and we adopted Julia in 2012. We had a perfect marriage, and Julia and our families were the focus of our lives outside of our professional lives."

"How did you handle Philip's death?"

"Not well. As Kevin said, I am somewhat emotionally fragile." Tears began trickling down Jason's cheeks. Kevin took a tissue and wiped his cheeks. "I still miss him terribly. Thankfully, I remain close to Philip's parents and brother and sister. Philip lives on in his parents, and in Paul and Anna, his brother and sister, and in Julia, whom he adored and influenced. Every time I look at them, every time I look at Julia, I look at Philip." Tears began flowing down Jason's cheeks. Julia turned around and hugged Jason.

Dr. Gupta paused while Jason wiped the tears from his cheeks. "Are you okay to continue?"

Jason nodded.

"Does Julia remember Philip?"

"She doesn't remember him. She sees his pictures and knows who he was. But she only knows Kevin and me as her daddies."

"Dr. Green, you may or may not know, but CNN requested through the Freedom of Information Act, information regarding an incident in 2005 when you were an intern in Dr. Glassman's lab. What we found is like right out of a spy novel. Could you tell us about it?"

"You know, I was sworn to secrecy about that. I think I'm legally bound not to talk about it."

"You are free to talk about it now. It's public knowledge, and the whole story will be published by CNN in the next few days."

"Are you certain? I don't want to go to federal prison."

Dr. Gupta laughed. "I will go to prison for you."

"I worked with a Chinese National in Dr. Glassman's lab in 2005. He was brilliant and a great mentor to me. To make a long story short, toward the end of the academic year, in 2006, I discovered that he was stealing data from our lab and turning it over to the Chinese government. I also discovered that a US Congressman was involved with the Chinese, and that this data theft not only involved our lab but many other labs across the US. When they realized that I had discovered what was going on, there was an assassination attempt. I was shot in the chest, and it was only because I was near Sinai Medical Center and because a talented group of health care providers was nearby that I survived."

"Wow. What happened to all of these people?"

"I think the US Congressman is in jail. I'm not certain what happened to all of the Chinese Nationals. The Chinese National with whom I worked did return to China. I received a letter from him in 2012 apologizing for his involvement. He said that he did it only because he was coerced by threats to his family."

"I also understand that you met the president during this affair, and that you met Kevin at that time as well."

"That is true. When I discovered this, I was taken to Camp David to meet with the president. Philip, Philip's father, John Olsen, and Dr. Glassman were with me. We told the president and his top intelligence officials about what we discovered. Kevin was in the marines and was the president's aide at Camp David. Kevin and I had a short conversation in Mandarin at that time."

"How did that conversation come about?"

"Kevin can speak to that better than I."

Kevin calmly responded, "The president simply told me that a young scientist was coming to Camp David, that this scientist sounded too good to be true, and that he spoke fluent Mandarin. Since I spoke fluent Mandarin, the president asked that I come into the living room after everyone was seated and speak to Jason in Mandarin to see whether he was in fact fluent in that language."

"So what was the conversation?"

"I walked in and said to Jason in Mandarin that the president wanted to know whether he was really fluent in Mandarin. Jason stood up, told me in perfect Mandarin that I could assure the president that he was fluent, and that if the president ever hoped to get his vote, that he should reconsider his position on same-sex marriage since one day he might want to marry Philip Olsen."

"Did you tell the president what Jason said?"

"No, I never did. The president did know that I was gay, however, and despite his public stance, he was privately very sympathetic to LGBT causes. I have remained in contact with the president since I left the marines in 2008."

"I understand the president gave you the Medal of Freedom for what you did."

"That is true," Jason said. "When I was in the hospital, the president visited me, with Kevin, and gave the medal to me at that time. I read about that medal after I got out of the hospital. I didn't deserve it."

"When did you next meet Kevin?"

"It was after Philip's death, almost ten years later. He had moved to New York, unbeknownst to me, and started a security firm, which has become probably the most distinguished security firm in the country. About a year or so after Philip's death, I finally agreed to go out with him. As with Philip, I fell deeply in love with Kevin, and we too have the perfect marriage. I must be the luckiest person in the world."

"Kevin, when did you fall in love with Jason?"

"I fell in love with Jason in 2006 at Camp David. I know that sounds crazy, but that is the truth. When I moved to New York, by happenstance I became close with Philip's father and brother through my security firm. I learned from them that Philip had also fallen in love with Jason literally on their first date. There is obviously something about Jason that results in love at first sight."

"Kevin, how have you been able to handle Jason's continuing love for Philip. Has it adversely affected your relationship?"

"On the contrary, observing the deep love Jason has for Philip, and knowing he is able to love two people in the same way, has just strengthened our relationship. I feel Jason's pain every day, and Philip's family is now my family as well."

"Dr. Green, in 2009, an anonymous donor contributed three million dollars to Sinai Medical Center to establish the Human Rights Distinguished Professorship. It was stipulated by the donor that Philip Olsen hold that professorship until his retirement, and that only a gay or transgendered professor be given that honor after Dr. Olsen's retirement. It had always been assumed that John Olsen, Philip's father, had donated the money for that professorship. I had the pleasure of sitting down with John Olsen yesterday afternoon. He assured me that he had nothing to do with that donation, and that he is certain the money came from you. I have since confirmed that you were indeed the donor and that Philip never knew where that money came from. You were a resident training in internal medicine at that time, making maybe forty or fifty thousand dollars a year. I asked Mr. Olsen how you could have possibly gotten that kind of money since you did not come from a wealthy family. He just smiled and said that you were a genius at investing. Do you care to comment?"

"No."

Dr. Gupta laughed. "Okay. Last topic. Dr. Green, do you believe in God?"

"Dr. Gupta, I cannot imagine why any of your listeners would be interested in my personal beliefs. Do we have to go there?"

"I think there would be great interest in your beliefs. A brilliant scientist who has read all of the great books, quotes philosophers, has a deep passion for goodness and life, by all accounts, one of the most ethical and truly good persons walking this planet. Yes, we all want to know."

"Well, I'm flattered by your characterization of me."

"Well, do you believe in God?" Dr. Gupta persisted much to Jason's annoyance.

Julia turned her head and stared at Jason.

"What I cannot explain is how this all began," Jason said after a long pause.

"What do you mean?"

Jason realized that Dr. Gupta was not going to let the conversation end.

"I mean, I cannot explain how all of the galaxies, the billions of stars, the billions of planets, how all of this began. There must have been a beginning. I'm open to the possibility of a God starting all of this. But if there is a God, She long ago left this planet to do Her other works."

"Why do you say that? And why do you refer to God as She?" Dr. Gupta persisted.

"Well, women give birth, so if we are going to assign a gender to God, I think it more appropriate to refer to God as She. Look, I just don't believe there's a God mi-

cromanaging events and lives on this planet. Human be-
ings have long had a history of making a mess of things.
We are making a mess of this planet, we are destroying
our oceans and forests, we have killed off hundreds, perhaps thousands of animal species, and we have a long
history of killing each other in the name of God. The religious fundamentalists always excuse God's microman-
agement by saying that we simply don't understand the
ways of God. That is simply not rational thinking."

"So I gather you think religious doctrine, whether
Christian, Muslim, Jewish, Hindu, or other is irrelevant."

"No. I believe religion came about to help people or-
ganize their lives and to be good. And to the extent that
religion is helpful in doing that, I'm all for it. Let me
make my beliefs, for whatever they are worth, simple. I
do not believe that any of the great or minor religions
came from the word of God. I believe they are all
manmade structures. I do not believe that religions should
make judgments about those who do not subscribe to
their particular doctrine. I do not believe religions should
dictate civil laws, and I do not believe civil laws should
be religious based. To answer your question, I believe
religion is relevant to those individuals who need it for
help in organizing their lives and being good people. For
those of us who don't need religion to achieve those
goals, religion may be irrelevant except for the fact that
religion continues, as it has for millenniums, to interfere
with many people's liberties and freedom by dictating
civil law."

"So do you have a philosophy by which you live?"
Dr. Gupta asked.

"I'm not a philosopher. The way I live is dictated by
my nature and civil law. I suppose if I were forced to give
you my philosophy on how to live in ten words or less, I

would say I follow two principles: The golden rule and second chances."

"What do you mean by second chances?"

Jason smiled. "I'll leave that up to you and your viewers to figure out."

# EPILOGUE

The CNN special became a two part series, each two hours long, airing on a Saturday and Sunday night at eight p.m. Kevin and Jason sat closely together on their couch, arm in arm, watching both nights. The first part described the science behind Jason's revolutionary discovery, with well-done graphics making the concepts easy to understand. Dr. Gupta's interview with Jason was played in full, and there was an extensive interview with Eric Adelman regarding the revolutionary computer program that Jason had developed as an intern. There were interviews with several of his postdoctoral fellows and with a number of famous scientists from other institutions, all describing Jason's genius in the laboratory. The first night concluded with Dr. Gupta's interview of Jason and Kevin, regarding the definition of genius, and finally Julia's answer to whether Jason was a genius: "No, he's my daddy."

The second night was a two-hour documentary on Jason Green's personal life. Dr. Gupta had traveled to Mississippi and had interviewed his professors and track coach, describing his successes as an All-American track star and his success in research as an undergraduate as well as in medical school. There was a relatively long interview with Jonathan Green about Jason's early life. Jason was shocked that Dr. Gupta had gone to such lengths and sat silently, disbelieving that he could be the object of such attention.

The documentary went on to describe Jason's internship and residency with interviews from several professors, including Seth Goldberg, who described Jason as "the most brilliant, humble, and kind-hearted individual I have or will ever know." Dr. Gupta interviewed Dr. Harvey Glassman's wife regarding Jason's relationship with the famed researcher, who had described Jason soon after their first meeting as "shockingly brilliant." There was an entire segment regarding the Chinese espionage affair, including an interview with the past president, who described Jason as brilliant and brave. Another segment followed describing Jason and Philip's courtship and marriage, their adoption of Julia, and Jason's relationship with the Olsen family including interviews with John and Evelyn Olsen as well as Paul Olsen. There were video scenes from Philip and Jason's wedding, and of Philip playing with Julia. Tears trickled down Jason's cheek during that segment.

The final segment was an interview with Kevin, which had been done in the afternoon just prior to Jason's interview. Kevin described his close relationship with the Olsen family that dated back to 2008, and his insistence on not connecting in friendship with Philip and Jason because of his feelings for Jason. Kevin described his feelings when he had first met Jason at Camp David and subsequently when he saw Jason recovering from the gunshot wound at Sinai Medical Center. He talked about the pain he felt for Jason and the Olsen family after the tragic death of Philip. He concluded, with tears trickling down his cheeks: "But out of tragedy comes the opportunity for second chances. I came along and gave Jason a second chance. And that awful tragedy has given me a second chance as well, in so many ways. With Jason, with the Olsens as my second family, and to discover true happiness with an incredible husband and an amazing child." The segment ended with a picture of Jason and Kevin standing at Philip's grave. Jason broke down and began sobbing. Kevin held Jason tightly.

Dr. Gupta's finale was a sophisticated and beautiful justification for filming the four-hour special. He ended the program by stating, "It is unlikely that the world will have the opportunity of seeing in this generation such an important scientific discovery or such an intimate look at this young, brilliant, and kind scientist and human being, Jason Olsen O'Malley Green. I suspect we shall hear much more from him in the future."

Jason sat stunned and exhausted as the program ended. Kevin continued to hold him. After five minutes, Jason stood. "Let's go to bed. I'm drained."

"In a few minutes," Kevin replied. "I'm not quite ready. Come to the kitchen. I bought a bottle of champagne. Just one glass before bed to celebrate."

Jason didn't feel like drinking but did not want to disappoint Kevin, and he followed Kevin into the kitchen. Kevin opened the bottle and poured two glasses. "It was an amazing four hours of television," Kevin said. "I'm so proud to be your husband."

"And I'm so lucky to have you as my husband. I love you so much," Jason said. Just as they clinked glasses, there was a soft knock at the door. Jason frowned and as he opened the door, in walked Jonathan and Sophia Green, John and Evelyn Olsen, Paul and Amy Olsen, Anna and David Kramer, and Seth and Sheri Goldberg. They had watched the television special with Jonathan and Sophia, and all had puffy eyes and tears that had dried on their cheeks as they walked the ten minutes from Jonathan's home to Jason. They came with bottles of champagne and after the usual hugs and kisses they sat and talked about the show, Jason sitting and quietly listening. Jason felt embarrassed that he had been the focus of a television special, but he could see that for the Olsen family it had in some way partially filled the void resulting from Philip's death.

&#x204B;&#x0254;&#x204B;&#x0254;

Over the next five years, almost seven hundred thousand individuals with pancreas cancer had been treated with the new drug. Of the initial thousand individuals who had been treated, ninety-eight percent remained cancer free after five years. The two percent who had recurrences responded to a second course of therapy with complete disappearance of the recurrent tumor. Of the seven hundred thousand patients, ninety-nine percent had complete disappearance of the tumor after the initial treatment.

Over the next decade, Jason's labs discovered similar cures for breast cancer and melanoma and developed innovative technologies for studying protein structure and function. Despite attempts from every major news organization to write articles and create television specials about Jason and his research, Jason refused any further interviews and shunned all publicity. Jason did allow a highly respected historian who had published several important biographies to interview him over several years, and Jason furnished many of his important scientific papers to her. The historian agreed that the biography would not be published until after the year 2030.

Marcus Blumenthal moved to Ann Arbor and became a very successful researcher with major discoveries of his own. He dedicated every award he received to Jason Green and put Jason's name as a co-author on every paper that he published. Jason and Marcus remained close friends and visited each other yearly.

Craig Henderson finished his PhD and wrote one of the most brilliant PhD theses that Jason had ever read. He remained in Jason's lab to complete a postdoctoral fellowship, and, following the fellowship, he became a tenured professor at MIT, where he continued to have major successes in protein research. He wrote a letter that he gave to Jason on his final day at Sinai. In it, he said: *There are no words that could begin convey how grateful I am to you, and so I will not even make that attempt. What I can say is that any success I have going forward will be because you gave me a second chance. Please know that you will be forever in my thoughts."* As with Dr. Blumenthal, Craig dedicated every award that he subsequently received to Jason and placed Jason as a co-author on every paper that he published. Craig married and adopted a son, whom he named Jason, and a daughter, whom he named Julia. Jason and Craig remained close friends and visited each other often.

Jason's computer program was distributed to every major scientific laboratory in the world, free of charge. Because of that computer program, major new discoveries in protein chemistry were made, resulting in major advances in treatment for various other cancers and auto-immune disorders. The program became known as JOOG, for Jason Olsen O'Malley Green.

In 2025 Jason received the Nobel Prize for his creation of JOOG and the major discoveries that resulted from that computer program. Kevin and Julia, who was fourteen years of age, Jonathan and Sophia, and John and Evelyn accompanied Jason to receive the award. Jason's acceptance speech was short and brilliant. He ended his speech with these words: "I want to give thanks to the thousands of scientists who made these discoveries possible—to Harvey Glassman who stood on this very stage to receive this same award, who allowed me to begin my own research, and who taught me to ask the right questions. Most importantly, my research would have never been possible without the love and support of my dear father, Jonathan Green, my incredible and talented daughter Julia, my amazing and beautiful husband Kevin, who gave me a second chance, and my cherished second parents, John and Evelyn Olsen. Finally, as all important as these individuals are to me, all of whom I love so deeply, it was Philip Olsen who first loved me and made me the man that I am today. And so it is Philip Olsen to whom I dedicate this award. "

The End

## About the Author

John S. Daniels is an endocrinologist on the staff of Washington University School of Medicine in Saint Louis, Missouri. He was born and raised in Fort Smith, Arkansas, the son of holocaust survivors. He was married for nineteen years and has three daughters from that marriage. He has been with his partner, Lance Cimarolli, for the past twenty-one years.